Dream Across This Mortal Coil

Duke Droste

ISBN-978-0-578-28817-8
Cover Design: Duke Droste

Come visit my website/blog at:
DukeDroste.com

DEDICATION

This novel is dedicated to my family, with a special mention for my daughter, Megan. Her independent spirit provided the spice of life for certain characters within this work.

CONTENTS

To die, to sleep;

To sleep: perchance to dream: ay, there's the rub;

For in that sleep of death what dreams may come

When we have shuffled off this mortal coil,

Must give us pause: there's the respect

That makes calamity of so long life;

For who would bear the whips and scorns of time,

~ Hamlet, William Shakespeare

1 - PRAIRIE DOG STYLE

My scream shattered this reality, waking me. I found myself sprawled across the floor—a nightmare inside a nightmare. The last one, a snake, devoured me. I looked around the room as I pulled myself up. Everything appeared as I remembered from last night. An unfinished energy drink that miserably failed to keep me awake anchored the homework strewn across my desk. Stuffed animals stared with dull eyes as I scanned the room for anything unreal.

How could I be sure that I was truly awake and not buried inside another dream? A vision bubbled up of those nested Russian dolls, fitting one inside the other. How many dolls deep am I? The dream was so real— the second one more than the first. Trembling, I crept toward the bedroom door. What would be the next nightmare to visit?

A booming sound of someone running down the hall pounded louder, approaching my door. I braced for the new level to reveal itself.

The door flew open, and Dad stood there with his eyes bugged out, breathing hard. "What's going on in here?" he shouted. His face softened when he saw beads of sweat pouring into my already soaked pajamas. "Lucinda, are you okay?"

This was real, and I broke down in tears. "Oh, Dad!" I leaped into his arms.

As I cried into his T-shirt, he hugged me and softly patted my back. His huge hands felt like soft pillows as they comforted me.

"It was so real …."

Once I calmed down, Dad let go, took a step back, but held my shoulders. "What was real?"

He knew the answer but felt compelled to ask anyway.

"I'm in a dark tunnel … then I'm falling into a snake pit … next a big one tried to eat me."

"Mmm." He looked down, knitted his brow in thought, and sighed. Staring into my sweat and tear-stained face, was he clueless?

"I can't wake up."

Dad squeezed my shoulders and let go. "Don't worry … I'm here, now."

"But I'm alone in these nightmares."

He remained quiet a moment. "Look, it's almost six, and we're not going to get any more sleep. Why don't I make you some of my World-Famous Pancakes?"

"Okay," I whispered.

"You get ready while I make breakfast." He gave me one more reassuring hug and left for the kitchen.

I stood for a few moments, unsure of what to believe. Entering the bathroom, I flipped on the light. My hair was a red, matted mess, and I was sure this was what someone looked like after wrestling a giant anaconda. I warmed the shower, undressed, and slipped into the flow. I let the water run over me for several minutes and could have stood there an hour if the hot water had held.

In the kitchen, Dad poured his World-Famous Pancake batter from the blender into a frying pan. A packet of pancake mix, two broken eggs, and an open milk jug lay on the counter. My father's default meal was pancakes. He stood with a spatula in one hand and the other on his hip, leaning against the stovetop, watching the cakes bubble enough to flip.

He brought two plates to the kitchen table. My appetite was uncertain, but after the first couple of bites, my stomach took over. I washed the pancakes down with a large glass of milk. Dad ate but kept a worried eye. I caught his stare one too many times, so I returned it.

"What, Dad?"

Dad flinched at being caught. "What?" he mumbled.

"Why're you giving me that what-am-I-going-to-do-with-you look?"

"Luce, this whole summer … with these dreams. It's scaring the bejesus out of me. You sound like … ."

"Like who?" I knew the answer, but I wanted him to spit it out. He never does.

"Like some creepy Stephen King story with monsters and ghouls and stuff."

I rolled my eyes. More silence passed.

Dad doesn't like conflict, so he changed the subject. "How was your first week at school?"

"Fine."

"About a month away from gettin' your driver's license. Bet you can't wait to drive solo?" I felt him searching for a subject that would engage me.

"Yeah, that would be nice, but you'd still be in the passenger seat ... 'cause we only got one car."

Dad knowingly cocked his head and said, "Maybe yes ... maybe no."

"You mean you're going to get me a car?"

"Mmm, I like said, maybe yes ... maybe no."

He loved to play these games, so I played along as the frustrated daughter. "Come on. Dad, tell me. For real," I said, leaning forward. "Are we going to get a second car or not?"

"Let's see what the Magic 8 Ball has to say." He reached for something imaginary, raised it to his ear, and pretended to shake it vigorously with his tongue slightly out. Pulling his cupped hand back down to his chest, he imagined a triangular answer rising from the murky depths. He squinted as if hard to read. "It says ... huh ... can't make out the answer. Can you get my reading glasses?"

I laughed. "Dad, stop! You're being mean."

"There," he said, pointing to my smile. "That's what I wanted to see. Don't worry. I got this handled." An uncomfortable pause and then he spoke again. "Why didn't that boy show up in your dream?"

"I dunno."

"Mmmf, some friend he is."

~ ~ ~

Dad shifted the gears of his old Subaru: 1 ... 2 ... 3 ... 2, delivering an unwelcome lurch with each transition. I usually drove and switched with Dad at school, but the nightmare shook my confidence. I stared out the window and watched my neighborhood pass by with an occasional kid lumbering along the sidewalk.

Dad slowed and entered the circular drive to Park North High School, stopping behind the last car.

"Have a good day, sweetheart. Feeling better?" He gently slapped my knee.

I took a deep breath. "I'm okay." I got out of the car, retrieving my pack and lunch from the backseat.

"Love you," he said just before I closed the door.

"Love you, too," I said through the glass.

Making my way to the main entrance, I pulled my ID badge from my pack and slung it around my neck. I really didn't want to be here. I couldn't wait for it to be October. By then, I would have my license, my freedom, and be rid of this Dallas heat.

The echoes of students came from everywhere as they clambered up the stairs and down three feeder hallways. Loading up my books, I hurried into my first class, AP English. It was so tough that students called it EFL (English as a First Language). I took a seat in the middle of the room and got comfortable. Dr. Van Vogt glided in and called roll. Her silver hair cut tight, and her glasses provided an austere presence.

Fifteen names down, she called me. "Lucinda Locke."

"Here." I raised my hand in a half gesture. Dr. Van finished roll and droned on about our current reading assignment.

"We'll have a test on Thursday over the first four chapters of Moby Dick. Don't even think about using cheat notes. They won't help you."

"Then why does she freak about them?" asked a voice to my right, whispering through the clenched teeth of a ventriloquist. I gave a knowing smirk to my friend, Maggie. Her head never turned away from the front of the class. Her superpower was making me laugh.

Dr. Van would threaten to ferret out those she declared to be lazy. If the cheat notes didn't work, then why did she want to root them out so badly? I have never used cheat notes because English was a breeze, as were all my classes. I have a photographic memory. It goes beyond just eidetic. I can recall to the word or image, anything I see or hear. They say that a true photographic memory hasn't been proven, but I know better. I never flaunt this at school because no one really cares, and it doesn't make me any more popular.

English mercifully ended, and after being excused, Maggie and I dashed out the door.

In the hall, Maggie brought a hand to her head. "Luce, Oh God! I'm so bored with school, I wanna puke."

"Yeah. Mr. Wilkes's class puts me to sleep." I drop my head and give a fake snore.

Maggie squinted. "Wilkes is a perv. I always catch him staring at me."

"I think he's intrigued by your fashion sense." I did an exaggerated scan of my friend for effect.

She bristled at the suggestion. "I wear what I want, and I don't care what he thinks."

Maggie is fearless. Today, she wore red jeans with big, ragged holes at the knees. Her blouse was yellow with purple flowers. She held herself with confidence. Large, looped earrings danced as she swung her head back and forth, checking out the student traffic. She tucked her hair behind her ears to accentuate the hardware.

"Who're you lookin' for?" I asked.

She feigned indifference. "Oh … no one."

"Ah, huh. Brad, right?" I loved to tease her.

She turned to me. "Are you all right?" She raised an eyebrow. "You seem tired," said the master of diversion.

"Why? Does my face scream *exhausted?*"

Maggie cocked her head slightly. "No, but your face does look like it's carrying luggage."

"Excuse me? Please translate. I don't speak Magpie."

"Good one," she said, pointing at my face. "You have bags under your eyes."

"Oh … some bad dreams last night," I admitted.

Maggie's brow furrowed. "Are you still having those scary ones?"

"Yeah, but they're getting nasty ... dark tunnels and snakes."

Maggie shuddered. "Snakes. They give me the creeps." The bell was about to sound, and Maggie, running off to her next class, added, "See you at lunch."

"Okay, later."

Maggie strutted up the hall and out of sight. I spent the next two uneventful classes of Science and Social Studies. After lunch with Maggie, we headed for Mr. Wilkes's Spanish class.

Mr. Wilkes explained that every Monday would be language lab. He broke out the headphones, and we listened to vocabulary words and sentence structure used in the *vernacular,* as he would say. This was much more beneficial. He was a good teacher, but he butchered his Spanish with a heavy Texas accent. The words flowed more naturally through headphones, and I could visualize them better. All summer, I'd been watching cheesy afternoon Spanish soaps to get prepared.

The afternoon sun streamed through the window beside me, and the air became hot on my side of the room. I intended to be a good little student and pay attention, but the combination of the heat, the restless night, and lunch conspired to put me to sleep. I fought to open my eyes.

My vision blurred, and my head bobbed until my forehead smacked the desktop, which woke me. The cycle continued again until I was ...

~ ~ ~

Darkness is all I see—always the darkness. Trying to remain calm, I look for a way to negotiate this passage. The sound and noise come from all around. I take short, sliding steps, hoping to kick away anything at my feet before it has the chance to bite. I'm able to conjure up a pair of shoes, but I feel nothing but the gritty dirt between my feet and the floor. My footsteps echo, so I'm thinking the room is much larger. I hold my hands out as I shuffle, searching for walls. Ahead of me, I hear whispered voices.

I don't want to get any closer, but my curiosity compels me to understand what they're saying. I pick up only a few muffled words as I approach.

"She ... Never ... Soon."

The words come soft and raspy. The voices fade away as I approach. Shuffling a little faster toward where I hear them last, I reach out and feel something. It's flat and cool to the touch. I can't tell if it's metal or rock. My hand brushes something protruding from it. Is this a handle or a knob? I jiggle it and hear a click. The moment I realize it's a door, it shoots away with a swoosh that pulls all the air around me. I sense a presence. Something grabs a clump of hair and rips my head back. It's behind me. I fight forward, trying to wrench myself free, but it holds me tight.

Then in my ear, so close, I feel its breath as if to whisper a secret. I stop struggling.

"We must stop meeting this way, my sweet," it hisses.

"I ... I ... wasn't trying to spy—"

"Well, try or not ... you did ... and now you must pay the consequences for this little intrusion."

A coiling force wraps me; it's overwhelming and crushes my chest and legs as it squeezes. I can't breathe. Each time I exhale, it ratchets tighter around me. My head feels it's ready to pop like a gigantic zit.

"Wake up. Wake up," I scream at myself.

"I won't allow you to wake up. Little trespassers must be punished," the voice drips into my ear. My arms are pinned to my sides. Freaking out and struggling with every bit of strength, I scream as if being murdered. My body thrashes violently as I fall backward.

~ ~ ~

I smashed into the floor and continued to flail and scream. The crushing force disappeared, and I was someplace else. Opening my eyes, I lay sprawled out on my back across the classroom floor with my chair underneath me. My eyes adjusted to the lights and saw the faces of my classmates pop up, prairie dog style, in the periphery of my vision. Their mouths agape and their eyes bugged out—unblinking, so as not to miss a single instant of the scene in front of them.

Jerks.

"She's lost it," someone said.

"Are you all right?" asked Maggie.

I sat up, feeling the weight of everyone's stares. Managing to get to my feet, I kept my eyes downcast and noticed a large chunk of hair lying on the floor. I wanted to climb into a hole and die from embarrassment.

"Lucinda, why don'tcha go to the nurse's office?" said Mr. Wilkes.

And tell her what? That I'm a freaking lunatic?

2 - BLURRED LINES

I marked today as the day I died. Not in the literal sense, but something about me croaked.

The school nurse set up shop in a little space in the front office to the left of all the secretaries. I waited outside the clinic door. Soon, Ms. Dooley tottered up the hallway wearing a white frock that had to be as old as me. Her grey hair was cropped in a little Dutch girl style—straight bangs and all. She had to be ancient, like over fifty, and wore bright red lipstick.

"Miss Locke, come in. Take a seat." She gestured to a chair across from her desk. "What seems to be the problem?"

"I need to go home."

Ms. Dooley's forehead knotted up. "Can you be more specific? What doesn't feel well?"

"I … ah, got a huge headache." Damn it, I don't lie very well, but now mentioning it, my head did hurt. I wasn't sure if it was the suggestion or the stress.

"I have some extra strength ibuprofen that should kill it. Just need to call your dad and ask permission."

"Can I also go home?" I rested my face in my hands for dramatic flair.

She straightened up. "You hurt enough to be excused for the day?"

"Yes. Can I, please?" I raised my head and interlocked my fingers in my best beggar's pose.

"Okay dear, that's fine. Use my phone." She moved her phone closer to where I sat and put it on speaker.

I called Dad and got him on record giving permission to leave early and receive the meds.

"Don't you need a ride?" queried the nurse, twisting her head.

"Dad's real busy at work. Besides, it's a short walk home. Can I please have the ibuprofen?"

The nurse clicked her mouse a few times and studied her screen. "Well, you have a great attendance record, so you're not flighty. We marked you in attendance before ten o'clock, so we already got the state's money for you today." A slight grin curled up the edges of her face. "Let me get you that pill."

She stood slowly and left. Returning with a fat red and white capsule and a small cup of water, she handed them to me.

"Thanks, Ms. Dooley." I took the pill, popped it, and chased it down with the water.

Her smile now showed some teeth. "Sweetie, you're excused. Go home and get some rest."

I gathered my things and almost made it through the doorway.

"How is Charles doing?"

I spun around. "You know my father?"

"I remember both your parents when they went here. Must be over twenty years ago. "My…." She glanced at the ceiling. "Has it been that long?"

"You knew my mom?"

"Yes, lovely thing, your mother. Sorry to hear about her." Ms. Dooley's eyes left mine and focused on her bookshelf.

"Can you tell me about her?" I took a step closer, my attention rapt. I needed to hear something, anything about her. Dad never gave details. At least, none that satisfied me.

"Curious about your mother, though."

"What?"

"She had headaches as well. But she began seeing a doctor who made 'em go away."

"Really, what doctor?"

"Mmm." Ms. Dooley looked up again in thought. "A Dr. Rami Bosch, I believe."

There was that toothy grin again.

~ ~ ~

I got home, drank a huge glass of water, and chomped a small bag of corn chips. It was hot outside, and I knew getting dehydrated would make my headache worse. The pill took more of an edge off than I would have expected. I kicked up onto the couch and tried to lie still. The room spun, so I put one foot on the floor to anchor me. Managing to relax every muscle, I worked through my entire body until the only movement was the slow rise and fall of my chest as I breathed.

~ ~ ~

A brilliant green field flows around me with white miniature daisy-like flowers dotting across the hillside. I lie on my back under a giant oak tree with broad, spanning branches stretching out overhead. The leaves rustle softly and sway, letting tiny flecks of sunlight break free and glow around me.

"How're you doing?" The voice comes from high up within the branches of the tree.

"A little freaked out. Come talk to me." I want to make sure it's him. The recent series of dreams left me drained. I didn't trust this reality like before.

The shadow, at the top of the tree, climbs down to the lowest branch. He jumps, landing beside me with a soft thud.

"Hey, you." He walks over near my feet, so I can see him. His dark hair hangs long and partially hides his eyes as he looks down. His smile shines easy and warm with small dimples at the corners of his mouth. He runs a hand through his hair, pulling it away from his eyes. They sparkle with a hazel color, and like his smile, beam genuine happiness.

I sit up and wrap my arms around my knees. "David, I'm so glad you're here. My nightmares are worse."

He sits across from me, mirroring my position, holding his knees, and focuses, waiting for me to say whatever I want. "Go ahead, shoot."

I tell him about all the dreams I've been having and the latest one today in Spanish class. Absorbed, he brings his hand up to his chin as if concentrating deep on the information spilling out and asks not one question.

"That's about it," I say, and become quiet.

David blinks, leans back on his hands, and gazes up into the tree. "Whew! That's a truckload." He looks at me and then plucks a blade of grass, sits upright, and tears it lengthwise several times along the grain.

"Got any ideas?" I ask.

"Ah ... nope," he responds.

"Nope? NOPE? You gotta help me figure this out. First, it's my dad looking at me funny. Now, it's affecting my social. People stared at me today." I lean toward him, opening my eyes wide for effect. "STARED AT ME. As if crazy with some disease. I don't want to look at what they're posting about me online."

"You're blurring the line," he says.

"What?"

"You're blurring the line between your awake self and your asleep self."

"Yeah? And it's driving me crazy."

"Exactly. That's the difference between the sane and the insane. The ability to distinguish between what is, quote, real and what is imaginary—it's what separates them. Lately, your line has lost its definition, and it has become … uh … fuzzy." He places his hands on his knees.

"So, I'm going nuts."

"The way some people might define it, but here, you're as sane as the next person. Who can blame you? All of this?" He raises his arms from his sides, looking around him. "I'm sure this looks as real as when you're awake. You see this tree and hear the leaves rustling." He reaches out and puts his hand on my forearm. "You feel the warmth of my hand, and I feel a slight pulse from you."

"Yeah, but this isn't real," I say.

"What makes you think that?" he asks.

"This is just a product of my imagination."

"We're back to that. You're saying I'm not real." David's eyebrows rise, waiting for my response.

"Well, not exactly," I say.

"I'm telling you, I am. I'm as real as you." His eyes lock onto mine with a sharp edge.

"Now, who sounds crazy?"

"Exactly." He beams a huge smile at me as if I paid him a compliment.

I scrunch up my face. "You're confusing me."

"Come on, Luce. Maybe you're in a dream, but you're not stupid. Your brain still works in here."

"Tell me. Just spit it out."

"I can't. You gotta see it for yourself. There are some things here that I can't help you with because it's *your* journey. I've got my journey to follow, but I'm not supposed to intrude on yours." David looks at his hands. It's as if he were guilty about something. "I can tell you one thing: you have to take control. Don't let these dreams get away from you."

"I've tried all the things I know to wake myself up, but it doesn't work."

"Sometimes I think you assume that because you're in this reality, you're a passenger. Tell me. You recognize what all this is, right?" He's pointing up to the huge tree we sit under.

"Yes, but—"

"There you go. That's half the battle."

"What is?" Why is he talking in circles?

David sighs. "Okay, I guess I can also tell you this. Knowing you're dreaming—it's got you half the way there. You just have to figure out the other half."

I get to my feet. David stands as well and brushes the grass off his jeans.

"Halfway to where?" I ask.

"To there. Aye yah, talk about frustrating. You remember your dreams, right?"

"Yeah, I remember everything."

"Then you need to commit this dream to memory; write it down on your brain, whatever. Just study it when you're able to concentrate on the words."

David's face loses its glimmer. His head hangs lower, and he scratches the back of his neck in thought.

"Sorry, I'm not trying to frustrate you." I put my hand on his shoulder.

"Oh, it's not your fault. It's sort of mine. I want to comfort you and help you work it out, but I can only help up to a point."

"Do you represent some kind of dream symbol that my subconscious can't reveal?" I ask.

"Where did you hear that mumbo jumbo?" Now it's David's face that's scrunching up.

"I read it in some book on dreams."

"Some parts of your dreams you might treat that way but not …. Anyway, you need to think back on what I told you and what I didn't." He glances sideways at me.

"What does that mean?"

"You'll understand," says David. "One more thing. Steer clear of that darkness."

"How? You don't know what I'm going through."

"As I said, replay these words later and analyze them. Just stay away from that Dark Dreamer."

"Who?"

"The snake guy, that's who. He's no one to mess with." He looks up into the tree. "Luce, maybe I said too much. I need to go."

"Wait, you know who this thing is?" I reach for him, but he jumps up, grabs the lowest branch, swings his legs up to another, and pulls himself into the tree. He soon becomes a shadow, climbing.

"How do I avoid this Snake Dude?" I yell into the tree after him.

He stops climbing. "Need to figure that one out by yourself," he shouts back.

"Yeah, some boyfriend you are," I mumble.

3 – A DOCTOR'S TALE

Maggie drove me to Dr. Bosch's office. I had called there yesterday to see if I could find an appointment on his schedule. The receptionist said he had an opening at five on Friday. It happened so fast. I just wanted to speak to him about my mother, and I didn't even think about what I was going to say about myself. Usually, I invoked my anal-retentive right to check out references. I would have looked him up online and seen what I could creep about him. Thoughts of my mother caused me to throw all caution to the wind, landing me in his parking lot. Maggie pulled up outside a two-story nondescript office building.

"You sure you know what you're doing?" asked Maggie.

"Yeah, don't worry," I said.

"I'm not leaving you here alone. I'll be in the waiting room, so if he turns out to be some kind of crazy, then scream bloody murder, and I'll bust in."

"It's just a doctor's office. Nothing to get concerned about."

"I don't know why, but I get a funny feeling. Chuck doesn't know about this, and I'm worried he's gonna freak out on me if he finds out I drove you here."

"He's not going to freak out on anything. I'll completely insulate you. Just do the Reagan/Clinton thing we talked about," I said.

Maggie nodded. "Okay. Okay. If pretending I don't remember doesn't work, I switch to denying everything, even if there are pictures. Right?"

"Perfect. Don't worry, this is really about getting info about my mother and less about me," I said.

"Sure, but Chuck—"

"Information about my mom has been in lockdown for too long. My dad tells me nothing, so I'm taking this into my own hands. And stop calling my dad, Chuck."

"That's his name, isn't it?" Maggie looked at me, eyebrows raised.

"It's Charles, but when you call him by that nickname, it feels weird. Like you're channeling Peppermint Patty or something." I fidgeted in my seat because I knew I was being sneaky, and having Maggie be the one to point it out was like having a pig farmer tell me to wash my hands.

Maggie smirked. "Well, your dad is thin up top and does have some Charlie qualities."

"Stop giving me the business about this. The number of times I've covered for you. I've never made you feel this guilty." I crossed my arms and looked straight ahead.

"All right, you got me there, but I'm still goin' in with you." She crossed her arms and stared back at me, trying to imitate my face with her eyes crooked.

I smiled and couldn't contain my laughter. "You're the craziest friend."

"No, I'm the *best* of friends, baby, and don't you forget it."

We climbed out of Maggie's truck and approached the door. The stenciled sign on the glass read: "Dr. Ramiro Bosch, MD, Ph.D."

Upon entering the foyer, we saw a windowed section with a nurse.

I spoke through the round hole. "Locke. I have a five o'clock appointment."

"Here, fill out these New Patient forms," said the nurse, handing them to me through the open slot below. She seemed nice enough, but she didn't smile.

We seated ourselves in the waiting room. I completed the forms and turned them in. Maggie and I picked out some year-old women's magazines and played a game to see who could find the most obnoxious story to read to each other. It helped to pass the time. No one else was waiting, so I'm not sure what took them so long.

The door to the interior office opened, and the nurse called, "Lucinda?"

As I got up, Maggie mumbled, "Remember … scream, 'Fire'. I'll call 911 and come running."

I shook my head at her with a half-grin and followed the nurse. She led me into a large room that looked more like someone's den than a doctor's office. At the far side stood a long leather couch with comfy black leather chairs on either side. To the right was a huge mahogany desk. It had a fancy light and was piled deep with thick stacks of patient file folders. The walls were dark, picture-framed paneling with no windows. Although brilliantly lit, its décor screamed this is a manly man. I expected to see mounted dead animal heads hanging everywhere; instead, there were numerous framed diplomas.

"Have a seat. The doctor will be with you shortly," said the nurse.

I settled into the chair facing the desk and waited.

A few minutes passed, and a medium-built man in a dark suit with glasses strolled into the room carrying a folder. He walked past me as if I were invisible and sat down at his desk. He flipped open the folder, which I assumed was mine, and read it intently. He kept his head down while running his left hand through his thick dark hair. I could only see the top of his head. He remained that way for several minutes and turned the pages slowly as if memorizing every scrap of information.

I thought maybe he didn't realize I was there, so I cleared my throat to warn him he had a spy.

He didn't lift his head to acknowledge me but only raised a finger and spoke to the paper. "I'll be with you in just one moment."

The doctor read a few minutes longer, closed the folder, and stood from his chair. A beaming smile painted across his face. Was he a doctor or a sales guy? I waited to find out. He maneuvered around his desk and, with deliberate steps, approached me, extending his hand.

"Nice to meet you, Miss Locke. Call me Dr. Rami." He had a strong chin and piercing brown eyes. I found myself counting the number of teeth in his cordial smile.

I stood briefly, shook his hand, and sat back down. He took the chair opposite me.

"Now, what can I do for you?"

"I ... I need some help."

"Your patient form indicated you've had problems sleeping."

"Well, yes, that's part of it, but I also—"

"Do you know what kind of doctor I am?"

"Ah ... well, no but—"

"It's no matter. I believe I can help you. Your dreams manifest themselves in ways you are unable to control."

"How do you know that?"

"I received my doctorate in Physics from Princeton, and my medical degrees are from here, there, and everywhere. I'm kind of West meets East in my training, and I'm professionally qualified to assist." He pulled off his glasses and stared back at me, unmoving like a slab of granite.

"Yes, but you didn't answer my question. How do you know about my dreams?"

"Oh, well, I was answering my first question to you. On your first question to me … that you already know." He let me simmer in my seat for a few more seconds, and when I was about to speak, he added, "You look just like your mother."

I was speechless for a moment and hadn't planned to be so transparent.

"Is there anything about your mother you want to know?" he asked.

This was a lead-in question I had been wanting from Dad since she died. Shocked, I had a willing participant in a conversation about my mother. I blurted, "How did she die?"

"She died of a broken heart," said the doctor, as he shifted in his chair.

"Broken heart? I don't remember Mom and Dad fighting or talking about divorce." I looked at my hands and tried to remember if I missed anything. "Dad said she had an aneurysm."

"Technically, it could have been an aneurysm, but your mother was under a tremendous amount of stress. Her heart was heavy with several worries, but your father was the least of them. He loved her regardless of his misguided beliefs." Dr. Rami put his glasses back on and pinched the bridge of his nose before returning his gaze to me.

"What misguided beliefs?" I scrunched up my face.

"Your mother experienced a schism in her personality, and your father thought she should seek help from traditional medicine. The only end that served was to pump her full of chemicals and ultimately suppress her transformation. He didn't understand she was reaching a new level of consciousness. Either he didn't understand, or it was something else. I could never tell with him."

I couldn't help feeling the doctor was not too fond of Dad, but the information he provided was too good a drink to put down. No matter how much brain freeze it gave me, I needed to get as much out of him as I could. Later, I would sift through what was truth and what was manufactured. It hurt too much for Dad to talk about her. Regardless, I wanted to know—I needed to know.

"You mentioned a schism?" I kept the flow going.

"She developed a split personality. It manifested itself in what could be diagnosed as schizophrenia. She would get terrible headaches and nausea, but the real problems occurred when she lost touch with this reality. Her dreams felt real, and her life with you and your father became the fantasy."

"What kind of dreams did she have?" I edged forward in my seat. This was tangible.

"Your mother was on a path to enlightenment. Whatever you heard, she was never crazy. The path she traveled allowed her to develop a gateway to an alternate reality. I believe in some ways her dreams were a parallel universe to ours. The information she provided wasn't possible for her to divine on her own. Lara's a …." He paused as if remembering something. "She was a truly remarkable woman. I learned some amazing things from her as a person, as well as a patient."

Dr. Rami knew my mother way beyond what I would imagine his Hippocratic Oath allowed.

"Tell me about your dreams. Do they scare you?" he asked and crossed his legs.

This came out of left field. "Some do. Some don't," I replied.

The doctor pulled a red pen from inside his jacket, clicked the end, and positioned it in his notebook. "Have you met David yet?"

4 – UP THROUGH THE RABBIT HOLE

I emerged from the doctor's office, and Maggie knew something had happened.

"You look like a ghost. Did you let him suck all the blood out of you or somethin'?"

"He dropped a nuke on me. I'll explain on the drive home." I was in shock, and I'm sure I looked pale, but the data overload would take some time to work through.

Maggie began slow with her questions and let me process the experience. I recited my conversation with the doctor, and when I got to the part about David, her jaw dropped to her chest, and she bobbled the wheel slightly.

"You're sharing the same dream boyfriend … with your mother?"

"Ah, yeah … that's about it," I said.

"How is that even possible?" asked Maggie.

"The doctor believes my mother could cross over into other dimensions. He thinks I'm just like her." My eyes filled with tears. "Is this what's going to happen to me?" I said to no one. I broke down and sobbed into my hands.

"Oh … Luce, no," said Maggie. "You can't assume that." She reached into the center console, pulled out leftover napkins from a fast-food run, and handed them over.

"Thanks," I said, and wiped my eyes and nose.

"Promise you won't get mad if I say something?" Maggie glanced at me as she negotiated past a car on the highway.

"Okay," I said.

"I get the feeling this doctor was in love with your mom. Sounds like you remind him of her. The perv has got to be older than Chuck."

"I know what you mean. I thought the same thing, but it's different somehow."

"Well, if I catch him stalking you, I'll sneak into his office, open up his coffin, and put a freakin' stake through his heart." Maggie laughed, and I knew she was trying to cheer me up.

"But it wasn't the weirdest part. Next, he talked physics."

"What?" Maggie twisted her face. "Doesn't sound like any doctor I know of."

"The doctor told me he got his Ph.D. in Physics from the University of London. He was influenced by a professor who studied under Dr. Bohm."

"Dr. Bomb?" asked Maggie.

"No, it's spelled different, I think. Anyway, he said this Bohm guy did research on sub-atomic particles. Something about how the big objects of our universe act in a certain way, but as you go deeper into the smaller sub-atomic particles, things behave unpredictably. Down in those lower levels, there is no past or future, only now."

"Freaky," said Maggie.

"Then he started babbling more about how the universe is a huge hologram, and we all play a part in its creation."

"Hologram? Like those stickers, you find in cereal boxes, where the image moves?" Maggie's face looked like she smelled something rank.

"No, not exactly. Let me see if I can replay his words and make sense of them. He said that holograms are created by a laser beam that is split and reflected off an object from two different angles onto a special film. Later, if you shine a laser beam through that film at the same angle, then you create a three-dimensional hologram object. The film looks like a series of overlapping concentric circles as if a handful of gravel were tossed in a pool of water. The really weird part is that if you cut the film into four pieces, each piece can recreate the same image."

"Wild *and* freaky," she said.

"So, he believes the universe is a hologram and everything knows about everything else. The parts know about the whole. Then he got all philosophical and stuff, saying that within each of us, we know about the entire universe, and some people can tune their brains like a laser at different angles and tap into other places in the past, present, or future. He believes my mother could do that."

"And you?" asked Maggie, sensing the direction I was going.

"I don't know. There's too much to soak in. Don't tell anybody about this, okay?" I didn't need any more attention than I already got at school. My episode in Spanish was now legendary at Park North, and I'd gotten strange looks ever since.

"Hell no, I won't say a word. Trust me on this. I got a vested interest in you being sane. I'm your best friend—guilt by association, you know? If I rat you out, I might as well wear a shirt saying, 'I'm with Crazy'."

I hadn't thought of it like that, but she made sense.

"What's Chuck going to say about this?"

"My dad won't know what to say about anything 'cause I'm not telling him."

"Sure, but if he figures out you're seeing your mother's *doctor*, he's gonna flip."

I gave Maggie a stern face, and she saw it out of the corner of her eye.

"I'm not gonna tell him if that's what you're thinking," said Maggie.

It was the second time she had brought up what my dad would think. "It doesn't matter because that's the last time I'm seeing Dr. Rami."

Maggie nodded as if she agreed with me, but I noticed a definite sense of relief as she took a large breath and let it all out. I would see Rami again. The doctor was a gold mine of info; I just needed to figure out how to see him in secret. I kept the other part of my appointment to myself.

~ ~ ~

Later that night in my dreams…. It's a night on a moonlit field, and once again, I stand under the familiar huge tree with its sprawling branches. The shadows around me dance as the branches sway from the breeze. There are no stars, only a black sky with a full moon. I think it's strange the moon has no face; it's clear as a light bulb.

I look up into the tree and find a familiar shape climbing down. The shadow comes to the lowest branch and stops.

"I need to talk to you," I say up to David.

"I'm sure you do. Maybe this time you should follow me. I have something to show you," he says.

"Help me." I reach my hands up to the branch.

"Help yourself. Jump."

"Hmm, all right." It must have been a ten-foot vertical. I leap and land on the branch beside him. David grabs my arm to steady the landing. "Wicked," I whisper.

"You've got the ability. You just need to remember to use it. Come on." David leaps and climbs up the branches.

"But …" I realize talking is for later and match him branch for branch as I scamper after him. The coarse branches are sticky with sap, which is gross, but helps my grip as I pull and jump my way to the top of the tree. David continues to be a shadow until he's suddenly gone. "Where'd you go?" I call up.

"Just keep climbing," says David's voice, above me.

I keep moving upward, and then I stand at the top of the tree. Below me, the fields stretch away in all directions. Other trees dot the landscape, but each one is separated by an equal space in what looks like a grid that extends to the horizon. Everything remains colorless—an endless sea of various grays and blacks.

"Are you coming?" asks David, from the void above me.

"Where are you?"

"Reach up and keep climbing."

"What?" I mutter almost to myself. I reach up, and my arm disappears into the inky, black sky. I feel another branch and pull myself into the darkness above me. I see nothing, but I feel the branches just the same. The cloying darkness reminds me of the tunnel and the dark doorway from my previous nightmares. I imagine hearing the Snake Dude's voice in my mind and remember the panic. In this in-between place, I continue for a few branches, and it's like a light switch flip. I find myself now standing again at the top of a different tree. It's daytime, and once my eyes adjust to the light, bright green fields roll in waves below me. Hills undulate out with a similar grid of trees as far as I can see. It's a mirror image of where I had been, except it's day now and there are fewer trees.

"Climb on down," comes a distant voice of David from far below. I look down between my feet and see a tangle of branches and a small figure waving its arms to get my attention.

"Okay," I shout down. I descend through the branches slower but reach the lowest branch and jump to the ground below. As I fall, all the color of my clothes sparkles up, and I feel as though I'm again a being of substance and no longer a child of gray. David strolls up from behind the trunk and greets me with the usual beaming glow.

"Wild ride, eh? Don't even ask me to explain, 'cause I don't understand it either. You go up, then you're going down. Go figure."

I nod my head and remain silent. I smile, wanting only to study him more and choose my moment to speak.

"Are you okay?" David senses my uneasiness.

"As okay as anyone, when you rattle their world."

"What do you mean?" David tilts his head to the side.

"How long have we known each other?"

"Um, I don't know. Time doesn't mean the same here."

"It's been almost eight years. We met by the same oak tree just after my mother died."

"Yeah, okay. We were both about eight at the time. We've kinda grown up together." David looks at his feet and smiles as if replaying a memory.

"Is that really true? Have you been the same age as me? Or have you been a different age?" I stick my chin out further, delivering the accusation.

"What kind of question is that?"

I stare.

"Why're you looking at me like that, Luce? It's the same as me asking you if you've always been a girl."

"Answer the question."

"My age is my age. I grow older just like you."

"Did you know my mother?" I ask.

"I know a lot of people, but I don't know if I know your mother."

"Her name was Lara. Lara Locke."

"Your mother is Lara?" His eyes glisten as tears well within them. He grabs my shoulders. "Your mother's Lara. Oh, my God. That's impossible."

"What's wrong!"

He shakes his head as if he doesn't have the words to express himself.

"Why didn't you tell me you knew her?" I ask him.

"I didn't know she was your mother. I never made the connection." He wipes the tears away on the sleeve of his shirt. "You were grieving the loss of your mom when we met, remember? Do you recall what I was upset about?"

I take a moment to think. "Ah, you said you lost your … guide."

"Exactly, Lara was my guide. She helped to navigate my way through all of this, and then she disappeared."

"You've never mentioned her name. You only called her your guide."

"You never told me your mom's name. You only called her 'Mom'."

"How stupid are we? You always got sad when I mentioned your guide, so I stopped bringing her up."

"Same for your mother. You always reminded me of her, but I didn't connect the dots. Now, I understand why I've been so drawn to you. You look so much like her."

"I've heard that twice today."

David cocks his head and scratches his neck.

"Never mind, I'll explain later," I say.

"Luce, there's something you should know. It's what I want to show you. I heard her voice last night."

"Whose voice?" I ask, not daring to believe what he may tell me.

"Your mother's."

5 – AMAZING WITH GRACE

David leads me through lush, green hillsides. Beautiful purple flowers swoon as we brush by them and dance back upward. The sky is a pale blue with no clouds to mar its serenity.

"Where are we going?" I ask.

David turns, "It's not much farther."

I'm running after him, but it's more like bounding as I take huge leaps forward. I feel unaffected. If I did this in P.E. class, I would fall flat on my face and die from exhaustion. My breathing is slow, and the running is effortless. We approach this tall green and red wall, and I see it's a twenty-five-foot manicured hedgerow. It reminds me of the red-tipped photinia bushes lining my backyard fence, which appear dense and impenetrable. I run my hand against the red leaves that are soft and pliable, like I'd imagine the fur of a polar bear.

"We've got to find the entrance along here. The funny thing is, the doorway hides, so you must look close to find it," explains David.

"What am I looking for?" I ask with my palms up.

"You'll know when you see it. I'll take the right and you go left. Holler, if you find it."

"O…kay." I study the hedgerow and drag my hand against the leaves, walking briskly beside it. Nothing changes; it feels uniform in every way as I travel along. The row curves inward and outward at different depths. I soon lose sight of David. After what feels like forever, I feel a bump in the leaves. I stop and run my hand, again, across the hedgerow. It's a seam that goes all the way up to the top. Cupping my hands around my mouth, I yell for David and wait for a response. Nothing. I reach inside my pocket and somehow pull out a coin. I place it on the ground to mark the seam and bound after David. The wall is like a green and red blur as I streak to find him. A small figure appears in the distance. We close the gap quickly.

"Did you find it?" he asks.

"Yeah, it's back here."

"Show me."

We sprint along the wall. Running, I glance at the ground and watch for my coin, and I stop when I see it. "It's right here. There's a seam running all the way up."

David places his hands onto the wall of leaves and feels. "There's nothing here."

"What? I know it's there." I put my hand against the wall, searching for the seam. It's gone.

"There's a wrinkle I forgot to explain. Once you find the door, stay there, and just holler until I meet you. You can even put your hand on it if it makes you feel better. Don't leave. The door will remain, but if you go, it believes it's free to move again."

"How 'bout we jump over? It's not that tall."

David scratches the back of his neck. "Ah … I wouldn't. You don't know what might be waiting for you up there."

"What do you mean?"

"Let's just say there may be nothing, but there might be something. And there's no guarantee it's always nice."

"Oh, thanks for the warning." I'm a little more nervous about this place. Before the Snake Dude had terrorized my dreams this summer, I hadn't been afraid in dreams—especially when David was with me.

"Let's try again, and this time, if either of us finds anything, we wait by the door and call to the other one."

"I did, but you didn't come," I say.

"I heard you."

"Can you give a courtesy yell or something?" I ask, in an exasperated voice.

"You know what? Why don't you and I go this way, and I go that way?" His face reveals a smirking quality.

"I'm not sure I follow."

"Just have to multiply myself. I thought about it earlier, but I didn't want to big-time you."

"I've never seen you do that."

"Done it several times before; you just never knew. All these years together, you've only been interested in talking under the tree. It's only recently that you've shown any interest in exploring. Multiplying is a way to cover ground quickly. Picture's worth a thousand." David clasps his hands as if to pray and bows his head. His face relaxes and becomes blurry for a moment, and then a second, David steps out away from him.

"Wow," I say, and place a hand to my mouth.

The new David speaks, "Much more efficient than solo. I'll teach you sometime."

"Which of you is the original David?"

"We both are," says the Davids in unison.

"Can I shake hands with Dave One and Dave Two?"

They look at each other and shrug. I guess they didn't get my joke because they stepped forward, and each shakes my hand.

Dave Two interlocks his fingers with mine; his grip's strong but comfortable. "We'll go this way. I've got a good feeling." He points opposite direction from the way we came.

Dave One points the other direction. "I'll search this way. If I see something, I'll send an internal memo."

Dave Two nods, and then we're running along the hedgerow. I show Dave Two, using my hand, how I feel for the seam as I drag it through the leaves. He runs beside me, my other hand still in his grip. Glancing at me and the wall as we bound along, he is thoroughly enjoying our search.

Sometime later, I find the seam again and stop.

"Put your hand on it," says Dave Two. He lets go of my hand and stands off to the side.

Again, he clasps his hands in front of himself and bows his head. A few seconds pass, and Dave One appears beside him.

"You found it, eh? Good," says Dave One. He assumes the same position beside Dave Two. They look like two praying bookends. The shimmer thing happens again, and there's one David.

He raises his head. "Cool, huh?"

"Very."

"You know, your mother is the one who taught me. She was *really* good at it."

This information hits me with a mix of emotions: happiness we have this connection together with my mother, sadness she is not here to teach me, and jealousy she spent time with David in a way I never will. I say nothing and continue to stand there with my hand on the stupid seam.

"Let's get this door open." He steps forward and places his hand over mine. I feel a tingle. He bows his head again and says, "Concentrate with your mind. Imagine the seam separating and the door opening."

I focus my thoughts and visualize the wall ripping. Nothing happens. "It's not working."

"We need to do this together. Take my hand." He smiles. "Try again."

I grab his hand and we concentrate together. Soon, I hear a tearing sound, the seam separates, and the entire wall curves inward enough to allow entry. I move to step inside, and David's arm shoots out in front, barring my way.

"Whoa there … Cowgirl. You don't just step into there."

"Why? What's wrong?" I ask.

"In your neighborhood, do you just knock on someone's door and enter when it opens?" He's smiling, but his tone is admonishing.

"Well … no."

"Don't you ask permission first?"

"Oh, okay." I speak to the tear in the hedgerow, "Hello, can we come in?"

We wait.

"No one there. I guess we go in?" I ask.

David stops me again. "When a door opens by itself, do you just barge on in?" He doesn't give me a chance to answer. "Nope, you carefully look where you step and be ready for anything."

"Okay, John Wayne. Lead the wagon train." I extend my hand to offer him first access.

David takes small steps to the entrance and sticks his head in, turning it from left to right. He disappears for a moment and then comes back. "Everything's cool. Come on."

I follow him through the doorway, and it's full of grays and shadows— a hallway about ten feet wide. The walls are all hedgerows. David leads me to the right, and we travel along the wall. We run into perpendicular greenery going to the left. David follows the wall to his right and makes several turns.

"This is a maze, right?"

"Amazing perception," he says with sarcasm. "Yep, you figured it out." He grins.

"Where does it go?"

"It's different every time. Keep a wall to your right and you'll always solve a maze."

We move through the hedgerow hallways for what seems like a long time, weaving around dead ends, and all the while, keeping the wall to our right the whole way.

"Why don't you do your multiple personality thingy, and we figure it out quicker?"

"Nope. Not in this maze. If I lose track of my selves, then I become fractured. I can't risk that, or I'll never get out. Besides, there is only one right side of the wall. We'll get there."

We round another corner. It's dark ahead. The hallways remain empty until the shadow of something moves. Footsteps pound the grass within the darkness.

"What is that?" I shout.

"Well?" David looks at me.

"Well, what?"

"What are you going to do?" He looks at me with a question mark on his face.

"Why are you looking at *me*?"

"I think you know," he whispers.

A huge mass bolts out of the shadows, running on all fours. Snarling, it roars as it closes the gap. When it enters the light, I see it's a massive grizzly bear. Scared stiff, I'm unable to move.

"Are you going to do something?" David yells at me.

"What? WHAT?" I say, unable to take my eyes off the bear.

The bear gets within ten feet of me and puts on the brakes. It stops in front of me. Its mouth is open with long, sharp teeth festooning its grimace. But the eyes—the eyes don't match the face. They're sad and frightened—not angry at all. It roars again. Hot breath on my face, its maw is only a foot away from my head. This thing is so huge it could bite my head off with one well-placed chomp.

"LEAVE," the bear roars in a clear, deep voice.

I'm full of fear and confusion, but I stand my ground.

"LEAVE," it commands again.

"Why do you want me to go?" I ask.

The bear sighs and sits, still looking at me with those sad eyes but says nothing. It turns its head slightly and gazes for a moment at David, then back to me.

"Do you know what you want to do?" David asks. I see him looking at me from the corner of my eye.

"I want to continue exploring," I say.

"Then tell her."

I look at the bear and say, "Please, let us pass."

The bear drops its head and turns to the shadows. "You don't understand," it mutters as it lumbers down the hallway.

"Wait. What don't I understand?" The bear doesn't answer and disappears into the darkness.

"Nicely done." David claps. "I was afraid you were going to screw that up."

David's smile fills me with rage. "You're about as helpful as a toilet paper umbrella in a hurricane," I yell at him. "Stop talking in code, and stop being so damn vague."

David continues to grin. "Feisty ... Meow." He claws at the air in fake mockery. "You handled it perfectly. Why didn't you do that to the Dark Dreamer? I told you, you have the power."

His praise and unblinking encouragement make me lose my anger. "Is that what I'm supposed to do? I couldn't move."

"Yes, but your will was firm. That's how you deal with difficult situations. Be scared but be a rock. Don't ever waver."

"LUCE." I hear my father's voice.

"Dad?"

"LUCINDA."

~ ~ ~

I opened my eyes. My father stood over me, jostled my shoulder, and then patted my face.

"LUCE. Wake up. Are you all right?"

"Sure ... just lost in a dream."

"It's two o'clock on a Saturday afternoon. You're dreaming your whole day away."

"Two? I never sleep that long."

"I had to go into the office this morning, but I didn't expect to come home and find you still in bed." I hated my dad's worried look. "You scared me. I've been shaking you for over a minute, and you didn't respond. You looked dead to the world."

I thought I saw tears standing in his eyes. "Sorry. Dad ... I'm okay." I sat up in bed. "Why're you upset?" I could count the number of times, on one hand, my dad cried in front of me.

Dad turned slightly and covered his eyes with a hand. "Oh, dear God ... it's happening again."

6 – A CROSSROADS

"What's wrong?" I asked.

Dad wouldn't answer. Maybe he was waiting until his voice didn't crack and could compose himself. He turned away and wiped his face on his sleeve and sniffed. He turned back and looked at me with sad, painful eyes.

"This is how things began with your mother," he said.

"Dad, tell me."

He just stared, focusing on nothing. Fat tears rolled down his cheeks and splashed on my hands. His upper lip quivered as he started to speak but stopped.

"TALK TO ME," I yelled.

He flinched. "Now, Luce—"

"Don't shut me out anymore. You say this is how Mom died. Explain her to me. If I understand what happened, maybe I won't end up the same way." Now it was my turn to break down as I dipped my head and dropped my own tears into my lap.

Dad remained silent.

I threw my head back. He stared at the floor. I wanted to say something but couldn't. He looked up, and we locked eyes. "Dad, sometimes I feel like I'm losing my mind. It scares me, and I feel you don't care enough to tell me what I need to know."

"Sweetheart, I …." He looked away and squinted, his brow furrowed like he was reliving a memory. Then, as if realizing the memory replayed itself more vivid to the dark screen of his mind, he opened his eyes again and sat on my bed. "I hoped I could protect you from this. You and your mom are so alike in all the right ways. You're both smart, funny, beautiful. But … you're alike in many other ways, too." He took a deep breath and sighed. I was glued to my spot, leaning into the conversation to absorb every word. "Her dreams became real to her. She would sometimes have nightmares where she'd wake the whole house with her screams. Other times, she'd say the same thing you just said—that she became lost there. When she began sleeping all the time, we argued about how she couldn't sleep all day and had to make time for her family. She said she never slept—that she was awake, all the time, especially when she was asleep. She was sorry, but she had to do something—had to help someone."

"Help who?" I blurted.

Dad hesitated a moment. "This is all such horrible déjà vu. I can't take it."

"Dad, she had to help who?"

"What?" His head snapped back to me, and then he realized my question. "I don't know who it was. She never said."

Silence again. I kicked myself for interrupting his stream of consciousness. My greed for knowledge had pulled him from his trance, and now he clammed up. He held something back—had to be.

"Luce, somehow you've got to stop these dreams. They're going to kill you … just like they did your mother."

"How do I stop? It's like telling me to quit breathing. It's automatic."

Dad's face fell further. "Can I get you some help?"

"What kind?"

"Someone … like a psychologist, maybe?"

"A shrink? You want me to see a shrink? You think I'm crazy?"

"I didn't say that." He held his hands up as if to stop me. "Maybe if you talk to someone, it might help you analyze it. Get control of your dreams."

"Sure, Father. Do whatever you think is best. Because … you know what's best. You ALWAYS know what's best," I said, all prim and proper.

Ignoring my sarcasm, "Okay … I'll see what I can do."

"Yeah, you do that. I'm going back to bed."

"What? No, you're not."

"Sorry, you interrupted a dream. I was going somewhere when you pulled me out. There's something I gotta do—someone I gotta help."

The barb had the desired effect, and Dad lumbered out of my room.

~ ~ ~

After school, I took the bus from an intersection about a mile from the house and away from where any of my friends hung out. I found the bus schedule online and got the necessary transfer information. Making another appointment with Dr. Rami was a no-brainer as he was the only other person who had the information I wanted.

The doctor came to the waiting room to personally usher me back. He wore tan slacks and a dark blue dress shirt with his glasses tucked into his front pocket. His smile flashed several teeth.

"Ah ... Lucinda, I'm so glad you rescheduled with me. I was worried I had somehow scared you off last time."

"Oh, I wasn't scared. I had some, ah, issues to take care of at home."

"I bet you did and still do." The doctor held the door open.

He led me into his office and offered me a chair while he sat in the other. I sank into the seat. Its comfort beguiling, I found myself relaxed immediately.

"Doctor, I need to talk to you about my mother."

"Sure ... of course. Go ahead."

I explained to him what Dad had told me and about sleeping late on Saturday. He sat quietly with his head leaned against his fist and clicked absentmindedly a red pen held in his other hand.

"Lucinda, some of what your father says is correct. She was awake— always. When you enter a lucid dream, you are never asleep. Her body may have been resting, but her mind was conscious. Like I told you before, she was experiencing another reality."

"Said she was trying to help someone. Do you know who?"

"Yes, and you know him, too."

"David, right?"

"It was David, but there was someone or something else as well. I never got more out of her on that issue, but I know it was an obsession she couldn't shake near the end."

Silence.

The doctor spoke again, "You need to be careful where you travel. Unforeseen dangers come when you leave here."

"Leave here?"

"Yes, you're not entirely *here* and you're not entirely *there*. You're tethered to *here* like an astronaut on a spacewalk. You must understand that when you lucid dream in the advanced stages of that you're capable, you come to a crossroads. The two roads are the Explicate and Implicate Order, as Dr. Bohm would say. The road of the Explicate Order is what we all travel upon. It's this reality, this substance." He waves his hands to indicate where we were. "*Here* is represented as time with a past, present, and future. Space is unfolded as we comprehend it."

I was recording every word to replay it back to myself later.

"When you lucid dream, you're turning off the Explicate Road and onto the road of the Implicate. The Implicate represents the infinite. The whole of the entire universe is enfolded within itself and everything else. Time is no longer a prevailing force. When you draw near to this crossroads, and you make that turn down the road of the Implicate, be aware. If you stray too far, you may be unable to get back to the road of the Explicate, which leads back to this reality. You become essentially … lost."

"Is that what happened to my mother?"

"Yes, I believe so." The doctor grimaced and studied his pen as he clicked it.

"Is there anything I should do to avoid becoming lost?"

He stared. "That's left to be determined. I'm not sure if I can help. Just being honest. I only saw you for one session, which was eye-opening, to say the least, but I would need to see you more often to unravel this Gordian knot."

I didn't know what I thought of this. "Okay, then begin," I said.

"Let's try a visualization experiment," he suggested.

"Sure. Do you want me here or on the couch?"

"Wherever you feel most comfortable." The doctor shrugged.

I thought about Maggie and her vampire/perv comments. "The chair is fine."

"As you wish. Now, close your eyes." He gave me time to comply. "Take twenty deep breaths."

He counted softly with each breath and led me through several relaxation techniques until I floated.

"Clear your mind. Wipe it clean. You should see nothing. Only the black screen you're viewing. Now, picture yourself in a meadow, and in the distance, there's a forest. Walk toward the trees and tell me what you see."

"I see the forest ahead of me," I said. Everything was lush and vibrant. Dr. Rami's voice was a whisper in the back of my mind. If I wanted to, I could have turned him off altogether.

"Good, now walk into the forest and through it, telling me what you see."

"I'm approaching the edge of it." The tall trees blotted out the sky. Inside, it was dark and foreboding.

"Enter the forest," he politely commanded.

"I don't think I want to."

"You're safe. There's nothing to worry about. Go into the forest and describe it."

"I smell pine needles. I hear the sounds of birds." The wind blew through the trees and swirled its way among the trunks ahead of me to the right. "Oh, that's cool."

"What?" asked the doctor.

"I see a black and white bird flying around me in circles. It wants my attention."

"Follow the bird, Lucinda. When you see something, tell me."

After a few moments, I said, "There's a break in the forest and a clearing ahead. I'm walking toward it. The forest is behind me, and ahead I see a rock wall like the side of a mountain. The bird is leading me to it."

"Okay, good. Tell me what the bird is doing?" whispered Dr. Rami.

"There's a cave and the bird's flying into it. I'm walking up. I'm just inside the cave. It's pitch black. I … I don't want to go any farther."

"Visualize a source of light, Lucinda. Take control of your vision."

"I have a flashlight, now. It's bright enough to see where I'm going."

"Good … good. Remember you are safe, here, in my office," he whispered to my subconscious.

"I'm walking deeper into the cave. It's just a straight tunnel ahead. The bird is flying back and forth ahead of me." It opens into a bigger cavern, now. It's huge. Immense formations glistened, wet. "I hear water dripping."

"Head toward the water."

Approaching the cave's column formations ahead of me, I saw they stood in a pool of water spreading out against this whole end of the cave. "I see a pool of water."

"Go to the pool. Look into it and tell me what's there."

"All I'm seeing is water, but there's nothing. Only my reflection."

"Look hard. Stare into the pool. Clear your mind and let the images come to you. Gaze into your reflection."

~ ~ ~

I stare into my own eyes for a long time. My face seems to be changing. My reflection doesn't quite look like me. It's morphing into someone else. Mom's face replaces mine. She's frowning at me and mouthing something. I can't hear what she's saying but only see her lips move. She's saying it with more emphasis, and although I don't hear the words, she repeats them.

"Mom… MOM! What?" Great, I get the chance to talk to my mother for the first time in eight years, and I can't read her lips.

Once I calm myself, I understand the main word.

She's saying, "RUN."

7 - REFLECTIONS

Mom looks behind her like something is coming.

"What?" I scream at her image and drop to my knees, getting my face closer to hers. It's like yelling at a television. It must reflect a previous time. She can't hear me. I'm talking to a shadow—a figment of my own hopeful imagination. I concentrate, and now, I hear her voice. The funny thing is, she acts as if she hears me.

"Luce … LUCE?" she calls for me, and this time I hear her.

"I'm here, Mama." My tears drip onto her reflection, and the ripples distort her image. I wipe new tears with my sleeve to prevent more from falling.

"Run … RUN!" she shouts.

"Who's chasing you?"

"Not me … YOU. RUN."

"I don't understand."

She's looking behind her again. "Luce, get out of there."

A wave of panic washes over me. My mother's face morphs again, and for a second, it's David. Now it's my father. I've seen this before. I think of saying, "Auntie Em," when the image of my father disappears, the pool reflects nothing—not even me. Something's dark way off in the distance. It's getting bigger. It's black-on-black as the pool of water is murky, and I can't really tell. Then I see its eyes glowing yellow and malicious. Its mouth opens, and the teeth are wicked. It must be the Snake Dude. I continue to kneel, mesmerized, until I realize it's not a reflection. The surface of the water breaks as a horrible face shoots up to mine. It happens so fast. Even though I flinch and move away from the surface, it turns its jaws to the side, and its mouth clamps down on either side of my face. The pressure of the bite is intense. It feels like my head is in a vise. The pain is excruciating. The monster thrashes its head, and my entire body shakes in the air.

Next, it pulls me into the ice-cold water. The visual shock and the temperature make it hard to breathe. All I see is the inside of its mouth, and it smells of death like a dead animal gives off when you find it squished on the side of the road. The water seeps in from the sides of its mouth. I reach up, dig my hands inside its lips, and attempt to pry it off my face. The monster continues to thrash me about like a ragdoll. I scream for Dr. Rami to pull me out of the dream, but no sound comes. I don't hear his voice anymore.

A rage builds within me as I struggle to rip this thing off. I'm staring down its throat; the bad breath makes me nauseous, and frankly, it's pissing me off. The anger burns, and at that moment, I hock a loogie and spit it down the monster's throat. It gags a little, and for some reason, the absurdity of it makes me laugh. I hear my laughter echo in its maw. Claws dig into my shoulders, and it coils around me, squeezing. This may sound gross, but I suck in every bit of mucus from my sinuses into my mouth and shoot another load of snot down its throat. I visualize it like acid, and the Snake Dude chokes on my little gift. I imagine it burning and destroying flesh all the way down, causing unbearable pain. The monster struggles to maintain its hold on me. Next, I projectile vomit down its throat, pumping gallons of caustic nastiness into it. It triggers a gag reflex, and it wants to release me. Uncoiling itself, it releases my face and pushes away. I break to the surface, struggling to swim to the edge. The cave floor becomes slick as I'm soaked. I slide away from the pool. Behind me, the water whips from the Snake Dude's thrashing, and painful roars erupt. My body shakes from shock and feels sluggish like running through a vat of Jell-O. The monster sounds like it's getting closer. I don't want to turn around and look at it for fear it may paralyze my will to flee.

I see my flashlight on the floor ahead, and I pick it up. The black and white bird flits back and forth in front of me to get my attention. It cries and hurries toward an opening behind me, away from where I entered. The bird wants me to follow.

"You're done. When I catch you, you're going to beg me to end your miserable life," hisses a voice behind me.

This snaps me out of my stupor, and I move with more immediacy. I follow the bird into a new part of the cave. The floor is gooey. A murmur of a thousand little ticks and chirps fills the ceiling of the cavern. Bats. It gives me an idea, and I imagine I, too, am a bat. My body shrinks, and my wings flap upward as my flashlight crashes to the floor. I find a formation and grip it with my feet and wings, peering around it to watch the opening. The snake monster bursts into the cavern and roars. It slithers with its head high over the ground. It could look me in the eye if I stand there with it. Two small arms near its head, claw at the air as it moves. Looking like a strange T. rex, it slinks, roaring through the cavern searching for me.

"Where are you, my dear? I am unable to find you. It would be so nice to slowly rend you to pieces," it hisses.

I'm frozen with fear. My heart beats so hard, I'm sure the thing hears it. My grip fails on the slick stalactite, and I slowly start to fall. From behind me, the bird appears. It dive-bombs the monster and pecks its head as it flies by. The monster is too slow to catch it, and its little arms are too short to grasp it.

"You ... I'll use your skull to pick her meat from my teeth when I get a hold of you," says the snake, as it becomes more enraged.

The bird continues its attack until it chases the monster away. My muscles ache, and I begin to tremble with exhaustion while maintaining my hold on the stalactite. The roars of the monster become dim. Letting go, I fall and flutter my way toward the floor near my flashlight and imagine myself returning to human form. I land with both feet. Turning my head, I listen for the monster. Nothing. The bird returns and helps lead me out.

The bright sunlight blinds me, for a moment, as I emerge from the cave. I shield my eyes and squint while I trudge across the break and back to the woods. Once inside the forest, I find a rock to rest upon and keep an eye on the cave opening in case the Snake Dude comes out. I reach up and touch my face and feel ragged holes where it bit me. Rubbing my finger over the wounds, I imagine them healing.

"Yak, yak, yak," comes a call from a branch behind me.

I swivel my body around on the rock and find the black and white bird. About the size of a small crow, it cocks its head to stare at me with one eye and repeats itself. I don't know if it's admonishing me or saying hello. I take a good look at it. It has a hood of pure black and a dazzling white belly. The wings are black with a thick white stripe, and the tail is as long as the body.

"Thank you, bird. You saved me."

"Yak, yak," it cries, still eyeing me, and hops to a branch in the sunlight. The bird then reaches its foot over its wing and scratches its head a few times. It's unafraid.

"My, my … you take yoga to do that?" This bird makes me smile.

It throws its beak up and turns the other way to check me out with its other eye. Then it does the strangest thing. It splays its tail feathers and wings out to the side, dips its head, and turns its back to the warm beams of light.

"Oh yes," I agree with the bird. "The cave was chilly. Great idea." I stand slowly, not to frighten my new friend, and find a spot in a patch of sun beside the bird. I lift my arms out from my sides and absorb the rays of light. The bird sits beside me with its eyes shut, absorbing the heat. Feeling safe with my friend next to me, I, too, close my eyes and enjoy the moment.

~ ~ ~

I woke up and stared at an empty chair inside Dr. Rami's office. I was alone and soaked with sweat. Where the hell is he? I got up from the chair, crossed toward the door, and exited the office. I made my way down the corridor, and when I entered the Waiting Room, I found the doctor with his feet kicked up, reading a magazine.

He looked up, rose to his feet, and set the magazine down. "Ah … Lucinda, I gave up trying to wake you."

"Where were you? I kept calling for you to pull me out, but you never answered."

"I was there the whole time. At first, you could hear me, but then you tuned me out."

"Why are you out here reading a magazine?" I yelled at him.

Dr. Rami produced a faint smile. "I gave up after three hours."

"What do you mean, three hours?"

"It's been five hours since you went under. I periodically checked on you for the last couple."

"Five hours? What time is it?"

"A little after nine," said Dr. Rami, looking at his watch.

"Nine? I gotta get home. Dad's going to kill me."

"Before you go, tell me what happened."

"You left me alone with a monster, that's what happened. I had to fight for my life."

"I thought I heard you say you saw Lar—your mother. Let's not overlook that."

"Yeah, she was there as a shadow. It really couldn't be her. Just some bits of imagination whipped up into a frenzy."

"Mmm … yes, this could be true, but did you think about the other possibility?"

8 – NIAGARA FALLS

Dad freaked out as expected, and then I did something I hadn't done in a while. I told a bald-faced lie about going to the library to do some research for a science paper. He asked why I didn't call. My excuse: I was so engrossed in my work that I lost track of time. He didn't comment on why I went to a library when I could have done my research online. Suspicion might have been raised for a moment, but our relationship was so open, he let it go. In addition to being shaky after my induced nightmare, I felt bad for lying to Dad.

School today would be tough, as I didn't get much sleep. Refusing to let myself sink into a deep state for obvious reasons, I tossed and turned until morning. Before I knew it, I stood at my locker with one class left, spinning the combination dial. Once I pulled the door free, I heard her.

"Lucy, had any more accidents lately?"

Looking behind me, I spied a tall, dark-haired girl wearing a twisted smile, cradling her books, and regarding me with torturous pleasure. Kimmy. Great, I go from Snake Dude to Snake Bitch. This is exactly what I didn't need today.

"Hello, Kimmy. I'm not up for dealing with you right now. Don't you have some rock to crawl under?"

Not missing a beat, Kimmy cocked her head to the side, "My … who got up and peed in your cereal this morning? I'm concerned about you and wondering if you've received the help you so *desperately* need. I can get you a nice long white coat with arms that tie in the back. It might be a fashion upgrade from what you're wearing today." She scans me from head to toe with a pouty look of consternation. I guess my jeans and t-shirt didn't fit her idea of fashion.

Her two cronies, Janice and Francine, sidled up on either side of her, wearing the same smirking grins. Kimmy and I have been at odds with each other since elementary school, when I beat her in the Spelling Bee. We were the last two left, and she couldn't spell the word 'anabolic'. She had used two **N**s. Insecure and a hater like her friends, they can't stand for any attention to come my way, and if it's the wrong kind, they become a little *too* happy. I had avoided her since the news of my freak-out session in Spanish class.

She opened her mouth and was about to say something nasty when I saw two hands span across the shoulders of Janice and Francine. Maggie's face appeared just to the left of Kimmy's head.

Glancing at the backs of each head in turn, "Hello, Larry, Moe, and Curly," said Maggie.

The color drained from their faces.

Maggie bellowed, "NIAGARA FALLS ... Slowly ... I ... turn." Maggie spun and did a wide arc around them, running up beside me. I knew what she was doing, and I tried to suppress a grin. "Step by step ... Inch by inch," she continued as she approached Kimmy. "I crept up on the jerk messing with my friend." Maggie stood in front of her and reached her hand up in front of the side of Kimmy's head and said, "First, I yanked out an earring." She pulls her hand down, pretending. The three girls' mouths opened in shock. Maggie raised both hands inches in front of Kimmy's face. "Then I clawed her eyes out." She does a mock rake to her face. Kimmy flinched. "Next, I punch her in the gut." Maggie swings a fist at Kimmy's stomach but stopped. Kimmy and her two friends backed away with their mouths agape.

"Margaret, you're crazy," said Kimmy. "What have you got against Niagara Falls?"

"NIAGARA FALLS," I shouted, and then spun in a tight circle and stopped, facing my locker. I then turned to them while saying, "Slowly ... I ... turn. Step by step ... Inch by inch." I stomped toward them and halted beside Maggie. They each did an about-face and hurried away from us. A few boys watching laughed.

Maggie turned to me. "Those girls obviously don't have older brothers."

"Or best friends with older brothers," I murmured and smirked. "You're definitely her kryptonite. She doesn't know what to do with you."

"Kryptonite? Are you suggesting she's Supergirl and I'm Mags Luthor?" She rolled her eyes in an exaggerated, crazy way.

"You crack me up."

"That's my job. Besides, three against one makes me angry. I hate it when they gang up on you."

"I can handle Kimmy, but thanks for coming to my rescue."

"Anytime. I love messing with that chick. She's such a load."

"Are you providing protective services to Theatre?" I asked.

"Sure, I'm heading that way myself."

"Oh … how convenient."

We marched ourselves to class with hurried steps with the bell looming large in the next minute or two.

Theatre One was our favorite class. I loved being able to lose myself in a character and be someone else for a while. Maggie might even have loved it more than me as she had a flair for the dramatic. We looked forward to this class each day. So far, Ms. Thatcher only had us do drama exercises, but she hinted we would soon work on a play for later this fall semester. Maggie had been trying to figure out which play it could be based on whatever topic or exercise we did. She hadn't been successful from what I could tell, but it was entertaining to watch her try.

"Ms. Thatcher, question?" asked Maggie, her hands clasped in front of her—her body slightly swaying.

"Yes, Maggie." Ms. Thatcher must have felt the latest attempt coming.

"Your last name … Is it related to the former English Prime Minister?"

"I guess there could be a connection somewhere down the line, but given our racial differences, I would assume we have very distant ties." Ms. Thatcher referred to her darker complexion.

"Oh well, I thought maybe you had some affinity for English plays … like Shakespeare?"

"Actually, I do enjoy Shakespeare very much."

"Oh … so you do." Maggie glanced my way and gave me an imperceptible wink.

"Nice try, Miss Twenty Questions," I whispered to her.

Ms. Thatcher nodded her head. "If you're asking if we're doing one of his plays, the answer is no. They're too complicated.

"Our first production should be simpler. The play we are going to do is called *Our Town,* by Thornton Wilder. It's considered one of the great American plays. The advantage is we don't need any elaborate sets because the play was designed for minimal props.

"The narrator is the Stage Manager, who'll describe the scenery and will verbally set the stage throughout the play. The characters will simply mime the objects they need." She picked up a stack of paperback books off her desk and handed them to me. "Here is a copy for each of you to familiarize yourself. Lucinda, please pass these out."

I handed them out, and when I gave Maggie hers, she gazed at the cover with reverent awe.

"Wow, our first play," she whispered and turned to the first page.

Ms. Thatcher continued, "*Our Town* takes place at the turn of the twentieth century in the fictional town of Grover's Corners, New Hampshire. It has three acts: Daily Life, Love and Marriage, and Death and Eternity. We will read and analyze each of these acts in the next three classes. Please read this at home and be ready to ask questions. Later, we'll have auditions."

We spent the rest of the class going over the first act. It was interesting how the props were all make-believe. We just needed tables, chairs, and ladders. When the closing bell sounded, we all felt relief as this was the last class of the day.

"I think I want to audition for the lead role of Emily," said Maggie.

"Maybe you should read the whole play first. The last act, 'Death and Eternity,' may be a killjoy," I warned.

Then I heard footsteps come up behind us. "Yeah, the last act is a tear-jerker."

We turn around to see the new kid, Evan. He carried himself well, tall with brown hair, and had a nice face. He seemed a little nervous as he addressed us. Girls in packs of two or more were intimidating. Glancing at something on the floor, he then looked at each of us.

"You've read this play before?" I asked.

"Naw, my older sister did this play a few years ago at my other high school. I just remember it was sad at the end. Made you appreciate life a little more."

"I'm surprised you would admit this play made you cry. Boys don't cry," said Maggie.

Evan shifted, a little uneasily, from foot to foot and looked to the door.

"She's not being mean. You'd have to know Maggie to understand that she loves to pry into the emotions of others. That's just what she does," I explained to Evan.

He perked up.

"Hey, don't be revealing my womanly secrets to the opposite sex." Maggie turned to me with a grin. "You play for our team, girl. A lady has to project an air of mystery and aloofness." She gave a playful flip of her hair. The corners of her mouth tilted up. "I am revealed and stand before you naked ... metaphorically speaking, of course."

Evan squirmed a little more after the 'naked' word was thrown out. Maggie once again was trying to manipulate the boys. She had a knack for it. I glanced at her and was about to say something.

"Don't say it," she admonished me, holding up a finger.

"What school did you come from?" I asked instead.

"Ennis."

"It's nice to meet you, Evan from Ennis," said Maggie, extending her hand.

Evan probably didn't get girls offering up handshakes in Ennis. Once again, he didn't know this was one of her patented girl-to-boy moves. He reached out and shook her hand with an amused face. I saw Maggie measure the physical contact, then she gave me an elbow to follow her lead.

"Ah ...Yes, Evan, welcome to Park North." I extended my hand as well. He was more nervous taking mine. When I got the impression he was about to serve up a dead fish, I squeezed harder to make him return the pressure.

"What's wrong? You don't shake hands with girls?" asked Maggie.

Evan rubbed the back of his neck and gave a partial laugh. "Well, come to think of it. No ... not so much. At least, I can go home and tell Mom I held hands with two different girls today."

Maggie laughed. "Good one. You're alright. Say, I got an idea. Maybe later we can form a little Theatre study group together. Read lines and stuff," said Maggie. Then she gave me a look. "Right, Luce?"

"Oh ... sure sounds great," I said.

"Okay. Sounds good." Evan glanced at his watch. "Oops ... I got to get to my ride."

"You drive?" asked Maggie.

"Uh, well, not for a couple of months, my mom is waiting for me. Nice to meet y'all." Evan exited the classroom door.

"Tsk, Tsk. Younger men. Mmm ... so rate his handshake," said Maggie.

"It was okay. Don't bring me into your games," I said.

"The grip was so-so and a little clammy, but the kid seems nice and has *real* potential. Get it. Real ... like flesh and blood," offered Maggie.

"What are you getting at?"

"I want you to have a date for the dance. You can't take your dream beau, David. Pick someone from this planet. Someone ... tangible." She reached out and grabbed my shoulders, shaking them for effect.

"Oh, I get it. This wasn't a shopping trip for you but for *me*." I feigned disgust and put my hands on my hips.

Maggie saluted me. "Thank you, Captain Obvious, you've figured out my ploy. Look, we're not suffering through another dance like last year. Let's be clear on that.

"Our sophomore year *has* to be great."

9 – PIECES OF EIGHT

Tonight, I let go of my troubles. I climbed into bed early after finishing my homework. I lay on my back and stared up at my ceiling fan as it slowly spun. I focused my dream on taking me to David. Putting his image into my mind, I willed myself to connect only to him.

~ ~ ~

A door opens, and David steps into my dream. With caution, he walks toward me, watching his feet as they kick at the dust of nothingness on the ground. In fact, there is no ground. It's as if he's projected against a white, hovering screen, and I remain there as if in a cloud from Heaven, waiting.

"Nice detail, here," he scoffs and throws his hands out to reference the imposing white.

"Sorry, I guess I focused so hard on you, I left room for nothing else."

He flashes the brightest of grins and gives me a big hug. He rarely does this, and it startles me.

"What was that for?"

"You … I am so proud of you. The closer you get to your multiple, the more you're becoming self-sufficient."

"Multiple?"

"Multiple of Eight." His face has a matter-of-fact expression.

"Eight what?"

"Eight Earth years, silly. Didn't you connect the dots and realize you saw me only after your eighth birthday?"

"Oh, I thought it had something to do with my mother's death."

"Mmm … maybe a little of that, but it was when you hit your first multiple. That's when you could see me. As you reach the second multiple, you cross deeper into your own self-awareness."

"My sixteenth birthday? What does that have to do with anything? It's not like I'm Percy Jackson or something."

"Your cycle is eight. Things will become clear once you reach the next level. Who's Percy? Is he someone you met here?"

"Oh … never mind about him. So, you're saying I'm getting more than a driver's license in a couple of weeks?"

He scrunches up his mouth and nods. Something about his reaction bothers me.

"What's going to happen?" I ask.

"Hell, if I know. But it's something. Good, bad, or ugly … we'll see." He shrugs.

"We'll see? WE'LL SEE? Why … why do you do this to me? Can't you just talk to me without all this mystery crap?" I throw my arms down straight at my sides.

"Luce … I told you before; this is *your* journey. Truly, I don't know."

"You're the same age as me, right?" I point my jaw at him.

"Give or take, yeah," says David, putting his hands in his pockets.

"What happens?"

"I'm not sure. My multiple is nine, and I don't hit my next one for a couple of years when I'm eighteen. Maybe then, I'll be strong enough to find my way out of here."

"How do you know your number is nine?"

"Remember about a year after your mom died, I disappeared for a while? I'd just turned nine and was called to another part of *here*. I took myself to the next level and transcended beyond what I thought I could be."

"What did you learn?"

David says in a sing-song voice, "That if I ever go looking for my heart's desire … I'll look no further than my own backyard. Then click my ruby red slippers three times …."

I cock my head to the side. "Stop it … I'm serious."

"Okay … Okay," laughs David. "I learned even though I was alone, I had others. What you provided me was a friendship even words are too weak to express. Whether you realize it or not, when we first met, I was in a death spiral. I'd lost my guide, your mother, and wandered around here until you found me. I needed you more than you'll ever know."

I fidget, staring away from him, then I see his face. "I had no idea. You know, you were just as important. Mom had died and I was afraid. Dad is great and all, but he was so sad that I felt guilty talking about her. I remember when you came back, you were confident and happier." I rocked back and forth on my heels. "Who are these *others* you're talking about?"

"Others?"

"Yes, others. You implied you have other friends here besides me."

"Ah ... well ... I'm not supposed to talk about them."

"Not even with your best friend?"

"Ah yeah ... I guess I kinda let that slip."

"You did, and now, you need to explain."

"Maybe now I should take you there. I'm surprised you haven't been summoned, being so close to your next multiple. Didn't you get an invite when you turned eight?"

"Invite? What invite?"

"It's hard to miss. It's a loud bell that rings only for you. You just follow the clanging, and it leads you there. I've figured out easier ways to get there since then."

"Wait ... I heard a sound like that. It was some time after my eighth birthday, like you said. I thought maybe it was the television in the den or something trying to pull me out of my dreams, so I ignored it."

"You mean you heard it and then ignored it?" David says, with a look of disbelief.

"That's what I just said. It was loud at first, but got dimmer to the point I didn't hear it anymore. Besides, it was just after we met, and you were a new friend. I couldn't talk to you about any of this."

"Oh, this is not good. Not good at all. I wish you had told me this before. I definitely need to take you now."

"First, take me to where you heard my mother's voice?"

David shook his head slowly. "Can't."

"Why not? We were heading there when my dad woke me up."

"I would like to, but it's not there anymore. After you dissipated from our dream, I continued without you. I tried to get back to where I heard her, but I could never find it. It was ... gone."

"What do you mean, *gone?*"

"It moved, or hid from me, or was just flat out gone. Sorry, Luce, maybe the others can help you."

"Where're we going?" I ask.

"The Twin Gates."

David grabs both my hands. "Close your eyes and concentrate on my words."

His hands are warm with a firm, yet gentle, grasp. I shut my eyes and instead of the suffused red color you see through your eyelids during the day, I am enveloped into a sea of vibrant blue.

"Concentrate and conjure a picture of an old-timey key. Like a skeleton key that would fit in an old door somewhere. Tell me when you get the image."

Closing my eyes tight, I focus my energy on visualizing a key. For some reason, it's not materializing in my mind's eye. I get glimpses, but it's fuzzy and poorly formed.

David, sensing my trouble, says, "Let it float up from the background. It's got a fancy curvy end. The key head is split. It's shiny and made of brass."

It works. The image of the key floats into focus and crystallizes into a bright brass key, revolving slowly to reveal itself in 3-D. "Got it."

"Is it spinning?"

"Yeah ... how did you know?"

"You got the right key," says David. "Keep that image. Hold it tight in your mind."

The key continues to turn lengthwise. The blue color surrounds it as it turns to an intense yellow and then shifts to fluorescent green. I feel no changes around me.

"We're here. The Twin Gates," says David.

The first thing I see is a huge double-wrought-iron gate with black bars going up forever. On the other side of the fence, a sprawling green and rolling hillside extends out to the horizon. I grab the bars of the gate and shake it, but it's locked tight.

"So, do we use the key we imagined to open the door?"

"Nope, that's just how we got here. The key to open the door is different." David just grins at me. "You'll see. Wait."

"For what?"

"Patience ... he'll come." David stares out across the hillside. I do the same and glance at him to check if he reacts to anything. We stand there for what seems like a long time.

"There," says David, pointing away toward the horizon. "Here he comes."

A figure, way out in the distance, looking like a speck, meanders at a snail's pace toward us. A few minutes later, I see a figure robed in black.

The hood hangs low, and his head is bowed. He's walking so painfully slow; it hurts to watch. I keep hoping he's going to pull a Willy Wonka: stop, do a somersault, and wildly jump to his feet. But I'm afraid it's not the Willy Wonka from the nineteen seventies but the freaky new one with the crazy eyes and the serial killer voice.

"Can the dude walk any faster than that? Who is he?"

"Shh, don't talk. Be quiet or he'll walk slower if you complain," whispers David, so low I have to focus on his lips to hear him.

The robed figure slowly approaches the gate, and I notice he tucks his hands together inside his sleeves out in front. The last twenty feet are excruciating as he shuffles in baby steps. My calves and feet cramp up, even though it's only a dream.

At last, the monk person reaches the gate. He's over six feet with a thick build and no facial hair. With a slight tilt of his head, he smiles at David.

"David, how good of you to return. We've missed you." It's as if he doesn't acknowledge me and will not look my way.

"I've brought a friend with me," says David, pointing.

The hooded figure refuses to look at me. "Yes, so you have."

"Hello, um … Mister … ah. My name is Lucinda." I move along the gate to get closer.

He turns to look at me with a sullen, blank face like I'm worthless. It's as if he's regarding an ant crawling along the ground.

"Yes, so it is."

It's worse than the freaky new Willy Wonka. He's Oscar the Grouch. The image of the nasty puppet flashes into my mind, wearing the trashcan lid for a hat. Monk-dude squints his eyes at me as if he smells something rank, and then turns back to David.

"Ready to enter?"

"Sure." David puts his hands together as if he's praying. His body trembles and quakes, and then he steps away from himself and turns into Dave One and Dave Two again. The gate opens, and the Daves stroll in. I try to follow through the gate, but as I attempt to cross the threshold, the gate swings and slams shut in my face.

"Hey, what gives?"

Monk-dude looks at me from the corner of his eye, trying not to acknowledge me again. Dave Two turns to me with an apologetic face. "Oh, sorry. Luce, you need to split."

"Split? You brought me here."

"No, not get lost. Split. Multiply yourself like I just did. These are the Twin Gates after all. You must traverse these grounds as a multiple entity and demonstrate you can at least split yourself into a twin to get through the door. It's kinda like potty training your dog before you let him run loose in your house. They have to make sure you're able to handle the basics."

"I don't know how to do that. No one's taught me ... and I hate the dog analogy being applied to me." I must be scowling as Dave One spears Dave Two with a look.

"I thought I showed you last time?" says Dave Two.

"You demonstrated it to me, but you never explained how." I could swear Monk-dude rolls his eyes.

"Yeah, I thought you'd practice on your own time," says Dave One.

"Who taught you?"

"Your mother, remember?" says Dave Two.

There we go. I'm pissed at him—them—all over again. The Daves seem to connect to my mom more than me, and I feel like I'm losing my cool.

"You're almost to your second multiple, and you cannot do a basic turn of a first?" says Monk-dude, serving me a condescending look.

"Sorry, I guess I'm the girl who rides the short bus in this reality," I say.

Monk-dude gives a hushed sigh.

"Hey. Why don't you have to split?" I ask.

"I already exist as a multiple in this realm," answers Claude with condescension.

Dave One pipes up, speaking to me through the iron bars between us. "Luce, I'll walk you through it. First, put your hands together like you're praying."

He waits for me to get into position.

"Close your eyes again and pretend your hands represent you. Now imagine them stuck as if they're glued together. Picture yourself pulling your hands apart, and as you do, your consciousness splits. You'll feel your body shake if you're doing it right," says Dave Two.

I do as he says and visualize myself splitting into two equal halves. I pretend my hands are glued together, and I'm ripping them. Pulling them apart, I open my eyes, but I'm still just one of me. Monk-dude, who walks as slow as a turtle covered in molasses uphill in winter, gives me another impatient look. I want to scream.

"Try again. Your body's cells do this all the time. You have to focus and visualize yourself as if you are a cell dividing itself into two equal pieces," says Dave One.

I try again and feel a slight tremor, but there's only one Luce. This goes on forever. Sweat drips off me as I struggle, with no luck.

"Focus your eyes on a point on your forehead between the eyebrows," says Monk-dude. He stares at me and almost wills me to make this work.

Sorry, Oscar, doing my best. You're such a ... freak-a-zoid. I roll my eyes back into my head and point them up and concentrate between my eyebrows. This time, I feel a quaking sensation from my palms and out along my arms. The shaking continues through my shoulders and hips, and up each leg until it meets at the center of my body. The trembling continues until I feel myself rip in two. My eyes are closed, but I sense I'm not exactly me. I'm me, but I'm more than me if that makes sense.

When I open my eyes, I see the Daves smiling at me and Monk-dude the Grouch. To my right is an exact copy of me. I remove my hands from the prayer position, and she does the same.

I finally did it. The voice echoes in my head as if I said it, but it was the other me.

No, I did it, I say. I'm Luce One, and you're Luce Two.

No, I'm Luce One, my other self says to me.

Quit arguing with me, or you ... us. We did it.

This is so weird. As the other Luce walks forward to the gate, I sense what she's seeing at the same time I'm seeing it, and I guess—well, I know—that is what she—or me—is experiencing as well.

The Twin Gates open, and we can pass through them. Monk-dude waits for me standing next to the Daves. He has a hint of a grin on his face.

"The name's Claude. Not Monk Dude, Oscar Grouch, or Freak Zoid."

Both of our consciousnesses shudder at the revelation that he hears everything we think.

"Your mind is like a sieve ... you leak thoughts all over the place. And it is the first thing we must fix."

10 – SHE'S A REAL NOWHERE GIRL

Claude guides us through the grounds and over an uncountable number of hills. His stride is long, and I/we find it difficult to keep up with him. The Daves aren't fazed by the pace. It's a strange feeling to walk with oneself. I see my own path, but I also experience a parallel trek that my other self takes at the same time. Our collective consciousness links, but we think independently. The moment I glance at her, she does the same thing. I'm not sure if I'm Luce One or Two. It doesn't matter anymore. I am now 'We'.

"Not too much farther," says a Dave.

"Where are we going?" one of me asks.

"NoWhere," says Claude.

"Huh? Where?"

"NoWhere ... but really, it's 'NowHere'," replies Claude.

"What? We're here? I don't see anything."

"It's really, NowHere, but we call it, NoWhere," says the other Dave.

Oh, our heads. Has this multiple thing scrambled our brains? "You're all talking nonsense, but I think I understand. Who's on first, Claude?"

"What?" asks Claude.

"Nope ... he's on second," we respond.

"Who?"

"Exactly what I said, Who's on first."

Claude glances back at us, his forehead knots with questions. The Daves give us lopsided smiles.

"Just wanted a little payback. You don't watch old television shows," says the me to the left.

"What's television?"

"O ... kay. Let's just quit there. What does NoWhere look like?" we ask.

"It looks like nothing until you're there," says Claude.

"Ah ... makes perfect sense. You sure you want to go *there* again?" says one of me.

"Where?" asks Claude.

"NoWhere," says a Dave and silently chuckles. One of me winks at him.

"Correct, that's where I live," says Claude.

We continue to trudge along, hill after hill. Claude stops and reaches forward to grab at something. When he connects, a ten-foot arched wooden door appears standing in the middle of a grassy countryside, with him grasping the handle. He pulls it toward him, and the door swings open to reveal only darkness on the other side.

"Close the door behind you," Claude says, as he disappears into the inky blackness.

"Ladies First," say the Daves, standing on either side of the door to let us pass.

"Such Gentlemen ... NOT," says one of us, while the other one thinks it.

The Daves shrug in unison. We pause a moment, and like when we climb the trees with David, we each put our arms into the darkness to test it. The black swallows us to our elbows. We each feel one of our wrists in a grip, and a force pulls us through a cloying gloom. We break through into a bright light. Claude stands, holding each of us by a wrist. He releases us.

"Welcome to NoWhere." He has a grim face, but we think we detect a hint of a wink to the Daves.

We look behind us and see the Daves follow, closing the door with nary a sound. We turn back to Claude and notice we stand on a dirt road leading to infinity ahead of us. There is an intersection a thousand feet farther. The roadways have scattered groups of more monk-like figures passing along them.

"How did you know where the door was?" we ask Claude.

"I counted the steps. Didn't you?"

"We didn't know we were supposed to."

"How else are you going to get here by yourself unless you count your steps?"

We don't know what to say, so we keep quiet. When we can't win an argument, we give people the quiet treatment and let them rail at us. Sooner or later, they get the hint we're not playing their game.

"Good choice," says Claude.

We forget we broadcast our thoughts too easily, and we decide to leverage our auditory gift. Once a conversation, movie, radio show, newscast, or whatever is read, heard, or seen, then we can replay it nearly word for word. We take turns playing an entire episode of an old program—complete with dialogue and sound effects. We picked an episode that was on the other day while surfing cable channels of old shows. We hope it drives whoever eavesdrops on our thoughts crazy.

Claude keeps straight on the infinite highway and moves at a steady pace. He kicks up no dust on the road as he passes. Dave One and Two do the same. However, we notice a small dust cloud kicks up as we shuffle along.

...

We each select an old television show within our minds and broadcast it loud as if shouting in our minds.

...

Claude glances back at us with another confused look but doesn't say anything. The Daves do not react.

We travel along the road for what seems like a long time. There's a building on our right. As we get closer, it reveals itself to be a wooden shack. Claude barges right through the small wooden door, followed by the Daves. We approach with caution. There's no creepy darkness—only a white hallway, so we follow our companions. Once we reach the end of the hall, a huge room opens. Monk-dudes walk with very calculated steps in all directions. We cut a direct swath through them and approach a half stadium where rows upon rows of dark-robed figures are seated. They all look down at their hands. The hoods of their cloaks obscure their faces.

We advance toward a large green circle about fifty feet in diameter in front of the group. People mill around the circle, but none cross into it.

"May I enter?" asks Claude, bowing his head.

"Enter," comes a voice from everywhere and yet no place.

Claude proceeds into the center of the circle.

The Daves also step to the edge of the circle and request permission. They bow their heads and wait. The voice tells them to enter, and they walk forward and join Claude in the circle. Repeating the process, both of us step to the green boundary.

"May we enter?" we ask. Waiting for several minutes, there's no response.

We ask again, "May. We. Enter … please?"

We look up and notice Claude and the Daves staring at us.

"Patience," the voice responds.

We watch Claude and the Daves talk to the council of monks. We cannot tell exactly to whom they speak; there is complete silence. It appears that once anyone steps inside the green circle, the conversation becomes private. We try to read Claude and the Daves' lips since we don't see any others' faces. We only pick up a few words: 'Nonsense', 'She', 'Dream', 'Snake', 'Trial', 'Lara', and 'Behind'. I know they're talking about us, but I don't know what. It's like in school when Kimmy's talking to her friends and glances our way and whispers whatever trash she spews. We know they're talking about us, and not being there to defend ourselves, really burns us. The same anger builds. It's almost at rage level, so we decide to distract our thoughts again with more of the old TV show.

The dialogue continues for several more minutes until I hear the voice.

"Enter the Collective."

Together, we step over the green circle, and a flood of voices fills our minds.

Claude waves me toward him. I stop after I stand next to the Daves and Claude. Then, as if on cue, the entire panel of robed figures snaps their heads up and all look at us. Their body language telegraphs little, but I could swear I almost heard a crack when they whipped their heads back.

"Explain yourself?" a voice bellows. Who's speaking? I don't know.

"We … we're not sure what you mean," one of us says.

Silence for several seconds. "Why are you nearly eight years late?"

We have nothing to say, so we play more of the show dialogue to hide our thoughts.

"You have put yourself in a difficult position. You approach your next multiple, and you're far behind. It's left you … vulnerable."

We're still trying to see who's speaking, but none of their mouths move, as if their thoughts are projected upon our minds. Are they talking about the nightmares?

"We're sorry. We didn't realize the bell was calling for us," we say.

"You are the first one who has been this late."

"We heard the bell but didn't understand what it meant. It got so loud it drove us nuts, so we turned it off."

"Impossible," came a voice. A monk down in front pointed at us. "You cannot turn off that invitation. You insult us by ignoring our call. It's what I would expect from the daughter of—"

"Well, excuse us for not reading the manual. No. One. Told. Us." One of us glances at a Dave and scowls.

The Daves look at each other and grimace.

"Silence. Both of you." I detect a figure in the center front row whose cowl is directed at me. The voice is female.

"Claude has explained your situation to us. We are carefully considering what to do with you," she says.

"It sounds like you consider us criminals. The dude giving me the finger over there seems to have a problem with my mother."

The silence that follows is deafening. We notice the monks turn their heads ever so slightly to look at one another.

"Your mother was a lightning rod for the Collective. This is true. Some saw immense potential while others saw her as a threat to our existence. She had a purpose, and some are disappointed with her. You being her daughter is representative of her legacy. You require greater scrutiny," the female spokesperson says.

"We're sorry if we insulted anyone by ignoring your call. It wasn't our intention. It just happened at about the same time we lost our mother."

"We understand ... but ..." The woman whose empty stare was burning a hole into me, as well as the finger-dude and the rest of the Collective, appear uneasy in their seats. "Stop that, please."

"What?"

"The noise your mind is broadcasting is very disconcerting. The three-hour tour with a ... Movie star ... the Professor and Mary-Anne. Who are these people?"

"Claude reprimanded us that he could hear our thoughts. Our mind leaked like ... what did you call it? A sieve?" We look toward Claude. He takes a deep breath. "We don't like anyone eavesdropping on us in person or through our mind. We decided since we are so leaky, we should turn the spigot on full blast and let it gush out nonsensical drivel, so you won't hear what we're thinking."

"She's a witch, I tell you," says Finger-man. His head moves ever so slightly. We stare at him, but he refuses to make eye contact.

The spokesperson, front and center, speaks. "Interesting. You have managed to cope with your inabilities quite well. You adapt. Impressive. In such a short time, you prevent all of us from reading your mind. Even you, Roman." She stared, but her lips remained frozen together.

"Send the witch away. She's too dangerous for our order to control," says Finger-man, who must be Roman.

"Yes, too dangerous. Too dangerous," bubbles up from more voices in the gallery.

It's the spokesperson again. "Too dangerous for *us* means she's too dangerous for *them*. I believe we have no choice but to train her."

11 – THE WATCH

We leave the Collective. We're surprised the experience didn't shake us from our dream. All the things they say are still rolling around in our heads. They're scared of us, they think we're a witch, and they're afraid of our mother. We're so confused. Once we get outside the shack again and on the road, the discussion begins.

"Where did that come from?" asks a Dave to Claude.

"Lara did say things as a member of the Collective. I cannot discuss them at this time."

"When will you discuss them? Seeing as they don't trust us," one of me says.

"When you're ready and not a moment sooner," responds Claude.

We sigh in unison. "Awesome. We really appreciate that. Now we're freaks inside our own dreams, and there's not a damn thing we can do about it."

"We will remedy that. I am afraid there are some things that if revealed too soon, might spoil your potential or change the path upon which the fates have set you," says Claude.

"When do we begin and what'll we learn?"

"You have already started, and you have already learned. Be patient."

"Ahhh," we growl through clenched teeth. "You and your talk of patience. Are we going to learn double-speak? 'Cause, that's all we get from any of you." We glance at the Daves and Claude in turn.

Claude chooses to keep his mouth shut.

"Good choice," one of me repeats back to him.

We travel upon the infinite road for a few moments longer and then Claude stops.

"Now, for your first lesson. To attend training, you must first know where to go." Claude kneels on the road and uses his finger to draw a symbol in the dust. First, he draws a horizontal football shape, and then an overlapping vertical oval on top of it. "Visualize this symbol while in a lucid state and you'll appear where you're supposed to be."

"It looks like a strange eyeball," we say.

"Correct ... think of it as the Third Eye. When you conjure this symbol, it will take you there. Let's try and see how you do."

We stare at the symbol on the ground to burn it into our mind. After we think we have it memorized, we close our eyes to bring it into focus. It's a little fuzzy, but we concentrate harder and make it three-dimensional. The eye comes slowly toward us until we're effectively swallowed. We open our eyes again, and we stand together in the middle of a desert. A flat, barren landscape of sand stretches out in all directions.

I realize that I am me again—just one of me, but where are David and Claude?

"Close," comes Claude's muffled voice.

"Where are you?" I ask.

"Just a little closer," David says.

"What? Closer to where?"

"Just a moment," says Claude.

I feel movement at my feet, and I look down to see two arms come through the sand and latch onto my ankles and drag me down. I'm sinking to where only my head is exposed. Letting out a final scream, my head passes underground. I expect to suffocate, but there's more inky black space, and then I land on my hands and knees on the shores of a lake. The water has no ripples, and it's as smooth as a mirror reflecting a blue, cloudless sky. I look over to see Claude and David standing.

"You could've warned me before drowning me in quicksand."

"What would be the fun in that?" asks David, grinning.

"What is this place?"

"It's 'The Watch'. This is where you need to come for training. As I said, you are way behind. You have made good progress on your own, but you approach a level that makes you dangerous. You're in between," says Claude.

"What levels are you talking about?"

Claude pauses a moment to collect his thoughts. "There are several levels of lucid consciousness. We can discuss a few of them. The first level is the Physical, which means you experience ordinary standard dreams with no order or direction. The Etheric level is where you have experiences outside of your body. Astral is where you can travel to the past. Mental is the state you're currently traipsing over. The Collective considers you dangerous because you've had no guidance. You have somehow stumbled upon the ability, yet you have no idea what you're doing."

"So, I'm like a toddler with a Uzi," I say.

"I'm sorry, I don't know what that means," says Claude.

"Pretty close, Luce," says David. "What's worse about your situation is you're firing in all directions, and someone might get hit."

Claude continues: "To attain the true Mental state means you have the power to visit the future as well as the past. It's the level a shaman or mystic reaches. This is the most dangerous state because beings at this level have the power to actualize fantasy, demons, anything. It leads you down the false road of the dream-self."

"Are you saying I'm mental?"

"That's one way to look at it," says David. "Remember when I told you about the line between your dream-self and your awake-self is blurry? Crazy people have trouble telling the difference. If you're not careful, you'll go nuts."

"Is that what happened to my mother?" I ask Claude.

"I cannot say anything more than Lara was conflicted," he answers.

"Okay, then you're saying the Snake Dude is my creation?"

"I cannot comment further about him," says Claude.

I drop my gaze down to Claude's feet, realizing I won't get any further information.

He wriggles his toes.

"Wait," I say. "I don't ever remember traveling to the Past or Future, and I don't have out-of-body experiences."

"Don't have OBEs? Are you kidding me? Look around. You think anyone can come here?" asks David, flashing his trademark grin.

"Regarding time," says Claude, "maybe you don't realize it when you are traveling through it. Or you don't remember. Who knows ... you might be all over the spectrum? Without the training, we won't know. We would be powerless to help you." He holds his hands up in a questioning pose.

"And you want to avoid getting dragged down with me," I say.

Claude raises his eyebrows, twists his mouth as if I hit upon a truth.

"Let's start," I say.

"I think you've had enough excitement for one dream. Class

dismissed." Claude claps twice like he's clapping off a light.

At that instant, I find myself flying away from the beach, over the water receding from them. I try to spin in a circle to maintain my lucid state, but I've lost it.

~ ~ ~

I thrashed about in the covers of my bed. No light came through the windows. Good, it was still night. I rolled over and saw my father staring at me. He sat in my desk chair and rolled up beside my bed. He wore a sullen expression, leaning forward with his elbows on his knees and his fingers interlocked together. Not sure if he was thinking or praying.

"Dad, what's wrong? Why are you in here?"

"What's wrong? Saturday night is what's wrong. I've been trying to wake you all day. I was this close," he held up his thumb and forefinger together, "to calling an ambulance."

Half my weekend—gone. "Dad, I don't know what to say."

"I hope whatever you're doing in there is important because I'm at a breaking point. My heart can't take this."

I didn't know what to say.

"I'll cook dinner." He slowly got to his feet and exited my room, wearing a worrisome aura of defeat.

"It won't happen again, Dad. I promise," I yelled after him.

He didn't respond, but I heard his footsteps trudging along the wood floor down the hall toward the kitchen.

12 – ALL THAT'S GLAM…

"Dad, I'm sorry about scaring you, but I'm called to my dreams. I've got to find out what happened to Mom." I sat at the kitchen table and tried my best to explain about David and where we went and why.

Uniquely unimpressed with my explanation, Dad stood over the stovetop burner and silently stirred a pot of soup. He set the spoon on a paper towel and turned to me.

"I understand how you believe you can make sense of your mother's death through your dreams. But I think it's dangerous. She's gone and there's no fixing it." His eyes had no sparkle and were deeper set.

"Aren't you listening to me? In my dreams, I've seen her. She's alive in there somehow. She's trying to contact me. Every time I get close, something interrupts me or sends me in another direction."

"Luce, I don't want to argue with you about this. If she were alive in some other realm of consciousness, then wouldn't she have contacted me?"

"Oh, I get it. Since your science brain can't understand it, it's all BS to you. I know it's hard to believe, but it's real. It's as real *there* as it is *here*."

"What?" His face is scrunched up in confusion. "It's as real as reality? Do you know how stupid that sounds?"

"Yeah … even if you don't understand it, you're going to have to believe me," I said.

I caught him rolling his eyes, and then he stared at the pot of soup.

We sat down together and consumed our late dinner in silence. After finishing his soup, he raised his head and looked at me.

"I do have something for you." He got up and walked over to the cabinets. Reaching into one, he pulled out a plastic bag with what appeared to be a box inside it. "I haven't wrapped it, but I thought you might like it now. Consider it an early birthday present."

He set it on the table in front of me. I pulled the box out, and when I saw the familiar apple-with-a-bite-out-of-it logo, I tore into it as if I were a ten-year-old at Christmas. It was the smartphone I hoped for. The latest and greatest version.

"Dad … this is awesome." I clutched it to my chest with both hands.

"Our phones were getting so old, I thought we needed an upgrade. You have a data plan with unlimited everything."

I could hardly contain my joy and squealed uncontrollably for several minutes. Dad knew he had struck a chord with me. My old phone was in shambles. It had tape holding things together like some nerd with broken glasses. Now, I was techno chic.

I hugged my dad and quickly helped him clean the kitchen, so I could go set up my phone. Getting all the apps I thought necessary, I called Maggie to make sure I hadn't missed anything. The phone kept me distracted from the nagging questions I had about Mom, David, Claude, and my upcoming training. I played these thoughts through my mind a few times but couldn't bring myself to go there in my dreams tonight. My brain needed time to collect itself and come up with a plan.

Sunday afternoon, Maggie arrived at my house to take me to the mall.

"You got to bling that thing up before you take it to school," said Maggie, nodding toward my phone as I put it in my purse.

"Yeah, maybe a little … a case or something to protect it," I said.

"It needs rhinestones."

"What is your obsession with glittery things?" I mused.

"Honey, I'm so glam, I sweat glitter. Anything I carry … *has* to match." Maggie slid her head from side to side, Egyptian style, and then snapped her fingers with both hands to make her point.

The mall was busy. Multiple levels all bustled with activity. Maggie managed to find some new earrings even more eye-catching and dangly than her usual selections. I marveled at how her earlobes took the punishment. She helped me find a case that suited my style, but with enough glam to match Maggie's minimum glitter requirement to be cool. We grabbed some takeout and settled in the Food Court to talk.

"What about him?" asked Maggie, her eyes pointing at a guy walking by, glancing our way.

"Huh? What do you mean?"

"Is he the type of guy you'd go with to Homecoming?"

"I don't know. He looks all right, but I don't know him."

"Oh ... I'll take care of that." Maggie started to get up from the table.

I put my hand out. "No ... please don't."

"Luce, I'm going to find you a date if it kills me, you, or the entire student body. We talked about how this year was going to be great. The first major dance is Homecoming, so if you can't find a date, I need to step in."

"What makes you think I can't? I'm just picky, is all."

"Yeah," said Maggie, drawing the word out. "You know, when it comes to everything else, you're fearless. But a dance or interacting with boys, and you're a noodle—all soggy and blah. Why won't you let me help you?"

I sighed. "Maggie, I love you. You're my best friend, but some things I have to figure out for myself—my way." Luce couldn't believe she was quoting David.

Maggie cocked her head to the side and took a long draw from her drink. "Fine. I hear ya, but since I'm your best friend, I'm not giving up on you."

"I don't expect you to. Keep pushing me. Motivate me. Whatever. But understand that I have to make the final move for myself."

"Okay." Maggie's eyes tracked a new target passing behind me. "What about him?"

I glanced to the side and caught a glimpse of a clean-cut guy in frayed jeans and a T-shirt, looking at our table. "He's cute. Not my type, though."

"Not for you ... practice for me. Watch and learn while I work my magic." Maggie set her cup down and slowly rose from her seat. She sauntered past the guy without the slightest hint of acknowledgment. Hooked like a fish, her catch followed.

"Amazing," I mumbled.

Settling in for a commercial break from the Maggie Show, I finished my sandwich and surfed for more apps to download. After a while, I noticed a familiar face that surprised me. It was Dr. Rami with a food tray, making his way in front of me.

"Dr. Rami," I said, loud enough over the din of the crowd around me.

His head swung around, and he raised his chin in acknowledgment. He adjusted his trajectory and landed at my table.

"Lucinda, how are things with you?" His glasses were in his pocket, and his wavy hair was tousled and fussier than normal.

She assumed that this was the weekend look.

"May I sit for a moment?" he asked.

"Sure." I pointed at the empty chair beside me.

He sat down and took a bite of his burger. He chewed it thoughtfully. I could tell he was compiling a question or comment, so I remained silent and watched him.

He put the burger down. "I'm glad I ran into you. I've been giving our last session some thought, and I realized you were upset. And rightfully so. What happened was something … I hadn't quite experienced before and wasn't sure of the best way to discuss. It's not an appropriate excuse, but it is all I have. I hope you will consider scheduling another office visit. You're a special girl. You have a unique gift that I want to understand better."

Not sure how to respond, I threw out, "That's okay, I've been freaking out a lot of people these days."

"Which is why I want to discuss things further with you. I have a real fear for you if we leave this untreated."

"What do you mean?"

"It was a simple visualization exercise I've done thousands of times, but it went completely wrong. You went in so deep and so fast that I lost control of you to the point you were unresponsive. It was like you were in a coma. Frankly, it … how did you say it? … freaked me out. I wasn't sure what to do, so I left my office to think when you found me. I'm sorry for my nonchalant attitude, but I didn't want to admit I wasn't in control. I had not seen anything like that since … your mother."

"She's alive somewhere," I blurted.

The doctor's mouth dropped open for a second. "Lucinda, what makes you think that?"

"Not physically, but her spirit is alive. I've gotten so close to her at times, and it's more than just a dream."

The doctor smiled a little. "Yes, I'm sure it feels that way."

"It is more than just a feeling. I wish I could explain it, but it's real."

"Lucinda, I'm afraid the fabric that makes up your reality is tearing itself apart. You're going through some profound changes here, and as I said, I'm worried for you. Call my office next week and set up an appointment. We need to discuss this."

Stunned, I got the impression he thought I was a danger to myself or maybe even others. I couldn't tell if I wanted to talk to him or run away.

Maggie glided up and sat. She took another bite of her sandwich and reached a slurping end to her drink while staring at Dr. Rami. He looked at her and wrinkled his nose at the noise she made.

"It's him?" she asked, not taking her eyes off Dr. Rami. "Don't know if bringin' this dude would work." She leaned back in the chair and soaked in the scene. It was difficult to gauge whether she was angry with me, or Dr. Rami, or so intensely curious she became catatonic. She didn't utter another word and then picked up her phone.

"It was nice to see you again. I'll leave you to your company." Dr. Rami stood from the table and carried his tray away.

Once gone, Maggie slapped her phone down and shot forward in her chair. "Are you kidding me? Are. You. Kidding. Me?"

"It's not what you think. He walked by, and I waved him over. It's no big deal." I couldn't tell her what Dr. Rami and I talked about because I'd promised her not to see him again.

"How many times did he walk past until you noticed? The dude has an agenda. I don't know whether it's perv-driven or what, but something's wrong with that dude."

"Maggie, stop."

"I'm deadly serious. I get the wrong kind of vibes from him. He's stalking you."

13 – LIGHT MY WAY

Monday fell like a lone domino. Nothing spectacular happened, but it gave me a new week to get ahead on my studies. I'd been falling behind due to my sleep issues and needed to kick it up a notch or risk getting a **B** in something. Maggie was no solace to my paranoia because she didn't understand my addiction. I've had straight **A**s since the third grade, and I'll be damned if Snake Dude, David, Claude, or whoever was going to take my winning streak from me. Here's where I've used my OCD to my advantage to attain my goals. I couldn't be less than perfect. It has been a lot of pressure that I've heaped on myself, but it kept me grounded.

My record would have been perfect except for Second Grade Language Arts. I got caught forging my reading log and received my first **B**. Regardless, I'm grateful to that teacher because she woke me up to the perils of dishonesty by teaching it's better to get an honest **B** rather than a dishonest **A**. Even though I did the reading, I didn't want to bother my dad with signing stuff since Mom was having trouble, or maybe I wanted to rebel a bit. I'm not sure which. I remember being pissed off at everybody. The personal rule I learned from Maggie was that if you're going to forge your father's signature, you must commit to forging all his signatures. Even today, though Maggie receives legitimate excuse notes from her parents, she always re-does them in her version of their handwriting to maintain consistency.

My birthday was this week. September 27th was a day to look forward to and yet, now a date to dread. Although I would be eligible to take my driver's test and get my license, I knew sixteen was my multiple. I didn't know what to expect from my other reality. Would my nightmares get more intense, or would I be able to control them? Tonight, I will enter training for the first time. I had no expectations about what would occur, but there were doubts. Since being eight years late for training, I needed to cover ground as quickly as possible. But the reality of my mind was unpredictable.

School went mercifully quick until Theatre. That's when everything crawled to a halt.

"Evan, you and Lucinda read the lead roles of Emily and George today," said Ms. Thatcher. "You'll audition officially in a couple of weeks, but I want to get a sense of chemistry between different people to see who might work well together."

I looked toward Evan. He seemed pleased, with a faint hint of a grin. I had expected him to be as anxious as I felt. I'm so clunky with boys.

"Go get him, Madame Curie," whispered Maggie in my ear and gave me an encouraging shove.

I gave her a *stop-that* look and strode to the front of the class to take my place with Evan. Ms. Thatcher directed us to a scene in the play, *Our Town*. It was strange to pretend to be on a date in a drug store, drinking imaginary shakes. I was Emily and acting jealous while saying these words of suppressed adoration to Evan, in the character of George, saying similar words to me. It was a scene from the happy second act: "Love and Marriage". I tried to lose myself in Emily's character, but I kept getting lost in Evan's eyes. Somehow, I hadn't noticed he had the biggest, brightest, and bluest eyes of any guy I could remember. He was confident and secure in his role, carrying himself well. My performance was less than stellar as I was off balance and unable to concentrate. We finished the scene and looked toward Ms. Thatcher.

"Very nice, you two. Evan, you had consistent ease to your delivery that made your scene come off smoothly."

Evan beamed at me and then Ms. Thatcher. "Thanks," he said.

"Lucinda, you showed a vulnerability in your performance I hadn't seen before. Incredibly good. Bring more of that when you read this character again."

Being a little embarrassed, I dipped my chin and said, "Thank you."

This was the way the rest of the class went. Ms. Thatcher picked different people to read scenes together. Our class had a lot of personalities, so it appeared wise to look at everybody with a different eye. She could mix and match us to make sure we complemented each other, depending on what roles she might envision for us.

Class ended, and Maggie came over. "Looks like we know who's playing the lead roles. You looked like you were melting for Evan … I mean George." She gave a look that suggested she thought she knew more. I hated it when people analyzed me so easily. Was I that transparent? But that's how best friends are; they read each other. Maggie didn't know when to shut up, so I got nervous about what she might say in front of Evan. I could see him approaching us from the corner of my eye, but I refused to look until he was in front of me. Then I was forced to talk to him.

"Hey."

"Hi."

Evan glanced at the floor, then gazed at me with those blue eyes. "Pretty cool scene we read. Ms. Thatcher's right. You were completely into character. How'd you do that? You didn't look at the script one time."

"I dunno. I just have a knack for memorizing things," I said.

Maggie piped up. "Oh, she's being modest. My friend, Luce, here is a genius … she's wicked smart," she said, using her best Boston accent. "She reads things once, and it's locked in." Maggie twisted an imaginary key to the side of her head and then pretended to drop it into her blouse.

Evan kept grinning and regarded me with curious glances.

"Your portrayal was inspired. I thought you were great," I said to Evan.

"Thanks." Evan, now embarrassed, looked down a moment and kicked his foot at the floor. "You think we have a shot at getting cast as these characters? It would be awesome."

"More than awesome, it would be epic," chimed in Maggie, smirking.

"Okay." I gave her another look to stop.

"What?" said Maggie, incredulous, but her eyes still shone. She knew what she was doing. "Say, Evan … Fair Day is next Monday. I'm going with my friend, Brad. Why don't you and Luce come with?"

I gave Maggie a look.

Evan turned to me. "Sounds like fun. What do you think? I haven't been to the Fair in years."

"I … I—"

"Sure, she will. We can celebrate your birthday." Maggie patted my shoulder.

"Your birthday's this week?" asked Evan.

"Yeah. I told Maggie I didn't want to make a big deal of it." I gave Maggie a wide-eyed look to make her stop. It never works.

"Oops … sorry," said Maggie with fake humility. "I only say that to people when I *do* want them to make a big deal."

Nothing came to me, and I imagined standing with my mouth hanging open.

"Okay, then that settles it. Evan, text Luce your address and we'll stop by and pick you up Monday at, say, ten o'clock?"

Still unresponsive, I kept staring at Maggie, slack-jawed.

Maggie sighed. "Here, give me your number," she said to Evan, and then with a swift motion snatched my phone, dialed his number, and hit send.

"Maggie, I'm perfectly capable of managing my own telecom, thank you," I said, secretly relieved this awkward exchange bypassed me.

Evan's phone rang. "Got it."

"Text her your address, and she will send it to me. Sweet, now you two have each other's numbers." Maggie stepped forward, pretending to accept an award, speaking to no one. "No need for applause. Any one of you would have done the same thing."

Evan and I clapped. Sometimes you just must feed the monster.

Maggie held her hands together at her chest and gushed, "You like me. You really … like me."

We said our goodbyes to Evan, and he departed down the hall.

When he was out of range, I turned to Maggie. "I thought we agreed to let me pull the trigger on my own love life."

"Um … not really. You mumbled something. Then, when I served one up for you so easy a three-year-old could hit it, you just stood there. Duh." She mocked my paralysis with hunched shoulders and her mouth open wide. "Life happens fast, and if you don't recognize your moments, then that's what busy-body best friends are for."

Maggie's smile was so genuine I couldn't be angry.

"Yes … busy-body-A-type-personality best friends," I laughed.

~ ~ ~

I got ready for bed. Needing a way to make sure I wouldn't oversleep, I decided to set the alarm tone on my phone to the duck quacking. For some reason, my brain has an aversion to the sound of ducks. I'm not afraid of ducks, mind you. It's just when I hear that ringtone, it gives me the same screech reaction and goosebumps as running my nails across a chalkboard. Duck quacking … go figure.

Plugging in my phone to charge, I settled into bed. In my mind's eye, I concentrated on the strange Third Eye symbol Claude had drawn in the dirt.

It would take me to The Watch, and ....

~ ~ ~

A few clouds float in the sky. I look down the shoreline to my left and then to my right. They both stretch out to infinity. I'm unsure which way to go until I hear a voice.

"Behind you."

I turn and see dunes. Claude stands on top of one of them with his arms crossed, staring at me in front of a huge lighthouse tower. He's wearing a scowl like he hasn't had a bowel movement, or dreamed of one, in days. I climb up the dunes to meet him and stop when I'm standing in front of him. He stares at me for several long seconds, drops his arms, turns, and walks to the lighthouse. I follow him.

The lighthouse is an enormous and imposing white monolith rising from the beachhead. There are no rocks or jetties to warn anyone about, so I'm uncertain of its purpose. The tower is capped with what appears to be a solid glass cage with a copper cupola. A black spire tops it all. He opens the door and strolls into the lighthouse ahead of me. I hurry, maintaining only a couple of steps behind.

He ascends the spiral staircase. After traveling several feet up, we pass a sign on a door that reads: *Watch Room*. Shortly afterward, we pass another called: *Service Room*. We continue upward to the door marked: *Lantern Room*.

Claude opens it and strides through. When I step over the threshold, the light is so brilliant I'm blinded. I walk forward with caution. Even with my eyes closed, the light's so bright it blasts through my eyelids. It doesn't hurt, but it incapacitates me. I feel a kind of vibration. It would be a humming sound if it made any noise at all. It calls me like the song of a Siren.

"Follow my voice," says Claude.

"Wow, I'm blind in here."

"In more than one way …"

"You could warn me," I say.

"Oh, I guess I forgot. It must have slipped my mind."

Next, I smack my head on a wall of some kind. "Ouch."

"Oh yeah, watch your step."

Things are peachy for me and Claude. I wonder when David will get here and save me from this torture. I turn toward where I heard Claude speak last and extend my hand in front to feel for any other wayward objects.

"Keep coming this way," says Claude.

The light gets less intense as I walk toward him. I stumble over a threshold and fall to my knees.

"Oops, a daisy, watch out. The threshold tends to trip." He's insincere. "Anytime, now. Could you stop playing on the floor?" Claude sounds as if simmering with amusement at the situation.

I slowly rise to my feet, keep my mouth shut, and travel to where I see his outline. Like walking through a fog of light, my vision adjusts the closer I get, and his features become clearer.

When I reach him, he moves into the remainder of the room. It's a brilliantly lit space with sets of tables and chairs spread throughout. We are alone. It has a library feel to it with some bookshelves. The walls are transparent and look out over the water to the left and the shore to the right. The land stretches to the horizon with no other landmarks of consequence.

Claude walks to a large chair made from rough-hewn logs with cushions strapped to the seat and back. He sits and adjusts to a comfortable position, then points to a chair across from him. Once I'm seated, he remains silent for a while.

"What took you so long?" asks Claude, cocking his head and leaning backward.

"So long for what?"

"To attend your first training class. I thought we established that you were approaching your next multiple, and you are woefully unprepared and behind. Eight years to be exact."

"Oh ... well, once I woke up, I had to smooth things over with my dad and then school—"

"Excuses, excuses. I don't care about the responsibilities you have in your other life. I'm concerned about you *here* and how *here* affects you *there*."

"Sorry ... I live in both places. I must maintain a balance. The last time we saw each other, I lost a whole day."

"Balance: an interesting word choice. You don't seem to grasp the power you unwittingly wield and how it will spill over into your world. You should be more careful."

"Mmm, I hear you say these things, but I don't *feel* powerful. I can barely keep things together in my personal life. I really only have two friends: one there and one here." I hug myself and rub my upper arms as if some chill creeps there. "When will David join us?"

"He won't. We decided his presence might be too distracting."

"Glad you included me."

"Lucinda, you need to stop this whiny attitude and get to work. We are wasting valuable time."

Once again, I shut my mouth and wait for Claude's instruction. He closes his eyes and appears to sleep. Great, he's taking a freaking nap during my training. I slouch in my chair and cross my legs. I notice a shadow out of the corner of my eye. Turning my head, I catch a glimpse of something sliding out of a chair across the room. It's dark and about the size of a medium-sized dog. It skulks from one chair to the next, using them to hide behind, always maneuvering between chairs, getting closer to me. I cannot see its face.

"Claude," I whisper. "There's something here."

Claude's shoulders roll as he stretches his joints, but he chooses to ignore me.

"CLAUDE," I say louder. "Something pissed off this way comes." I try to sound literary and maintain a sense of humor, but my facade starts to crack when I hear it gurgling, and its breathing is raspy and wheezing.

"It's nothing," says Claude, as if in a dream.

"That *Nothing* looks creepy, sounds creepy, and *is* creepy."

As if on cue, the black mass jumps to the back of one of the chairs and then leaps out across to the table nearest me. It has a kind of dog head, but its body is wrong. It paces back and forth on the table, eyeing me like a snack. Its legs are strange and bend and move wrong for a dog. They're spider-like. The eyes glow yellow, and it opens its mouth to smile or breathe or something. It has a maw full of long dagger teeth—hundreds of them.

"Unless you want to be munched, you might want to open your eyes," I scream.

"Is it black and walks like a spider?" asks Claude, his eyes still closed.

"YES," I yell.

"Does it look like a dog with a lot of sharp, nasty teeth?" he asks, now mimicking the monster by grimacing and gnashing his teeth at the air in front of him, eyes still closed tight.

"Yes. Hell, yes." I retreat deeper into my chair, trying to hide from it. It continues to pace and regard me with malicious intent.

"Good," says Claude, sounding pleased. He opens his eyes and looks at the table. "Oh, nice. It's exactly what I wanted."

"What you wanted? Are you crazy?"

"It's nothing," says Claude, with a nonchalant air.

"Looks real to me."

"Stop feeding it," says Claude.

"I'm not feeding it."

"Yes, you are," retorts Claude.

"What am I feeding it?"

"You."

"I'm not feeding it me."

The thing leaps to the ground and slowly stalks toward me, wheezing with its horrible gurgling breaths.

"Lucinda, listen to me. Stop feeding it."

"I don't understand you. Help me ... it's coming."

"Look at me."

I turn my head slowly away from the monster. I hear it coming up behind me.

"Don't look at it. Look at me." Claude's pointing to his chest.

I want to turn to look at the thing, but continue to watch Claude.

"You're feeding it your fear." He leans forward in his chair. "Stop feeding it," he commands.

"How?" I squeak.

"Remember ... it's nothing," he repeats.

"Tell that to its teeth," I say and slowly turn my head to see it a few inches from me, snarling.

"Don't look at it. Don't think about it. Look here," he yells, and I snap my head back to him.

"The more fear you feed it; the more real it gets. Give it no more attention. Don't think about it." He puts his hand out and drops it. "Close your eyes," he whispers.

I do as he bids, even though I feel the heat of its breath on my face.

"Give it none of your energy. The thing's not worthy of your emotion."

I listen to his voice, and for some reason, I get a vision of an old comedy called *Mister Ed*. It's about a talking horse. I let the sitcom overtake me, and the episode plays in my head. I'm voicing all the characters and reciting the words out loud. "Hello, Wilbur." The monster's breathing quiets. I'm not sure if it's the voices playing in my head drowning it out or what, but I sense the presence of the thing waning.

"Good," says Claude. "You can open your eyes now."

Putting *Mister Ed* on a commercial break, I open my eyes. I slowly turn my head and peek at where I last saw it. It's gone. I get up out of my chair and look all around me. No sign the monster exists.

"Where did it go?"

"It dissipated. It was nothing like I told you."

"The thing scared the snot out of me."

"Good. Not bad, if I say so myself. I'm glad you liked it."

"What do you mean? The thing is yours?"

"No, it was yours. I gave birth to the idea of it with my mind, but you gave it substance."

"Was I in danger?"

"Most definitely, but you handled it well."

I wanted to rail at him, but I knew it would just make him happy.

Quack. Quack. Quack.

I shiver and feel myself flying from the room. Claude has a look of exasperation as I exit The Watch.

Claude points at me and yells, "Here. Tomorrow."

14 – DRIVE ME CRAZY

My birthday was today. A bittersweet day I shared with the anniversary of my mother's death. I woke up wondering if I would feel different, but it was the same as any other day. After completing an intense training session last night with Claude, I got ready for another day of school. The funny thing was, although emotionally drained, my body felt rested. It was almost as if I had done brain exercises, and my mind had adjusted, enjoying the activity. Claude had run me through several sessions to neuter numerous kinds of dream negativity. I employed my fallback method of concentrating on something else, like reciting a sitcom or practicing my lines for *Our Town,* to sever any fear binding me to whatever host, ghost, demon, or wayward entity Claude created.

He had tapped into my inner fears and came up with some truly ghastly creatures. One was a snake with huge fangs. Another was a cute kitten that morphed into a saber-toothed tiger with a penchant for redheads. Claude helped me successfully remove everything.

He taught me another technique that involved just the opposite way of thinking. He had me clear out my thoughts and become completely devoid of anything, whether it be fear, happiness, or anger. I focused on being in a small boat in the middle of the sea during a dark, moonless night with only the starlight for illumination. Imagining, as far as my eyes could see, there were no waves, I concentrated on the surface of the water and maintained it to appear like glass. If I held that image as it stretched to the horizon in all directions, it had a similar effect on whatever monstrosity haunted me, but it was more abrupt and cut it off at the knees, disappearing with a pop. It was more satisfying than evaporating.

School went well enough. Even Kimmy and her friends didn't hassle me. For that matter, they didn't seem to notice me. What if I were the monster, and they're banishing me using my own techniques? I sat in the cafeteria in my usual spot.

"Hey Birthday Girl," said Maggie as she dropped down across the table.

"Hi," I said, and tried to sound happy, but I guess my sour attitude shone through.

"Why the long face?"

"Oh, nothing. Guess I'm a little tired this morning."

"Nightmares again?"

"No, they've pretty much stopped."

"Whoops, now you did it. Better knock on some wood." Maggie rapped her knuckles on the cafeteria table.

I didn't know if the laminated particleboard counted. Claude and my training were subjects I kept to myself. I didn't need to worry Maggie with any further dream discussion.

"I got something for you." Maggie reached into her purse and pulled out a two-pack of cupcakes wrapped in cellophane. She opened the package, pulled out a candle, and stuck it in one of the cakes. Removing a lighter from her purse, she lit it. "Quick, think of a wish and blow it out before anyone sees."

Choosing a generic wish, I blew out the candle.

"I hope you get your wish. You don't look all that happy to be turning sixteen. When do you take your driving test?" asked Maggie.

"I don't know. Maybe I'll do it after school."

"After school? Did you make a reservation? I don't think you can just walk up. There are only so many open slots. I had to reserve mine almost a month ahead."

"A month? I can't wait that long."

"Mmm." Maggie dipped her head in thought. "You might be able to go to Waxahachie."

"Great." I closed my eyes and shook my head at my stupidity.

~ ~ ~

The last bell sounded, and I was making my way to Maggie's car for my usual ride home when I got a text from Dad that he was waiting for me out front. Why did he leave work so early? I parted ways with Maggie and walked out front and looked along Senior Lane for his car. I didn't see it, so I paced back and forth along the sidewalk to wait.

Hearing a car horn, I looked up to see Dad waving to me but not from his car. My heart skipped a beat. No way. It couldn't be possible. He bought me a car for my sixteenth birthday. It was new, sleek, and blue. Hurried feet took me to the car, and I jumped in the shotgun seat.

"What do you think?" asked Dad.

"It's beautiful."

"Took a half-day off and bought it this afternoon."

I reached across the seat and gave him a one-arm hug and squealed a little. "Dad, you're the best."

He hugged me back and then pulled away from the curb. He looked again at me, and this time his face told me he just experienced an "Oh-no" moment. "Luce, I'm sorry. I think you may have misunderstood. I got this car for me." He had a failed smile after he said this.

"Oh ... so to celebrate my birthday, *you* bought a new car?" I tried to look happy. I knew it was selfish of me to expect a new car, but it was one of those happy dreams you hoped would come true.

"Well ... do you remember reading about President Reagan and his *trickle-down* economics?" asked Dad.

"Yeah ... but wasn't it also called Voodoo Economics? At least that's what the teacher said to Ferris Bueller. But I get your drift: supply-side economics. Give tax breaks at the top, and it results in more jobs and spending money for the people underneath."

"Good. The 1980s were economic good times, and so is your sixteenth birthday."

"Dad ... what are you saying?"

"I'm saying the trickle-down effect of this deal is you get the old Subaru."

"Really? That's awesome." It wasn't the same as getting a new car, but it was the next best thing. It meant I didn't have to share my wheels. I had freedom.

"I left it at the dealer, and they are doing a bumper-to-bumper safety inspection. Then they'll detail the whole thing. It'll look as close to new as they can get it."

We stopped at the light, and I gave Dad another hug. "Thank you. That's a great birthday present."

"You're welcome, Sweetheart. Now, on to the next present."

"What?" I whispered with rapt attention.

"We're going to the Department of Transportation for your driving test.”

“I think it might be a waste of time. I was supposed to make an online appointment four weeks ago.”

“Actually, I made the reservation over a month ago. Maggie gave me a heads-up at the end of the summer. Did I do okay?”

A smile lit up my face. “You did great. I’ll thank Maggie later, too.”

Dad drove me to the Carrollton DoT, and when we walked into the office, we found it full. We checked in and got a number to watch for our turn on the screens at both ends of the room. After a few minutes, our number popped up and instructed us to go to Service Desk C. We were greeted by a female clerk. I did the best I could to make myself presentable. Dad paid for the test and license fees. She directed us to an even longer line to wait for my driving test.

Twenty minutes passed, and a gruff-looking lady in uniform called my name.

Dad and I approached her. “I’m Officer Velázquez. Are you ready?”

“I hope so,” I said.

“Your father must wait in the lobby.”

“Okay, here are the keys. Be careful,” said Dad.

I followed the officer through a side door outside.

“Take me to your car.”

I unlocked the doors with the fancy remote key, and we climbed in.

“All right, let’s start it,” said the officer.

I turned the key, and the radio blared some new pop single. I didn’t remember the radio being turned up that loud. The instrument panel was new to me, so I was unsure which button was the volume.

“Please turn it off.”

“Yes, ma’am.” Her sour attitude and the new controls made me so nervous my hand shook as I turned knobs at random. It felt as if the music went on forever as I frantically searched for a way to turn it off. Finally, I found the right button and was rewarded with silence.

“Nice car. It smells ... new.”

“Yes, ma’am, my dad got it today.”

“And he’s letting you take it for your driver’s road test?”

“Um ... I guess so.”

“Ah ... a man of great faith, then,” said the officer. “Pull around to the back,” pointing to another car to follow.

I adjusted my mirrors to fit my driving position while Officer Velázquez scribbled something in her notebook. I put the car in reverse.

“Seatbelts?”

I put on my seatbelt. When we entered the backside of the complex, she pointed toward four tall flagpoles with diagonal yellow and black decals and said, "Park inside the poles, please."

Oh no, the dreaded parallel parking test. I knew I had to be careful not to hit a pole or the curb, or I would flunk immediately. My plan was to get as close as possible and not hit anything. It was better to get points off rather than fail altogether.

I pulled up ahead of the lead flagpoles. I could have sworn I heard a soft growl from behind me. Glancing in the rear-view mirror, I glimpsed a shadow. I attributed it to maybe being my instructor's stomach and clouds moving overhead. I put the car into reverse and twisted around to look at the flagpoles through the rear windows. Resting my right hand across the back of my instructor's seat, I eased my way back.

I turned the wheel and concentrated on what I was doing. A giant shadow appeared in the back seat and morphed into a huge black dog. Fangs bared, it lunged and snapped its jaws shut an inch from my forearm. It shocked me so much I whipped myself back around to the front, but goosed the gas pedal, hitting a yellow and black flagpole behind me.

"What the hell," I said, turning again to look in the rear seat. Nothing was there.

"Shame ... you were doing so well," said the officer.

Yeah, Happy Birthday to me.

15 – WELCOME TO THE STATE FAIR …

Monday was Fair Day, which meant school was out. I convinced Dad to take a half-day and drive me to Waxahachie for my driving road test. Otherwise, I was going to have to wait a month for another chance. The Waxahachie school district had its Fair Day next week, so I didn't have to compete with the local kids.

An appointment was available, and I easily passed parallel parking. The officer administering the driving test then took me down Main Street as his idea of a small-town speed trap. Thinking I might not notice the drastic speed limit changes, he didn't realize that this summer I drove through Weatherford, where they have a 30 mph sign only three hundred feet from the 45. I was not fooled. That and no ghost dog attacks meant I walked out of there at ten o'clock with a license.

I had just enough time to get back to Dallas and get ready to connect with my friends at the State Fair this afternoon. I called Maggie and told her I would pick up Evan and meet her and Brad at Big Tex around one o'clock.

Ringing Evan's doorbell, I waited only a moment before the front door opened. He saw me through the storm door and burst over to my side.

"Great day for the Fair," he said, running his hand through his hair and looking at something in his lawn.

The sun was out but it wasn't hot. Blue skies. Birds singing.

"It is a nice day. Ready?" I asked.

Evan must have noticed Maggie missing and deduced it was only me.

"You got your license? Congratulations. How does it feel?"

"I didn't think I would care, but I didn't realize how much my dad chatters in my ear about everything on the road. The drive over was so quiet. It was awesome."

"My mom is the instructor in our family. You ain't heard no chatter until you've been driving with my mom riding shotgun."

"Is that a dig at women drivers?" I asked with a hint of a grin.

"No. Not at all." Evan tried to recover.

"Just kidding with you. You don't mind me driving?"

"Nope. I don't think walking is an option."

Evan and I arrived first at Big Tex, a huge cowboy statue erected near the entrance of the Fair. He stood over fifty feet tall, looking snazzy with a huge hat, pearl-snap shirt, jeans, and boots. He's been a part of the State Fair for as long as anyone can remember.

"Howdy folks. Welcome to the State Fair of Texas," boomed Big Tex. It made me jump, standing right next to him. During the Fair, an announcer in a little room inside one of Tex's giant boots delivered the State Fair news of the day.

Maggie and Brad showed up, holding hands. Brad was a tall, muscular type of guy who played receiver for our football team. The way Maggie talked about him, he must be good. I hadn't been to a game to see for myself, but he was friendly and able to co-exist in Maggie's world, which was no small miracle.

Maggie let go of Brad and hugged me and Evan. "I'm so glad you two could make it. Today's going to be a blast. Do we go to the Midway for games or catch some rides?"

We looked at each other for a second. Then Brad spoke, "Why don't we hit some rides first, then get something to eat. We'll hit the Midway games last."

"Why, baby, do you have a weak tummy?" said Maggie, in a smothering mommy voice.

"If you want to push your luck and get pre-digested corn dogs down your blouse, then be my guest." Brad smiled back, but you could tell he was serious.

Yeah, Brad was exactly right for Maggie.

"Sounds like a good idea to me. Going on some rides first, I mean. However, seeing Maggie fish chunks out of her bra and boots might be fun as well," I said.

Evan gave a muffled laugh.

Maggie put her hands on her hips. "Okay, enough of the puke-talk.

You're going to jinx one of us."

"Agreed, let's get some coupons," said Evan.

We walked over to the booth and each plunked down forty dollars for coupons. Money had no value here as they tried to trick you by paying for rides, food, and everything with coupons. Evan tried to pay for mine, but I told him he could buy me something to eat later.

We waited in line for almost an hour to ride the Texas Star Ferris Wheel. Then we followed it up with the Zilerator, Fast Track, and Stratosphere. Now hungry, we made our way to the food stands positioned near the Midway. As we got closer, the assault on our senses began: the sounds of baseballs striking metal jugs, plastic rings bouncing off bottle tops, carnies hailing you to stop by their booths, and the smell of all the notorious fried foods.

The food was the worst: fried bacon cinnamon rolls and fried jambalaya. One could chase it with a fried Coke or a fried latte. It was horrible and wonderful in the same breath as we ingested the scent of grease and sugar. After scoring some more coupons, we each got our main course. Brad got a corny dog. Maggie and Evan began with a sausage on a stick, and Evan bought me a smoked turkey leg. We each bought some lemonade and found a bench to rest and enjoy our late lunch.

We wolfed our meals and were about to leave in search of some fried dessert when I heard something familiar.

"Yak, Yak, Yak."

It was faint, as if far away, but I heard it again. "Yak, Yak, Yak."

It sounded like it came from the trees on the outer edge of Fair Park.

Maggie must have noticed me straining to see something and asked, "What is it?"

"Oh, nothing, I guess."

Now it was louder, and I looked out into one of the live oaks and saw a familiar black and white bird.

"Yak-yak-yak. Yak-yak-yak-yak-yak," it cried, in an agitated staccato.

"You hear that?"

"Yeah, sounds like Maggie when she calls late at night while I'm trying to get some sleep. Yack. Yack. Yack," said Brad with a smile.

Maggie playfully slugged him in the upper arm, and he grunted with fake pain.

I stared at the bird, mesmerized by it. It flew from a tall branch and landed on the chain-link fence ten feet away from us.

"You see it, don't you?" I asked.

"Yeah, it's one pissed-off bird. Like it's yelling at us," said Evan.

The bird was flustered and flapped its wings in a flurry, lifting slightly off the fence and then back down—all the while crying.

It couldn't be the bird from my dreams, could it? No, I know I'm awake. It must be a similar bird because it looked and sounded like the one from my dreams.

"Maybe we're too close to its nest or something. Let's go to the Midway and see if we can win some games. I want a stuffed animal or souvenir to remember this day," said Maggie to us all, staring at Brad the whole time.

When we got up, the bird flew back into the trees. "I guess Maggie's right. We were too close to something," Brad said.

We arrived at the Midway, where there was all manner of games underway.

"Hey, y'all," cried a carny, "Want to try your hand at a water balloon race? Every game's a winner."

Since it was only us four competing, we agreed. Brad ended up winning.

We were happy we could rest easy knowing Maggie had her stuffed animal, and Brad didn't have to keep trying to win something. Maggie chose a big stuffed Panda bear. I found a game I liked and challenged Evan to a BB gun shoot-out. We were each given a BB machine gun and a target with a red star in the middle. We had a limited amount of ammo to shoot out the star. I'm a good shot and won. Evan lost graciously, although it was a rip-off as the carny claimed there was a point of one of the stars still showing.

We meandered about the Midway for a while longer, and then Brad noticed a sign. It was small and red with an arrow that said, "Freak Show - This Way". There was a small path running between some old buildings.

"C'mon, let's check it out," said Brad.

We all followed. The path led between the buildings and around behind an old warehouse. It looked creepy to me. Ahead stood a huge, closed tent with a carny man positioned outside, waving us in. He was tall with a painted face and wore an old-fashioned suit that matched his bowler hat.

"Welcome to the Freak Show of Texas. Come on in, young people, and see things you've only heard about. Why, for only eight coupons, I say, a measly eight coupons apiece, you can witness the impossible," said the carny.

We paid the admission and walked into the tent. It was cool and dark. There were four chairs set up in front of a curtained stage, so we sat in them.

"Strange that nobody else is here with us," I said to no one.

"Maybe this venue is so far off the beaten path, nobody knows it's here," answered Evan.

"You know what's weird?" asked Maggie. "I don't remember ever seeing a freak show at the Fair. I'm surprised they'd allow it."

Big Tex started up again. "Welcome to the State Fair of Texas. Be sure to visit the State Fair Auto Show, the BMX Bike Show, and the Birds of the World." Then in a whisper, I heard Big Tex say, "Stay away from the Freak Show."

Did I imagine that? I was about to say something when the carny man appeared from behind the curtain.

"Welcome to our little show. We have some truly freakish freaks here for your entertainment," exclaimed the carny and threw his hat offstage. His thin hair, almost like wisps of smoke, waved in the air above his head.

I glanced at Maggie. Her eyes were like saucers, and her mouth hung open. She didn't return my gaze.

"Our first Freak is *The Dragon of Inchon*. Be careful ... his bite has heat to it."

The curtain pulled back, and a man wearing only a loincloth came forward on the stage. Every inch of exposed flesh was festooned with colorful tattoos, including his face and bald head. He snarled at us, baring his teeth, which were filed to points. Then he reared his head back and blew a burst of flames at us. I didn't see him bring anything to his mouth to ignite it—a pretty good trick.

"Watch out for his breath, young people," called the carny off stage.

The dragon blew more flames, and the curtain fell again. All of us remained riveted to our seats.

The carny glided back on stage. "Ladies and gentlemen, *The Dragon of Inchon*." He flung his arms outward to invite applause.

We each clapped a smattering of times.

"Now, for something truly amazing. This next freak is from the Far East. It is not known if his deformity is a genetic mishap, accident, or whether we should classify him as human at all. Welcome to the stage *The Serpent of the East*."

Big Tex played his announcements again. This time, I heard him clearly say, "Lucinda, please report to the main gate. Lucinda, you need to get out of there."

Panic crept in from the corners of my mind into a tunneled vision of only the stage. I couldn't move. The curtains opened, and *The Serpent of the East* stood in the center of the stage. He wore no shirt and stood with his arms crossed. Scales covered his entire body. His yellow eyes had slits for pupils, and they burned with rage, locked onto me.

"Lucinda, LEAVE," called Big Tex again.

The Serpent looked off stage. "Dragon, please shut that big guy up," he hissed.

The Serpent turned back to me, uncrossed his arms, and put his hands on his hips. "Ah, Lucinda, my sweet. It is so good of you to invite me here."

"I didn't invite you."

"Luce, do you know this guy?" asked Maggie.

"Yes, it's the Snake Dude. The one I told you about. Don't worry. Somehow, I fell asleep after lunch. It's all in my head."

"That dude looks pissed," said Brad.

"Like I said. I'm dreaming, so you guys are safe. They're just figments of my imagination. They aren't real."

The Serpent now smiled at me but made no effort to approach.

"Not REAL! What are you talking about?" cried Maggie.

"I just need to wake myself, so we can finish our day at the Fair and leave Ugly up there to simmer in his own juices."

The Serpent's smile widened, and he laughed. "Tsk, tsk. Poor, stupid girl. You have no idea, do you?"

I held my seat. My training with Claude countered my knee-jerk reaction to run. I would not give this thing any of my fear or the satisfaction of rattling me.

The Serpent sauntered to the front of the stage, jumped, and landed on the ground below with a thud, positioning himself in front of me.

"Anything you want to say to your friends before we begin?"

"Yeah. They can disappear and let me deal with you."

"Disappear? How do we disappear?" asked Evan, alarmed.

I turned to look into his eyes. He was visibly shaken, and sweat rolled down his face. It amazed me how real he seemed.

The Serpent took a step forward.

"Yak-Yak-Yak-Yak," came a cry behind me, and my friend, the black and white bird, flew into the tent and dove at the Serpent's head. It fluttered about, diving at the Serpent.

"That's not going to work this time." The Serpent used his full-sized arms to swat at the bird. He connected on the second swipe and knocked the bird across the room. It hit the side of the tent with a smack and slid down the tent wall to the ground.

"Hey, you big bully," I yelled.

"This time I'll fix you." The Serpent unhinged his jaw wide enough to swallow a small goat and lunged at me.

Maggie shot forward and shoved her big Panda bear into its gaping maw as deeply as she could. "Choke on this, Bitch."

The Serpent gagged a moment, then backhanded Maggie, flinging her backward over her chair. She landed in a heap and didn't move. Brad backed up. I felt Evan's hands on my shoulders, trying to pull me away from the thing. The Serpent spat the Panda bear back at Maggie, and it landed beside her with a moist thwack.

What is Maggie doing in my dream still? Why are Evan and Brad still here? I sent them away. What if what happens in my dream is happening to them in real life?

"You are going to taste wonderful," said the Serpent, and opened his mouth to swallow me.

Using Claude's technique, I closed my eyes and concentrated on being on my imaginary boat in the middle of the sea. There were no ripples or waves. The ocean was like glass.

"Ahahhahhaa," I heard the Serpent scream. Next, I heard and felt a loud explosion that knocked me backward.

Sleep …

"Luce. Luce. You okay?" It was Evan's voice.

Keeping my eyes closed, I thought how great it was going to be to wake up and enjoy the rest of the day at the Fair with my friends. I've got to stop nodding off. I opened my eyes, expecting to be somewhere on a picnic bench or a ride, but I was lying on my back on a patch of grass behind an old warehouse. I looked up into the eyes of a paramedic leaning over me with Evan standing behind him.

"Miss, are you all right?"

I sat up. "Yeah … did I faint or something?"

"According to your boyfriend, you were attacked."

"Attacked? No, I just fell asleep."

"Then what happened to your friend?" asked the paramedic, pointing over my shoulder.

I looked behind me and saw Maggie on a stretcher being loaded into an ambulance.

16 – CROSSOVER AFTERMATH

Maggie lay in a hospital bed for the rest of the afternoon.
The doctors said she suffered from a concussion. Medical tests suggested she would be all right, but she might have to spend a day or two in the hospital for observation. I felt as though I were walking through a fog. My senses dulled by the trauma, I kept hoping I was nested in some horrible nightmare that I would wake from, but relief never came. Brad and Evan were unusually quiet—especially once the police showed up.

"Okay, so let's go over this one more time. You say some freak made up to look like a snake attacked you and your friend, here?" asked the officer.

"Yep," I said.

"You realize there's no evidence of any freak show. It doesn't appear on any vendor list." The officer remained silent to entice someone to fill it. No one obliged. "You have anything more to tell me?"

"Nope," I said.

"Mmm, we'll see what she says when she's awake," said the officer, jerking a thumb at Maggie. "Funny thing is, we got the 911 from y'all almost at the same time a call came in reporting Big Tex was on fire. Now that's a strange coincidence. Don't you think?"

Brad and Evan looked at their feet and shifted side to side. They couldn't look guiltier. It must have been the Dragon who started the fire.

"I have no idea." I looked him in the eye, unblinking for several seconds. The twenty-question routine was getting frustrating, Maggie was hurt, and the rest of us were in shock. Besides, I had some questions of my own.

The police left, and Maggie's parents arrived. We hung out together and fought through some awkward moments until the three of us decided to leave Maggie in her parents' care.

The ride home with Evan was solemn. I was curious what he remembered. How much had my dream world crossed over into his reality?

I broke the silence first. "What happened?"

Evan looked forward through the windshield as he spoke. "It's all a little fuzzy to me. I remember some scaly guy attacking us, and Maggie got the worst of it. I woke up in the grass somewhere with the rest of you sprawled out around me. You and Maggie looked really hurt, so Brad and I called 911."

Thank God. If that's all he remembers, then I'm golden. There was so much craziness that maybe he's unsure if he dreamed it or not. "I think she'll be okay," I responded.

"Uh-huh ... I hope so," he managed to force out.

I decided to leave him alone as he was a little drunk with stress. We arrived at his house. He got out of my car and started to close the door, but then opened it again and stopped to talk to me.

"What were you saying about us being imaginary? And ... uh ... how did you make them all disappear like that?"

Frozen in my seat, I reacted in no way to alarm him. "You know I'm fuzzy on everything, too. It's a blur to me," I lied.

He twisted his mouth up to the side, which I took as a sign that he didn't believe me. I didn't know what else to say. "Okay, we'll talk later. Night. Thanks for the ride."

He closed the door with only a minor glance just before he went inside his house.

I could crawl under a rock right now and die from embarrassment. I hoped to never talk about this but knew I would. Once home, I managed to skirt around the issue of being late with Dad and went to bed.

~ ~ ~

I stand on the beach in front of The Watch. Instead of climbing up the dunes to the lighthouse, I stare out across the water and ponder. I sense a presence behind me and find David a few steps back, kicking at a shell or something in the sand.

"When were you going to say something?" I ask.

"When you were ready to talk," he says, his attention focused on his feet. Then he looks up at me with concerned eyes.

"I need to tell you about something that happened to me today. It's not pretty, and I don't know what to do." I relay my story about the attack at the Fair, and he remains quiet.

"It's your multiple. Claude tried to tell you about the unpredictable nature of it and the power you unknowingly wield."

"Yes … yes, I know. I'm a child waving around a machine gun. But on my sixteenth birthday, nothing big happened, so I thought I was in the clear."

"But you told me about the ghost dog. I had hoped your training helped you recognize the danger."

"All my training is done inside the confines of my dreams, so I thought I was safe."

"I guess Claude didn't make it clear that when your multiple happens, it puts you into a different class of danger. You know, having a multiple of eight … is … rare. Most multiples are at ten, and only a few have them at nine, like me. Add in the fact you didn't receive your training on time, it makes you unpredictable."

"No, it makes me dangerous just like the Collective says. I can't be trusted with this gift. It's beyond my control. I almost got my friends killed when the Snake Dude and his buddies crossed over into my world. The really scary thing is he's stronger, somehow."

"But you did handle it. Your training saved them."

"Is there some way to diffuse me? Neutralize this ability?"

"Not that I'm aware of. Let's go talk to Claude."

He grabs my hand, and we trudge up the dunes. Climbing the winding staircase of the lighthouse, we cross through the blinding light foyer of the Lantern Room into where I train. Claude sits in a chair at the other end of the room, looking out the huge windows and across the lake. He doesn't appear to notice my approach.

When we get to within ten feet of him, we stop, and he speaks with his face in profile. "I hear we had an episode on your side of the fence?"

"How do you know?"

"I have my sources. I really blame myself for your training. I didn't think something like this was even possible at your level. It makes me wonder if there is anything else I have underestimated. You should not have been able to open any door big enough to allow that much through. I am puzzled." He tips his head down in thought.

"If this crossover event was never supposed to occur, then what happened?"

"I think the strength of your multiple went well beyond what was anticipated. You must consult with me if anything like this occurs again or anything else strange, for that matter."

"What's the Collective going to say? Some of them already think I'm some sort of witch. I can only guess what they're saying."

David still holds my hand and gives it a squeeze of support. "Don't worry about them. They don't understand what they don't understand."

I smile internally as David continues to talk in doublespeak, but I know it's just the way he is.

"Claude, any discussion of this?" I ask.

Claude is silent for too many seconds for my comfort. "They are calling for a conclave soon to deliberate." He sighs.

"About me?" I let go of David's hand.

"Mostly, it deals with my negligence in your training."

"Negligence? Why? I've learned so much in the last couple of weeks I can't think of what more you could have done. I'm in here almost every night while asleep." I throw my hands out. "I'm mentally exhausted."

"It has more to do with what I've yet to instruct you."

"Can you give me some details?"

"Although I believe you have a right to know, I am forbidden to discuss this any further with you until I am cleared."

I want to rail at him, but I know he's only doing what he's told. "I understand. When does the Collective want me to appear before them and swear allegiance?"

Claude lurches, and I know the truth.

"Soon."

17 – OBE MEETS NDE

The couch had a comfy disposition. I leaned back and read an article from a women's magazine about how to get your man to do the laundry and not ruin your favorite clothes. It had an interesting premise, but it didn't apply to me. I might never get to try these manipulation techniques on any man. My fear was that guys would probably think I'm a freak. And freaks do their own laundry.

I felt anxious as I hated waiting. The assistant behind the glass appeared preoccupied and unresponsive to my stares and facial machinations to end my suffering.

The room held a strange odor, even though it represented the stereotypical scent for offices of this type, I couldn't place it. The smell, mixed with the outdated décor, gave me pause to second-guess the owner's design influences.

The music that seeped in from the cheap ceiling speaker was bland and left no room for inspiration, so I got out my smartphone and played my own tunes. I launched into the next magazine.

The door opened. "Ah ... Lucinda, so good to see you."

"Hi, Dr. Rami."

Dr. Rami sported a fresh haircut. The curly hair on the sides was sufficiently tamed, which made him appear less crazy than the last time we met. He waited at the door, holding it open. I put down my magazine and slid between him and the door jam. He gave a soft pat on my shoulder as I passed and followed me to his office. I entered first, choosing one of the matching high-back chairs. Dr. Rami sat across from me.

Opening the thick folder, he casually flipped to a page and clicked his red ball-point pen to the ready. "Do you want to tell me what happened? Or … would you prefer I tell you what happened, and we'll see how close I get?" He leaned back into his chair and peered at me over the top of his glasses.

"Be my guest," I threw back. I was curious as to what he thought he knew, or was he just being a smart-ass.

"Good, I love doing this. Mmm … let's see. You … had another episode with your dream world that was far too real for you to fathom." He stopped to perhaps get a reaction from me. I gave him nothing but a cold stare. "However … it was too real because it happened while you were awake. Yes … yes … it was a full waking nightmare which … affected you and the people around you. And … someone close to you got hurt."

I must have twitched involuntarily during his blind assessment as if he'd struck a chord since his eyes narrowed and he leaned farther back into his chair, looked up, and waved his pen in the air like some magic wand with which he was divining the truth. I tried to maintain my poker face and gave him nothing more with which to work.

The doctor continued. "It's more than just this episode. You have a distinct … fear of yourself and for what you're capable of doing. Before, you were just afraid to sleep, but now—now you realize this other reality can, at any time, step forward into the one you share with your family and friends. You have absolutely no clue how to stop it. You're probably wondering if someone is going to die. Well … most certainly someone will perish. Should I take a guess at who? I spy with my little eye and would most likely say it's—"

"Enough," I said, and felt my shoulders slump. "Your guesses are pretty close. Are you spying on me?"

Dr. Rami gave a deep sigh. "No. No spies. I let experience be my guide."

I told him about what had happened the last few days with the ghost dog and the attack at the State Fair but didn't share with him anything about Claude or my training at The Watch. I wanted to keep both sides in the dark, hopeful that maybe one or both could provide me the answers I sought. He listened intently and twirled his pen back and forth around his thumb like a baton. Every now and then, he stopped and clicked the pen out, scribbled something across his notepad, and then clicked it back in.

"Mmm … you're more advanced than your mother at this age. I have to admit I'm alarmed and excited all at the same time." Dr. Rami bent forward, put his elbows on his knees, and held his pen clasped in both hands while assuming a posture of thoughtful concern. For some reason, his whole demeanor and attitude soured me. I always try to give respect to adults, teachers, parents, doctors, but I couldn't help thinking—what a dick. I wanted to bite on his comment, intimating my mother had a similar experience, but I decided to stare until he asked a question.

A few more moments of silence passed. "So how do you want to proceed?" he asked.

This made me laugh. "You're the doctor." I played along. "What do you suggest?"

"Well, considering the only other patient with a condition like yours that I tried to help died, I have some doubts." He waited for me to respond.

With smooth deftness, I rose from my seat and extended my hand. "Dr. Rami, thank you for your time. I think I should leave now since there's nothing you can do." He must have expected me to cave in, beg for his keen insight into my problems, and plead for him to save me. Hell, he couldn't save my mother. I'd become a bit jaded and didn't want to spend any more time playing his games.

He left my hand unshaken and sat back into his chair, raising his hand to halt me. "Now wait just a minute, Miss Locke. I'm trying to give you my perspective and concerns. I guess it's my fault for portraying too grim a picture. Please ... please sit down, and let's talk about this."

I returned to my seat, crossed my legs, placed my arms onto the rests of the chair, and threw out my own attitude of don't waste my time.

My tactic worked. Dr. Rami didn't know I had been verbally jousting with Claude and David and had prepared myself to cut through this kind of crap.

"Lucinda, do you know what OBE and NDE are?"

"OBE, I think, stands for Out of Body Experience, but I don't know what NDE means."

"You're correct about OBE. NDE stands for Near-Death Experience. Think of the two as different sides of the same coin. OBE is what you experience as you travel to these other realities within the Uber-hologram that is our Universe. NDEs are similar, but you're more abstracted from your physical body. The way I see it, time is merely a mental construct our brains have created to make sense of what we cannot comprehend. But when we enter a realm where time is not a linear thing, then we must change our thinking and adapt. NDEs add the concept of spacelessness, where space no longer limits us any more than time. The trick about NDEs is not to push things. You've got to have the 'N', or you just have a Death Experience, and the tedious thing about that is you can't share it with anyone."

Wow. I tried not to show it, but he did have my attention by presenting some different dots for me to connect.

"What are you asking me to do? Be open to dream … suicide?" I asked.

"No, I'm saying we need to project you beyond just merely the Out of Body and into the sphere of Near-Death. I know it sounds scary, but it should be a gradual transition. We need to help you create a barrier that gives you more strength to deal with this other reality, so you remain in control."

"The last time you *helped*, you disappeared, and it scared the bejesus out of me." I raised my hands in frustration. He was talking circles around me.

"There's the rub I'm talking about. Somehow, you and I have to develop a kind of tether to make sure we stay connected during these episodes when we explore them." Dr. Rami stood and strolled behind his chair and then leaned against the back of it in thought.

"Are there any techniques you can teach me?" I asked.

"Exactly what I'm trying to consider. Your case perplexes me, but in a good way, like a puzzle. The direction chosen must make you stronger without putting you in danger. I'd prefer to embark on the more prudent course."

He paced around his chair for several minutes, clicking his ball-point pen, stopped, and stared at the pen. "Ah-ha, that should work." Going to his desk, he opened a side drawer and pulled something small from it. He returned to his chair and leaned forward to show me a small metal frog.

"Very cute. Is he a friend of yours?" I couldn't help but tease him.

"No, he's going to be your friend," he said, with a wry smile. He pushed its belly, and the frog emitted a metallic clunking sound. "This is what we'll use to keep us connected during our sessions."

"A metal frog," I said with deadpan coldness.

"Close your eyes."

I humored him and shut them.

He clicked the frog. "Concentrate on this sound." He clicked it a few more times. "When you hear this sound, you need to pull away from your dream and listen for my voice. This will be our proverbial tether." He went back to his desk and pressed a remote that rolled down a projector screen from the ceiling. He hit the lights and pressed another button, turning on an overhead projector mounted against the far wall. He returned to his chair with a laptop.

"Are we going to watch a movie with Froggie?" I tried to use humor to mask the dread I felt being alone with Dr. Rami in the dark. I kept hearing Maggie's warning that he was weird, he had a thing for me, and I should be ready to stake him if he tried anything. I maintained my composure, but my mind briefly touched on Maggie. I needed to visit her.

"We're going to help you focus on your pineal gland."

"My What-gland?"

"Pineal," he repeated.

"That somehow sounds gross. I don't think I have one of those." Now I was getting nervous that he might try to bite me.

Rami gave a soft laugh. "The pineal gland is part of the endocrine system in your brain. It regulates the hormone, melatonin, a derivative of serotonin that modulates your sleeping and waking patterns. It's also called the Third Eye. It is the doorway into the inner realities and allows you to do … well … what you do."

"I don't remember any such gland from Biology class."

"The gland is about the size of a grain of rice near the pituitary. It's buried within the center of your brain and has a pinecone shape, hence its name. Eastern philosophers believe that it's the source of mystic power. Something a biologist cannot verify, but it's the magic, if you will, within our minds. A trap door that opens to the infinite or the implicate, as Dr. Bohm suggested. The enfolded universe where we're all connected to everything."

"Claude said something about the Third Eye," I whispered to myself.

"Whose Claude?" asked Rami.

"Oh … a boy from fifth-period Spanish class," I recovered.

"Mm, I knew a Claude, once."

I didn't want to discuss this any further, as I wasn't a good liar.

"Anyway … the Third Eye," said Dr. Rami. "You have unknowingly activated and developed yours to some degree, or you couldn't travel internally as you do. What I wonder is, if we purposefully train that part of your brain, will it give you more control over this power you hold? You're like a three-year-old running around with a samurai sword, swinging it all over the place. Someone's going to get hurt." Dr. Rami shrugged.

"Interesting analogy. I hadn't heard that one yet." I took a deep breath and continued, "You think you can help train my Third Eye?"

"Your ability suggests that yours is very well developed. When I trained in the monastery, I witnessed students who took twenty or thirty years to reach even a fraction of the level you've somehow stumbled upon. Some would be highly jealous of your ability," said the doctor.

"Pineal Envy?" I guessed.

Dr. Rami smiled. "Yes, something like that. Now, let's get started." He opened his laptop and tapped a couple of keys, and a colorful round drawing displayed on the presentation screen. It had a pattern swirling around it like a flower with petals and a pair of eyes above it at the top. In the center was a depiction of three Indian people dressed in flowing garments. One had green skin. On either side of the circle were bookend mirror images of some dudes with multiple arms, but with different colored outfits: one green and one red. Below a dude was a person inside a little house or gazebo, but on the other side was the same house, but with a door inside it. All over the petals, and in the corners, were Sanskrit characters.

"This is a mandala," said Rami, with a laser pointer. "It's a Sanskrit word meaning 'circle'. They are used by Hindus and Buddhists to elicit the path of lucid dreaming. Students typically concentrate on these images while chanting a mantra. Later, they're able to summon these images up within their minds and use them to transport themselves whenever they wish. I'm showing these as an example. They don't necessarily pertain to you since you can achieve this state at will. What I want you to do is create your own mandala. It should have a personal meaning and reference. Doing this will help to understand where you're developed and where you're weak."

He flipped through several more mandalas and had me linger on them to attempt to absorb what I could. "Go online and look up more examples, then buy yourself a sketch pad and some colored pencils. Then draw your own mandala. It can be a gradual process where you add images and symbols as you go."

"Okay … do you want me to bring it to my next appointment?"

"No, this homework assignment is more for your development. You share it with me when you're ready. For the moment, I need to show you a visualization exercise for your Third Eye. Concentrate on the center of your forehead just inside the front-center part of your brain. When you close your eyes, roll them back as if you are looking at your Third Eye. You will feel a similar sensation as if you crossed your eyes, and you might feel a slight headache, but it will pass. In this state, you must practice visualization of your own mandala, so when I guide you through an exercise, you will be able to focus and tap into additional resources."

"This is a lot to digest. Let me think about it."

"Sure. And when you're ready, reschedule with me. But I wouldn't wait too long."

"Why is that?"

"Because what you experienced at the Fair is only the tip of the iceberg. There are worse things that can happen … other than dying."

"Like what?" I asked.

The doctor removed his glasses. "Like losing your soul."

18 – IN SHEEP'S CLOTHING

Maggie's house oozed silence like a church on Monday morning. I slowly lumbered up her front walk, filled with guilt of ditching her to recover alone, so I could see Dr. Rami. I couldn't hope to explain it to her. I rang the doorbell and waited patiently. The door opened, and Maggie's mother stood there.

"Lucinda, I wondered when you'd be by." Her mother shared Maggie's features, except for the wrinkles around her eyes from smiling and her long hair in a French braid.

"Sorry, Mrs. Williams, for not coming sooner. I couldn't get Maggie to answer her phone, so I figured I'd drop by. How's she doing?"

"She's doing better. Yesterday, she was still foggy, but she's getting stronger. Come on in." She waved me to follow her up the stairs to Maggie's bedroom.

Her mom knocked softly on the door and announced me. Tentatively, I entered Maggie's room. She was propped up in bed surfing on her smartphone. She glanced at me for a moment. Well, now I understand. She was so angry that she refused to answer her phone. I grabbed her desk chair and pulled it beside the bed and sat. She kept flipping through screens and didn't acknowledge my existence. Maybe she was so pissed that I exposed her to the Snake Dude, she couldn't speak to me.

"Are you going to talk to me?" I asked.

She continued to surf.

I sighed. "Sorry, I got you hurt."

Maggie stopped surfing and looked at me and said, "Is that why you think I'm mad at you?"

"You won't return my calls or texts."

"Exactly why I'm pissed at you."

"You're angry at me because you wouldn't return my calls?" I asked, frustrated.

"Luce, stop being stupid. Quit the literal interpretation of everything I say."

"What did I do?"

"You called me."

"Isn't that what friends do?"

"Friends maybe, but we're best friends, and you don't call best friends when they're hurt."

I just stared at her with my face screwed up into a question.

Exasperated, she huffed. "Best friends don't call—they come in person."

I put my hands out in front of me and scanned myself down from chest to feet. "As far as I can tell, I'm here. No figment of your imagination or anything."

"What about yesterday?"

Okay, now she had me; the guilt washed over me, but I tried not to let it show. "Sorry, I wasn't sure how you'd react. I had to understand what was happening to me. You probably don't even remember."

"I remember more than you think."

I shivered. Maggie was my best friend; hell, she was my only friend. If I'd scared her away by being a freak, then I didn't know what to do with myself. I couldn't decide how much to share with her. Where was the line that, if crossed, I would lose her friendship?

Maggie answered my question without me asking. "I remember the Freak Show, the fire-breathing thing, and especially the Snake Dude. He came at you, then I got in his way and got smacked. That about it?"

Shocked, I didn't think after a concussion she could remember any of it. I was ashamed to say that I hoped she might have lost the day to a reboot of her brain. I knew what I needed to do. "Maggie, I think you should stay clear of me until I figure this out. I'm afraid somebody's going to get hurt worse."

"What? There you go again—pissing me off."

I didn't understand.

"You're like a sister to me. Girl … don't bring me into this and then dump me just when everything's gettin' interesting." She smiled, her eyes flashing. "I can't let you do this alone. I'll just need to be … better prepared, is all."

"It's too dangerous. You realize I almost got you killed."

"No, I almost got me killed by confronting that freak," she whispered, so her mom could not overhear. "I probably should have grabbed you and ran instead."

"Do your parents know what happened?"

"Julia and George know nothing. They only know what I want them to know."

"What about Brad? I think he's in shock, but he could still tell somebody," I said.

"Nobody will believe him. Leave Brad to me. I'll think of something to distract him." She did a model pose, putting one hand on her hip and the other behind her neck, and blew me a kiss.

Maggie made me smile. "You are the biggest flirt."

"No, I'm not." Maggie faked indignation at my suggestion. "I'm a young woman using her God-given gifts to keep her friend out of trouble."

I sighed and slumped in my chair. "What do I do with Evan? He must know I'm a freak."

"You really like him, don't you?"

"Yes. But I don't want to drive him away with this stuff."

"You don't see the way he looks at you when he thinks no one else is watching. He's diggin' whatever cereal you're serving him. Even if you think it's *Fruit Loops,* I wouldn't worry about it. Let the fates take you where they will. You can only control so much, then you have to trust yourself to let him go if he becomes a dweeb."

"Such wisdom from a cracked skull," I mused.

"Hey, I try." She held her arms out from her sides in self-congratulation.

That night, I dreamed of The Watch. I needed to see Claude.

~ ~ ~

I appear on the beach and make my way to the lighthouse and to our training room. The entire facility is empty, but I notice a sheet of paper on a table near where we usually meet. It reads: *Come to the Twin Gates first. The Door is 2,323 steps directly forward. We'll meet at the shack.*

I focus my mind on the key symbol and arrive at the Twin Gates. I shake the gate door to see if it'll open, but it's locked tight. Then I remember that I need to multiply myself to cross through the gates. I put my palms together and imagine I'm splitting myself in two. The shimmering thing occurs, and *I* am now *We*. The gates open, and we begin our long trek to the doorway. The problem is that the door is only visible when standing directly in front of it. We count the steps, but it occurs to us that 2,323 of Claude's steps don't equal ours. While discussing this with myself, I lose count. The frustration with the additional stress of dealing with multiples builds into a roaring headache.

"Let's stop this multiple thing. It's hurting my head," I say to my other self.

"I know. I've got the same pain. But aren't we supposed to remain a multiple while we're here?" the second me asks.

"Screw it. We'll make something up," says the first me.

We each assume the praying position and come back together as one. To my relief, the headache disappears. Ah, this is a much better way to travel. I decide to stop the idea of counting steps and see if I'm able to visualize the doorway to get me there. I close my eyes and concentrate on the doorway that I had seen Claude conjure the first time. It works. When I open my eyes, I stand in front of the wooden door. I pull it open to a shrouded scene of inky blackness. I step into it, and I repeat the same trick to get to the shack.

I open my eyes to see Claude jump as I appear out of nothingness.

"You have figured out walking is a waste of time."

"Yep."

"Where's your multiple?" he asks.

"Oh, I ... I left her at the Twin Gates."

Claude's eyes narrow, and I think he's trying to read my mind, but I turn up the volume in my head and play a nonsensical sitcom to shoo him away. He retreats from my thoughts.

"Where's your multiple?" I question back to him.

"I have many multiples both inside and outside the Twin Gates and all throughout NoWhere or NowHere. You're not my only student."

"Really? Can I meet some of them?" I didn't know I had classmates.

"We'll discuss it later. For now, we need to keep moving."

We step into the shack, which houses the other reality that is the Collective. Claude and I decide to speed things up and concentrate on the auditorium and the collection of monks, and we are there outside the privacy circle, which is the stage of this crazy theatre. The monks wear their black robes with their hoods up and their heads forward, looking ominous as their faces are invisible except for an occasional chin, mouth, or nose—never their eyes. People mill about outside the circle, minding their own business and don't notice us.

We request entry. I hear the same woman's voice come from everywhere, and the more I think about it, the voice must be within my mind. It bids us enter. We step over the threshold of the privacy circle, and the crowd noise behind us is gone. There's only the Collective.

The Collective is silent. I feel the pressure of their gathering thoughts trying to creep into my head. They must have worked up a way to penetrate my mind, even though I play a complete sitcom there. My auditory memory is so good that I play parallel comedy show scripts in my head along with laugh tracks to push them away. The pressure increases. It's as if they believe they can break me. Maybe they're working together to subdue me. My headache is coming back, throbbing like a drumbeat. Panic grips me for a moment, and I think of my training. Visualizing my boat on the sea at night, there are no waves; the sea is glass. I do this while I focus on a pinpoint of light, which allows me to hear what's going on outside of me. I focus to hold these two things together.

My headache goes away, and the pressure subsides to nothing. I'm quite comfortable that the Collective cannot enter my mind.

"Very good." The voice from what must be the woman in the front row of the Collective. "Claude, you have done well on this part of her training."

"Thank you, Madam," replies Claude.

"Too bad you failed on the rest of it," says a voice I recognize as Roman, somewhere up and to the left. "She allowed them to cross over. Do you realize the damage they could have done?"

That Roman guy's a jerk. He's one of those whiny types—never happy.

"We understand," said the Chairwoman, "but the same training she uses to block us from reading her is what she used to mend the tear."

"She's still too dangerous. Why do you dismiss me on this?" asks Roman.

"Dangerous ... Dangerous ... Dangerous ...." The voices bubble up from different places in the auditorium.

"As we agreed before, we must weigh the potential positive against the potential negative. So far, the scales appear to tip in our favor," says Claude.

"Yes, but for how long?" drops in Roman.

"How long ...? How long ...? How long ...?" ask more voices from the Collective.

"Silence," said the Chairwoman. "We'll discuss this after we've heard from the emissary."

"May I enter?" It's a familiar male voice.

The Chairwoman's head turns ever so slightly to look at somebody behind me. "You may enter."

A white hooded and robed figure steps into the privacy circle beside me. He stops and puts his hands on his hips but refuses to look at me. Something about the way the figure's stance bothers me.

"Emissary, you accept the rules of the Collective?" asks the Chairwoman.

"I do."

"Then proceed with your deliberations."

I feel Claude tense beside me, and the figure turns to face me.

"Hello, Lucinda, my sweet."

I'm unable to see all his face through the shadows, but I can see enough.

"YOU!" I yell.

19 – EMISSARY OF KOODZIMA

"YOU!" returns the Snake Dude, mocking me. He faces me, pointing with a bony talon, and leans in slightly, whispering, "So cliché. You can do better than that." He wears a tight, twisted little grin, showing a single fang. Throwing back his hood, his eyes have a yellow glow with slits for pupils. The scaly exterior is gone, and his head is clean. He looks more normal, as if he's trying to tone down his creepiness. I'm in shock and have no more immediate words.

"Emissary, you accepted the rules of the Collective," barks Claude, rounding from the other side.

The Snake Dude raises his open claws. "I will do no harm to this one ... all in good time."

I find my voice. "Why is he here?" I ask Claude or anyone else who will answer.

"The Emissary of Koodzima requests an audience with the Collective, and we are bound by the Rules of Palaver to oblige him," says the Chairwoman.

"I'll oblige him with my foot up his scaly butt," I mumble.

"Ah, ah, ah," admonishes the Snake Dude, wagging a talon at me. He turns back to the audience. "Esteemed Collective." He makes a slight bow. "I have been sent here to discuss an opportunity."

"What kind of opportunity?" growls Claude.

"An opportunity to regain something lost to you." The Snake Dude scans across the auditorium, claws splayed with arms out from his sides,

"To all of you."

He has the ugliest jazz hands I've ever seen; no manicure could fix them. I'm seething at his little performance, but I remain silent as I'm curious as to what he will say.

"What is lost that Koodzima could give us?" asks the Chairwoman.

"First of all, 'give' is not the operative word here. Let's use 'exchange' instead."

"Exchange, then," she responds.

"Koodzima is willing to trade," the monster glances at me and smiles, "access to the Star of Larissa." He let that declaration smolder in the minds of the Collective. A few gasps bubble up from the audience. I have no idea what star this is.

The Chairwoman twists slightly in her seat. "How is that possible? That Star disappeared and is gone forever. How can Koodzima say it will provide us something it could not possibly have?"

"But that is where you are wrong. It has been hidden from you." The Snake slinks across the circle and comes to a stop in front of me.

"You mean Koodzima has hidden it," says Claude. His complexion darkens, and the muscles of his jowls do gymnastics.

"I'm not here to comment on that particular point of contention, but Koodzima is willing to return the Star to the light of your universe." He holds up one gnarly talon. "If … you are willing to trade."

"Trade what?" asks Claude.

The Snake Dude looks at me. His eyes gleam in the light of this place. "YOU!" He points at me. "Maybe I should reconsider. That one word *is* effective. You are now as white as my robe."

"Me?" I ask. "You want to trade me for a star?"

The monster flexes his claw into a fist and then relaxes it. "It's not just any star. If you would pay attention, you would understand."

"Regardless, we do not bargain with thieves," says Claude.

"Yes, but *you* do not speak for your order … do you?" asks the Monster.

"No, he does not," says Roman, standing. "We would entertain your proposal. Continue." Roman returns to his seat.

"Hold it. You can't barter me," I exclaim, holding my arms out.

"I guess someone needs to read The Rules of Palaver," quips Roman.

I whip around to face Claude. "What's he saying? Claude, what does he mean?"

"Calm yourself," whispers Claude.

"Calm Down! You brought me here knowing full well I had an issue with this," I say, flicking my hand at the Snake Dude, "thing,"

The monster snickers as I rail at my situation. His grin is so wide it cuts across his whole face. He's immensely happy with this scene, and it appears to nourish his nasty soul.

"Lucinda, please," says Claude. "I knew he might be here, but not about his proposal."

"Well, now he says I'm to be sacrificed by your monk friends. And some of you have the nerve to call *me* a witch?" I say this to the audience while looking at Roman.

"But you are a witch, aren't you?" sneers the Snake.

"You know what ...? I've had enough of you." I take a step closer to him, my hands curl into fists, and I raise them like a boxer.

The Snake backs up and raises his claws in fake surrender.

"Lucinda, control yourself." Claude grabs my arm. I shake his grip loose, but I stand down.

"Madam of the Collective," says the smarmy Snake, approaching his audience while ignoring me, "isn't it the decree of this order that all who enter NowHere must travel in multiple form?"

"Yes, it's an imposed construct to this realm as a protection."

"And no one can circumvent this?" asks the Snake.

"No, it's embedded in this space that no one can disregard the command, even if they choose."

I get a sick feeling of where this is going.

"As you see," says the Snake, pointing behind us to a figure in the distance outside the privacy circle. "My multiple is present. However, I ascertained during a lapse of Little Miss Lucinda's decorum that for some unexplained reason, she has no multiple."

"That is not possible," says Claude. "Lucinda, please call your multiple here."

I kick my foot against the floor three times where I stand. "Um, here's the deal. I got a horrible headache after I split into my multiple, and it was so bad I decided to integrate myself before I met up with you."

"You're not only forbidden, but it is simply not possible to integrate once you step inside the Twin Gates," says the Chairwoman.

"I don't know how I did it, but I had a feeling I would need to focus and—"

"See? I rest my case." The Snake takes a step forward. "She somehow cast a spell to integrate herself. Something no one here can do. She is ... a witch. Why do you insist on protecting her? It's a fair trade: The Star in exchange for this troublesome girl."

"The Emissary of Koodzima provides a compelling case. We should consider his offer," says Roman.

"One problem, Bubba. I won't allow it," I say, now in a full boil.

"We don't need your permission," says Roman, leaning back into his seat.

"You should be careful, or I might turn into a newt," I say.

Silence.

"Madam, she can't do that, can she?" Roman quietly asks.

The Chairwoman sighs. "Lucinda, you are not permitted to modify anyone."

I guess they didn't get my sense of humor. "I understand," I say.

More silence.

The Snake crosses his arms and appears amused at the verbal volleys we exchange. He stands, waiting with his body tilted.

The Chairwoman lowers her head. I don't know if she's thinking or resigns herself to some fate. It makes me nervous.

She raises her head. "Emissary, I speak for the Collective. We request more time to consider your offer."

The Snake doesn't appear pleased with this soft rejection. His smile fades, and he unfolds his arms. "Very well," he hisses through clenched teeth. "This offer will not be extended indefinitely."

"The Collective understands. You may leave."

The Snake Dude looks like he wants to say something else but catches himself. "So be it." He does a small bow and turns on me. "You might feel like you won, but I wouldn't rest easy. Anytime."

I catch his drift, but can't help but add, "Don't let the Twin Gates hit ya where the Demons of Hell split ya."

He approaches me and stops within inches of my face. His eyes narrow, and he speaks quietly. "You're on borrowed time. Spend it wisely. They won't last long. Soon they will *beg* me to take you away."

He laughs and marches from the circle, disappearing with his multiple.

20 - PALAVER

I turn to Claude, "What's that all about? I thought he was my imagination gone wild—some monster my fears had created. Now, I find out he's some emissary?"

"He is R A N D E," spells Claude. "I don't want to give that universe the pleasure of his name being spoken aloud."

"Randy? This thing that has terrorized me for months," I shake my head in disbelief, "is RANDY?"

"No, the 'E' is silent. He's from a different universe."

"Let me guess. He's from a dark universe ... far, far away. The emperor he serves is a heavy breather who's my real father, right? Give me a freakin' break."

Claude screws his face into a knot. "Yes, it is a dark universe but the rest. I don't follow you."

"Of course, you don't. Who could follow any of this?" I say, and spin in a circle of frustration with my arms out.

"Lucinda, we haven't dismissed this assembly," comes the voice of the Chairwoman.

"That's another thing. You know my name, but I don't know yours."

Silence.

"My name is Thekla."

I feel only a measure calmer. "Thank you. Thekla, please tell me what just happened?"

"I will do my best, but there are some things even words cannot complete the picture." She fidgets ever so slightly in her seat. "We are not exactly sure what Koodzima is or where it is. We believe it is a universe that has few, if any, stars. We haven't been able to discover much. They have been trying to get a foothold into our universe since we can remember. At this time, we are in a standoff. Rande is their latest emissary."

"Why are they interested in me?"

"That is why we requested more time. The Collective needs to properly explore this subject. Let me ask you the same question," replies Thekla.

"Not sure. I'll have to think on it." Why does everyone look to me for answers?

"She knows, but she's unwilling to say," pipes up Roman.

"You're such a hater. I don't know if you're jealous of me, scared of me, or too stupid to know the difference." I continue to stare at this monk, hiding behind his hanging hood. I still don't know what he looks like, and he doesn't appear to look my way.

"Forgive Roman's concern. He has been charged by the Collective to protect us from the nefarious interests of Koodzima," says Thekla.

"Excuse me for not pardoning his insensitivity and willingness to trade me away to the enemy against my will."

"Your will is irrelevant. It is the will of the Collective and the safety of our universe that is our concern," says Roman.

"Do you expect me to believe that *you* represent our universe?"

More silence.

I turn to Claude. "I need to leave. Be … before I say something I'll regret. I'll meet you at The Watch."

Claude nods that he understands.

"She must swear allegiance to this order before you allow her to leave," says Roman.

"Lucinda, we must ask you to take an oath you will not hinder the authority of this order," says Thekla.

I turn from Claude to again address the assembly. "I'll do nothing to harm you or our universe. I swear it. I'm not sure I understand all the consequences of any of my actions, so I'll need Claude to help me make sense of this."

The Collective is more at ease, relaxing in their seats. For some reason, they think they have control of my soul—my spirit; the idea really rubs me the wrong way.

The words, "It is good. It is good. It is good," rise up from the Collective.

I step forward. "However, I believe you need to understand that I *do* have free will. Therefore, I will continue to attend the Collective in singular form to remind you."

A collective gasp escapes from the assembly. I focus on an image of the training room of The Watch. I do not ask permission to leave and disappear from them.

I arrive at The Watch and take a seat in one of the empty chairs near the entrance. I look out through the windows of the lighthouse tower at the calm water below. The sky is clear, but clouds form low to the horizon. I lean forward and rest my elbows on the table. I steeple my fingers and stare at them in thought. Several moments pass, and I sense someone in the room with me. Thinking it's Claude, I turn my head and instead see David.

He nods his head. "Can I sit?" he asks, sweeping the hair from his eyes.

"Sure. Where have you been? It feels like forever," I say.

"I've missed you, too." David moves toward me.

"Why haven't you visited my dreams?"

"Claude asked me to give you space to focus on your lessons."

"Ah, Claude. I think I'll be taking a break from training. I just got back from an interesting and disturbing visit with the Collective."

"I heard." David glances at his feet.

I give him a who-told-you look and then follow it with a sigh.

"Claude filled me in."

"Then you know I got ambushed, and they tried to sell me to Randy."

He nodded. "Yes, Claude asked me to talk to you."

I jump to my feet. "Don't tell me you're in on this? Then I'll have no one to talk to."

"No. I'm not included in what the Collective does. Claude realizes you might be a little spooked."

"Spooked is not exactly the word." I sit back in the chair. "Can you tell me about Randy and Koodzima? You called him a Dark Dreamer before, but now I find out he's something more."

"No, nothing more. Koodzima is another dimension or universe folded inside or outside of our universe. Where? We're not exactly sure because no one has been there. Or if anyone has, then no one has returned to tell about it. Rande is a Dark Dreamer. That's what we've called his kind forever. He is the latest emissary in a long line of whom we have allowed to meet with us."

"Why is he such an ass?"

"He has an agenda, and obviously, it involves you. Koodzima wants access to all the worlds in our universe. This plane is a portal for them to get to these worlds. He's trying to disrupt the Dream Maker."

"Dream Maker? What?"

"Who? What? Where? Why? How? That's the point. No one is certain. You can think of the Dream Maker as the entity who created all of this, the stars, planets, solar systems, and galaxies of this universe."

"Like God?" I ask.

"From our perspective, yes." David shifts from one foot to the other.

"Why do they want to disrupt this Dream Maker?"

"They belong to a different universe—a different Dream Maker, so to speak. To put it simply, if they disturb our God, then they influence and twist what we *know* and what we *are* into something different. Possibly even destroy us. Koodzima is a dark place—devoid of much of the beauty of our universe."

"Sounds like their Dream Maker sucks and lacks imagination. Randy must be a child of a lesser god, and Koodzima just wants what they don't have." It amuses me to think of Rande this way.

"That's one way to look at it, I guess. Maybe they want us to share our universe with them." David shrugs.

"I know people like him back home. They never stop. Give them a micron and they'll want a meter."

David looks at me for a second as if he doesn't understand.

"What? I'm trying to use the Metric system more." I sit and rub my face. "My immediate problem is I now have trust issues. Thekla, Roman, and the rest of their cloaked cronies make it sound like I am their property to trade. They reference the Rules of Palaver and say they could do whatever they want."

"Mmm, the Rules of Palaver." David holds his chin in thought.

"What are they?"

"They are the rules that govern the truce between our universes. The Collective and Koodzima agree to abide by them. It has been that way for as long as anyone can remember."

"Can I see them?"

"Why?"

I put a hand to my chest, and in my best I-do-declare voice, I say, "So I may conduct myself in the way the Collective thinks proper, of course."

David shrugs and goes to a closed bookcase behind him. The glass doors show nothing inside, but when he opens them, I see volumes of books. David grabs a huge tome bound in a material of which I am unsure. It's cracked and dusty. He carries it over and drops it on the table in front of me.

"Here, knock yourself out. I know what you're about to do, so I'm gonna take off."

"Okay," I say, still looking at the book. I realize I must approach this like a lawyer and commit this volume to memory. I read out loud to myself.

As I slog through every page, I notice an interesting clause that leaves room for interpretation. I find one that really stands out from the rest.

I read that clause twice and sear it into my memory.

21 – OUR SCHOOL

Enjoying a more normal moment, I was glad to be in the mundane reality of good old planet Earth and to just be a simple high school sophomore. My other reality for the last few nights had caused some emotional distress.

Traveling the halls for my first-period class, I was uncertain if I was paranoid or just sensitive to the attention of others. It felt as if there were a force field around me—like a huge bubble. If I could step outside my body and look down on myself, I was sure I would look like a ten-foot boulder with a river of students flowing around me, but they never got too close. They parted away from me like the Red Sea for Moses. Now, I remembered why school sucked. Did Brad or Evan say something? Was someone's dad a cop who ratted me out about what happened at the Fair? I decided it was a culmination of things mixed with a sixth sense that my fellow students had developed: she's weird; give her space.

I didn't need any of them. I could get along fine by myself.

Who was I kidding? Like I said before, I'm a bad liar, so bad I'm unable to even lie to myself. I wanted to belong, but now that my other reality had encroached on this one, it was clear things would likely get worse.

I kept hearing my mom's voice in my head, "Get over it, Luce. Don't let anyone get you down, least of all yourself. Ignore it. Don't let the past define you because today is a new beginning." When I was a kid, Mom knew the right thing to say to pull me through this kind of stuff.

English class with Dr. Van was my first stop. I took my seat and waited for the fun to begin. Dr. Van had a poetry exercise for us. The class was supposed to write and share a poem. The assignment was to compose something capable of eliciting an emotional response. This was the third day, and alphabetically, I was next. The fun part was that the rest of the class was supposed to critique it. Awesome, now there would be sanctioned student abuse.

"Miss Locke, you're up," said Dr. Van.

Great. This morning I pulled an old poem I had written a while ago from my stash. It had some artistic flare and enough teenage angst to get me the **A** I craved. I took my place behind the lectern to the left of Dr. Van's desk and read my little gem.

I Don't Know

The water is falling through a miller's wheel.
Millstone is grinding the grain into steel.
The sun beats down so hard, it cools my soul.
I lost my mind; all that's left is a hole.

The kite has fallen. The string's in a ball.
I can't unravel it. There're knots through it all.
Could you please give me a hint or a guess?
And help me try and clean up this mess?

I sit and stare at the blue of the day.
Seeing the thoughts my lips won't say.
I tried to be the girl of his dreams.
Finally, I see how absurd it seems.

I don't know who I am or where I have been.
I don't know what to say or where I should begin.
I hope you'll listen and try to understand.
A teardrop is missing. Could you please lend a hand?

I shut out the room while I read, so I had no clue what their reaction might be. I looked up to the firing squad of my class and waited for the sniping to begin.

"Okay, who will be first to critique?" asked Dr. Van.

A few people raised their hands.

She pointed to a boy in the back row. "Simon, we'll start with you."

"Uh, I didn't get the grain to steel and the sun cooling her soul stuff. You can't grind grain into steel or have the sun cool you. It was confusing. Was she doin' drugs or somethin'?"

What a dolt.

"Yes, Miss Brown," said Dr. Van.

Great, it was Kimmy.

"I think the author has some deep-seated problems with depression. I do agree with Simon that the work appears to be fueled by substance abuse. She's groping around for teardrops. Like what does that mean?" said Kimmy, in her sing-song voice, sounding as if she were a valley-girl cheerleader. Give me an L. Give me an O. Give me an S …

Some people are just too linear to understand certain things. Maybe I hadn't thought through the content of my poem and how it left me exposed.

"Okay, everybody, stop right there," said Dr. Van. "This is a beautiful poem. The author is trying to express feelings that are difficult to put into words, so she juxtaposed the grain with steel and the heat of the day to cool her soul. Let's stop the drug references in your critiques. Lucinda, would you like to tell us about your piece?"

Not really. "I'll try," I said. "It's not autobiographical. I just imagined a girl who was in love, and she couldn't make sense of her feelings. That's it. No one's on a crack pipe. No one's suicidal."

"Very good, Lucinda. Anyone else have something constructive to say?" Dr. Van waited for a second. "Miss Williams."

Maggie held her hands over one another on the desk in front of her in a demure style. "I thought it was poignant and real. She captured the pain that dealing with boys can cause, and her poem painted an emotional picture for me." Maggie paused a second or two and added, "Luce is a good friend, and I can honestly say that no hemp plants were harmed in the writing of this poem."

The classroom burst out in laughter. I even noticed Dr. Van give a hint of a smile. Leave it to Maggie to smooth things over. Dr. Van ended my torture and moved to the next student.

The rest of the school day passed, and I headed for Theatre One. Today was the day we would find out the role assignments for the play, *Our Town*. Hoping I would get a good one, I was petrified at the same time. If I got the lead of Emily, it would be great, but then it would mean performing in front of my peers. English class demonstrated today that most students were not patrons of the arts. Did I want to put myself out there and be a further butt of jokes? Who knows, I might raise myself to a level above crazy redhead.

Maggie showed up out of nowhere and strolled alongside me. "Today's the big day. You ready?"

"I'm so nervous, I was tempted to skip class and call you tonight," I said.

"Why're you worried? Your tryout went perfectly. I got choked up when you performed that scene." She sighed. "My version of Emily wasn't near as good. I'll probably get the role of Mrs. Gibbs or something."

"Your tryout was just as good. I would be surprised if you didn't get the part. Your reading was bright and energetic."

"Luce, you don't realize how well you did. People listening behind me were impressed. You possess those same traits you think I have. You also portrayed a longing sadness in a matter-of-fact way that nailed the scene. I would be pissed at Ms. Thatcher if you don't get the part. The play won't be as good without you as Emily."

I knew how much she wanted the part, and it touched me to hear her say that. Most people, let alone friends in a competitive situation, might get jealous or bitchy but not Maggie. She was a true friend, and I loved her dearly. "You're the best," was all I could say as we took our places.

Across the room, Evan looked up, smiled briefly, and waved but didn't come any closer. I guess my nightmare friends blew my chances with him. Since the Fair and the attack, Evan had been acting a little strange. I didn't seek him out because I was afraid he would tell me exactly what he thought, and I couldn't bear the rejection. I was more fragile than anyone knew. If the wrong thing were said, I could fly off into a rage or bust down and cry a river. Since I couldn't tell what would happen, I avoided the people that could break my heart.

Ms. Thatcher came into the room a few minutes later. She held a sheet with our names and the roles we would play. "Okay, so let's get down to business. I'll call out your names and assign your roles."

She assigned the smaller roles first, and she got down to the bigger ones.

"The role of George will be played by Evan Grantford."

Evan had been looking at the floor, not even wanting to see what Ms. Thatcher said—only to hear it. When his name was called, his head shot up, and he beamed a huge smile.

"The role of Emily will be played by..."

Time stopped. Evan and I stared at each other. I turned.

"Lucinda Locke," said Ms. Thatcher. "You two will be great."

"I knew you'd get it," said Maggie, putting her hand on my shoulder. "That's awesome." She seemed upset.

"What's wrong?" I whispered.

"All the other female roles are taken. What's left for me?"

"Now," said Ms. Thatcher. "The role of the Stage Manager will be played by Maggie Williams."

"What?" said Maggie, maybe louder than she expected.

"You have a problem?" asked Ms. Thatcher with a faint smirk.

"Oh, no. No. I just assumed one of the boys would play the part since the Stage Manager also plays the owner of the drug store and the minister."

"Mmm. Don't you think you can play the part as a female?"

"Sure, yes. I just … I don't know … thought that role was beyond me, somehow."

Ms. Thatcher stopped and smiled a moment. "Geraldine Fitzgerald did it in 1976."

"Who?" asked Maggie.

"The *who* doesn't matter. Maggie, you did an excellent job at the tryouts. So much so, I thought you could handle it. The Stage Manager is really the lead role with the most lines and the most responsibility to drive the play. You have such a strong will as a person that I have faith in you for this part, regardless of what sex it was originally written for."

"Thank you, Ms. Thatcher," said Maggie, in a tone both reverent and grateful.

She would give her all to the role, and I expected her to be great. I returned the favor and gave her a hug. Once I released her, she launched into re-reading the play from a new perspective.

With all the roles handed out, we spent the remainder of the class going through each role and what Ms. Thatcher's expectations were for the production and our responsibilities.

After the bell, I approached Ms. Thatcher. "Thanks for the part of Emily. I won't let you down."

"I know you won't," said Ms. Thatcher. "Every time you spoke Emily's words, you channeled the spirit that Thornton Wilder breathed into that role as he wrote it. The third act, when you converse with the dead, almost brought me to tears. And for an old Stage Marm like me, that's not easily done."

Evan appeared beside me. "Thanks for George."

Ms. Thatcher looked to both Evan and me. "Both of you'll make a fine New Hampshire couple."

Heat warmed my face. I was unable to stop it. Evan had an aw-shucks look as he glanced at me. We thanked Ms. Thatcher again and headed for the door.

Once outside the classroom, Evan stopped. "How … how have you been?"

"Good," I said quietly. I could still feel my whole being flushed, and I imagined my face looked like a bright red apple.

"Missed talking to you. I called, but you didn't answer," said Evan.

"Sorry. I guess the whole Fair thing got me frazzled, and I don't know how to talk about it with you."

"Oh, look, *that* whole thing. I'm so embarrassed." Evan shook his head and closed his eyes as if in shame.

"About what?" I asked, disbelieving he should have any guilt.

Evan sighed as if he were admitting something horrible about himself. "I totally froze. The whole thing is a blur now. How can I be your boyfriend? I totally wimped out. I'm so sorry." Evan looked at me with eyes that pleaded for forgiveness.

I threw myself into his arms and gave him a gigantic hug, holding him tight. I fought the urge to drown his shoulder with tears.

"I thought I was going to lose you," he murmured.

"You sweet idiot," I whispered into his ear, "I'm not lost."

22 – TRAP DOOR

I had an appointment with Dr. Rami this week, so I wanted to work on my mandala. It would give me an image I could concentrate on during my sessions with him and hopefully allow me to focus better. I pulled together some sketch paper and my colored pencils and did some research online on how to create one.

In the center of the page, I made a huge circle. In the middle, I created the eye symbol for The Watch. I drew a smaller concentric circle around just the eye. Then, in the lower left and upper right, outside the main ring, I sketched the old-timey key for the Twin Gates. In the opposite corners from the keys, I drew my friend, the black and white bird. In the upper left corner, the bird flew toward the circle. In the lower right, I drew the bird again. This time, its back was to the circle with its wings spread and tail feathers splayed in the same position it had when it was sunning itself. In between the inner and outer circles, I drew pictures of the Twin Gates, the bear from the maze, the black doorway to NowHere or NoWhere, and the little shack that led to the Collective. I stared at my work for almost an hour until the mandala burned itself into my mind. I saw it with my eyes closed. Just like Dr. Rami asked, I had made it personal with those images from my dream world.

On Wednesday, I drove downtown to Dr. Rami Bosch's office. The nurse waved me to come back since the doctor was waiting. A dimly lit hallway led to the inner sanctum of the doctor's lair. The other offices were empty on my left and right. At the end of the hall was his office, and I knocked gently on the door. It opened almost immediately as if he had been lurking there, awaiting my arrival.

"Ah, Miss Locke, I'm glad you made it. Please have a seat." His arm extended to his chairs and couch.

I decided to be brave today and take the couch. Although the doctor had a strange vibe, I did feel safe in a weird way. He had never acted inappropriately that I could tell. I looked past my feet to a dark-paneled wall filled with hung degrees, certificates, and diplomas.

"Mmm, the couch. A different approach for our next series of office visits together?" Dr. Rami circled to the chair nearest my feet so he could face me.

"I figured I'd try out your couch and see if it was any better than the chairs," I said in a snarky tone.

"Oh, is it comfortable?"

"Yes, it will do."

"Let's begin." The doctor pulled out the green metal frog and clicked it a couple of times. "Remember our little friend? I want you to close your eyes and concentrate on the sound it makes."

I closed my eyes and focused my brain on the metallic clunk as Dr. Rami clicked the frog several times in a row in a slow, methodical beat.

"Lucinda, when you hear this sound, you need to stop whatever you are doing and listen for my voice. I don't want you to break your connection, just be aware I am here."

"Okay, but what if I get into trouble, and I want to abort your visualization exercise? How do I break free?" I asked.

"Mmm, a particularly good question. Is there something you have an aversion to? Something that you particularly dislike?" I peeked. The doctor sat with his legs crossed and leaned back. His glasses were perched on top of his head.

I thought for a moment, the only thing that popped up was … "Acorn squash. My grandmother would try to trick it up with cinnamon and orange juice so I could eat it." I grimaced and smacked my tongue as I could still taste it.

"Well, I guess you can think of the smell of cinnamon and orange juice. That could be your trigger. Keep your eyes closed. Try to imagine you're in a bakery with cinnamon rolls. Can you smell them?"

I focused on the image and tried to recreate the aroma of cinnamon rolls. I could smell them now. "Yes, I smell them."

"Okay, now pour a glass of orange juice and try to drink it. Smell the tangy orange juice."

I imagined trying to drink the orange juice in the bakery. As I drank, the two smells collided and made me gag. I sat up on the couch and bellowed a retching cough.

"Wow," Dr. Rami mused aloud. "You have a real talent. Just don't use it for anything dangerous, like say, bulimia."

I threw a glance at him and coughed a few more times. "Don't plan to," I said, annoyed.

"When you feel better, lie back down on the couch."

I cleared my throat a couple more times, lay down, and once again closed my eyes.

"Okay, so first let's talk about your homework."

"Homework?"

"Your mandala. Did you create one and burn it into your mind's eye?"

I opened my eyes. "Yes, I sketched it out and studied it for an hour yesterday."

"Perfect. Close your eyes, again. We are going to practice a technique you should be very adept at completing. It is opening the pineal door."

There was that word again. I was going to say something crude but thought better of it.

"Remember, it is the gland in the center of your brain that is the seat of your soul, so to speak. Roll your eyes back into your head and look at the center of your brain. Visualize your mandala there. Once you see it, shift to concentrate, and imagine a trapdoor you're trying to open. I will give you silence to focus."

I stared into the darkness of my mind and summoned the mandala. The eye of The Watch was regarding me with a curious stare. I felt it become more real as if it were going to blink. Once the mandala floated there, I slid into visualizing myself standing on a trapdoor as one would find in some gallows. I looked down at the square door. It was made of slats of solid oak. The hinges were visible behind me, and I focused on the latch directly in front of my feet. I willed it to open. I imagined lock tumblers that would fall into place, and the door would fly open from the weight of my body. The door rattled on its hinges as if it were about to burst open. It felt real.

"Click. Clunk," went the metal frog, and then I heard Dr. Rami. "You have any luck down there?"

I rolled my eyes forward, opened them, and looked at Dr. Rami with what must have been a face to match my aggravation.

"Oops. Sorry. Anything?" Dr. Rami had an amused look, like he really enjoyed this.

"Yes, I almost had the door open when your friend, Froggie there, inserted himself into the scene."

"Great! That is exactly what I hoped. I wanted to make sure the sound could pull you back. It worked even better than expected."

"If you had given me a moment longer, I would have been through," I said, irritated.

"Um, I gave you twenty minutes. Didn't want you to spiral down and become nonresponsive for hours. Remember?" He twirled his pen around his fingers and scribbled another note.

"Twenty minutes? It seemed like only a few." I sighed. "I guess you're right. The frog did the trick."

"Yes, the deeper you go, the less effective it will become. You were shallow enough that it pulled you out. I think the frog will do fine. Let's try again. I'll give you another thirty minutes before I click it. Listen and try to stay connected, but also, try to communicate with me."

"All right." I lay back and got my mandala focused, but this time I projected it onto the outside of the trapdoor. I got back into that state quicker than the last time. The door rattled again. It got violent like something was trying to get out. It lifted me as the door banged in place. The trapdoor went quiet. Muffled silence filled my ears like I was a hundred feet underwater. Everything calm. Wham, the door flew downward, and I shot through it into utter darkness with a whoosh.

~ ~ ~

I stand on the shores of The Watch, but I don't feel the same as before. It's spooky weird. Turning around, I see Claude at the top of the dunes, waiting. I make my way up to speak with him, but he doesn't react. I guess he's just being pissy the way only he can be. When I get close to him, he turns and walks toward the lighthouse.

"Claude. Claude," I yell. He stops for a moment, turns around, stares at the beach but ignores me and keeps trudging onward. I catch up and decide to follow him into The Watch.

We climb the stairs through the layers of the lighthouse. Claude crosses over the threshold of light and into the training room. I follow, but the light isn't as bright as usual. I find Claude sitting, looking out the window. I choose to sit in a chair opposite him.

He squeezes his face up like he smells something rank, looks right at me, and says nothing.

Fine. I can play this game and pretend to ignore him, too. I look at my fingernails and clean whatever dirt or stuff my dream reality has for me there, waiting for Claude to speak.

Soon, from the direction of the threshold, I see a figure approach. The figure gets closer. It's David. He steps right in front of me and talks to Claude. "She here?"

"No. I got the notice she was coming, but no one was there." Claude gives a small shrug.

I don't believe this. They're both playing with me—ignoring me. What's worse is I see only David's back as he speaks to Claude. Neither of their faces is visible; I only hear them as they cut me out of the conversation.

"What're we going to do, now?" asks David. "Koodzima's serious, and they want an answer."

"They won't like the answer we give them."

"Yes, but is the Collective strong enough to withstand them? Some are weak and susceptible to suggestion." David shoves his hands into his pockets.

"True, there are a few that are easily swayed. And there are others I do not trust. I have faith the majority will do the right thing," says Claude.

"For how long? We've got to tell her."

"Tell me, WHAT?" I yell at them. Still, they ignore me.

David glances behind him at me in the chair. Maybe they should take me more seriously. Then David backs up a few feet until he's right in front of my chair. When he starts to sit, I yell at him to stop and close my eyes, waiting for the impending crunch. But there is no crushing weight—only a strange sensation. I open my eyes, and David is not sitting on me or beside me but sharing the same space as me. He sat through me.

I jump out of the chair and float to the ceiling and softly land between them. They are both in thought. I stand before Claude and wave my hands in front of his face. He can't see me. Neither can David. I'm a ghost in this reality and having an out-of-body experience while I'm out of my body. Trippy.

I decide to have some fun with this and pass my hand through Claude's head. He looks over to David.

"What's wrong?" asks David.

"I had this strange feeling just now." Claude cocks his head.

"My whole body tingled a minute ago when I sat down," says David.

"Click. Clunk," chimes the frog, but this time I'm not pulled from the dream. I listen for Dr. Rami's voice.

It's a whisper. "Lucinda, how are you doing? Can you speak to me?"

"Yes, I hear you. You hear me?"

"Your voice is a whisper. You must have broken through the doorway. Where are you?"

"I'm in a dream, but nobody can see or hear me. It's like I'm a ghost."

"Oh my, you're nested. I've not known of anyone who could do that," says Dr. Rami.

"What do you mean?"

"Well, you're not just in another dimension of a different reality. You've somehow become enfolded in that reality. Most people who have an OBE step outside their physical bodies here. They see people and places they have no way of knowing, otherwise. But like you said, it's like you're a ghost and only tethered to their reality. It's as if you're an astronaut in another galaxy doing a spacewalk. Don't panic, though. Stay calm."

"Stay calm? Am I in danger?" I ask.

"I don't know. This is uncharted territory for me."

David stands and says, "I hear whispering."

"Me, too," says Claude. "Wonder what that means?"

"It means I can spy on all of you," I say.

23 – LAST LESSON

Being a ghost in a separate reality while my supposed guide sits helplessly beside me may send most people into a hysterical fit, but I feel fine. I readily accept that I have a power that didn't come with a set of instructions. It doesn't matter what I believe, so long as I believe in myself. Enough of assuming the role of pawn, it's time to take things into my own hands and stop putting my faith in others. Sure, I'll go along to get along, but I'm going to maintain my own agenda as well.

"Lucinda, are you all right?" I hear Dr. Rami speak inside my mind.

"Yes," I answer. I see Claude and David looking about them, trying to figure something out. I think of cinnamon and orange juice, and I choke and gag. I drop from my ghost state. Upon opening my eyes, I'm where I expect to be.

I stand on the shores of The Watch.

No longer a ghost within my other reality, I am an active element within it. "Dr. Rami," I say. "I'm no longer nested, but I need to work out an issue here. Can we go radio silent for a while?"

I hear a soft sigh. "Okay, I'll leave you alone. Maybe read a magazine. I'll check in with you shortly," says the doctor.

I climb the dunes, ascend the staircase of the lighthouse, and cross over the threshold to the training room. Claude and David are so involved with each other's conversation that I completely surprise both when I walk between them.

"Where did you come from?" asks Claude, taking a step back.

"Same place as always," I say, in a nonchalant manner.

David moves forward and puts his hand on my shoulder. "I thought you weren't coming."

"What makes you say that?" I ask.

"I got a message you were on your way, but you weren't there," says Claude, a strange look of doubt crossing his face.

"I guess whatever alarm or message center you use is out of sync somehow. I just arrived and came on up." I gave them no hint I had been spying on them.

"Mmm, that's not how it works. It's never wrong," Claude says, and then drops his head in thought.

Yeah, go ahead and ponder all you want. "What do you want to talk with me about?" I ask in my catty way.

"What makes you think that?" David tilts his head to me.

"David, it's the first time I've seen you in the training room with Claude. I thought you were supposed to let me train, uninterrupted." I cross my arms. I'm trying to reverse the suspicion. "Why else would you be here unless there was something you two need to discuss with me?" I step forward. "Spit it out."

"There's some trouble with Koodzima. They've been requesting that the Collective decide on the trade for you," says David.

"Requesting or demanding?" I shoot at Claude.

"That is not the issue. The problem is Koodzima threatens to demonstrate their intentions somewhere inside of NoWhere," replies Claude, rising from his seat.

"So not Trade? You mean Attack?" I say.

"Well, that would be a more specific way of looking at it," says Claude. "But we're not going to entertain any discussions with them. The Collective knows there is some reason Koodzima wants you, but they are afraid if they hand you over, they may be sealing their own fate."

"I believe they're right," I say with no reservations.

"Why do you say that?" asks David. "You sound like you know what they want." He runs his hands through his dark hair and sweeps it from his face. I notice his piercing eyes are full of concern.

"Not really. I have a feeling Koodzima thinks I can help them with something, but they don't realize I have no intention of cooperating." I shift my weight from one foot to the other.

"They are persuasive. Do not underestimate them," says Claude.

"Oh, believe me, I haven't, but I think they underestimate me," I say and approach Claude. "What is it you're not telling me?"

Claude rears his head back, trying his best to feign ignorance, but I know there's a truth hiding there, and I'm going to figure it out, one way or another.

"What do you mean?"

"Claude, I may be young, but don't take that for stupid. You know something and you're holding out on me." I jab my finger at him in an accusatory way. "What is it?"

Claude resigns himself to whatever truth he wants to release and relaxes his stance. "There are things you need to know about Koodzima and what they are capable of doing." He looks out the window a moment and turns to me. "We have maintained a cold peace with them for what would seem to you like a thousand years. When your first multiple arrived, things got more serious. Koodzima became more insistent we locate you."

"How did they find out about me?"

"We are unsure. Someone released that information without the Collective's approval."

"So how long have y'all known about me?"

"Since you were born," says Claude.

"Since birth? And when my multiple hit on my eighth birthday, your call came for training." I say this to no one in particular, talking to myself.

"Yes, which you promptly ignored," says Claude. I couldn't tell if this fact irritated or pleased him.

"The Collective was concerned with more than just my attendance?"

"This is true, but there were factions of the Collective that did not want to find you—to keep you hidden," says Claude. "I do not know whether it was a ploy to hide you or stunt your growth. Either way, it was best you did not reveal yourself."

"Why didn't you say something?" I ask David.

"I did, but Claude told me to keep our friendship a secret," says David.

"For eight years? What faction were you a member of?" I ask Claude. "To hide me or minimize me?"

Claude holds himself to attention. "Let's just say I did not want to give Koodzima or the Collective the satisfaction of your presence."

"You had suspected their motivations?"

Claude nods.

"Things must have gotten interesting as I approached my second multiple."

"Indeed," says Claude. "That is when Koodzima took matters into their own hands and initiated a search for you. The peace went from cold to lukewarm, and it continues to heat up."

"About the same time, Randy started to attack me in my dreams."

"Interesting thing is, it wasn't all his fault," says David.

"What do you mean?" I ask.

"You found him as much as he found you."

"Wait a minute, I did nothing to invite that dim bastard into my dreams."

Claude shrugs. "Not consciously, but somehow you were able to surprise and catch them unaware of your presence."

"You pissed them off, as much as you intrigued them," says David.

"David and I have been working to shield you from them and everybody until we could better understand your situation," says Claude.

"What have you learned?"

"We've learned there is so much more about you to understand that it boggles the mind." Claude cradles his chin in his hand.

"Ah, flattery won't allow you to change the subject. What do they want? Why are they chasing me in my dreams and crossing over after me?"

"It's a mystery, and that is why we want to keep you close, but it has something to do with your mother and whatever talents you inherited from her. They believe you are the missing piece to their plans."

"Or a threat to them in some way?"

Claude looks at David. "Mmm, we hadn't thought of that, but it definitely has a ring of truth to it and could explain some of their actions."

"What actions?"

"They're about to start a war," says David. His face is stern.

"Why?"

"They want the resources from our universe: power, light, stars," says Claude. "They are all related. It is an age-old struggle between the haves and have-nots. They believe we have been selfish and not willing to share with them. This is true, only because they are ruthless and poor stewards of what we provide them." Claude throws his hands up. "They are not trustworthy."

"Why am I the one in the middle?" I ask. "I just want to run home and let y'all deal with them."

"But there is no place you can hide. They'll just follow you and create havoc in your home reality," says David.

"What am I supposed to do? I'm behind in my training."

"That is not entirely true," says Claude. "You have one last lesson, and then I will release you from your training. Multiple Multiples. You may find it necessary to preserve yourself by partitioning your consciousness into many copies."

"David told me the side effects could cause me to become fractured. I could lose my mind."

"Yes, I did. This is way too dangerous," says David to Claude as David steps between us.

"I have considered that. However, everything else she has done up to this point has been fraught with peril, and she hasn't wavered in the least. My concern is what happens if we don't go over it. What then?" Claude stands rigid in his spot, waiting for David's reply.

David drops his head, nods at his feet, and then backs off a couple of steps. "I still don't like this. It could get out of control."

"We will discuss all the aspects with her. Lucinda, are you ready?"

"I … I guess so. You two are scaring me."

"Nonsense, you are an excellent student, and I am confident in your abilities." Claude is brimming with assurance in me.

I glance at David, his head is still tipped, and he looks at me with such sad eyes. I'm torn. I know what's coming is inevitable, so I must prepare. "Ready."

"Creating multiple multiples is pretty much like splitting yourself, but you have to visualize each one of your multiple selves splitting as well. Here is the key piece. You must also embed within your vision that they are tied together with the *Silver Cord of Lucinda*."

"Huh? Silver Cord of Me?"

"Yes, this is the part I cannot teach. You must develop that cord in whatever construct you choose. It must be strong enough to pull them together, no matter how far apart your multiples are. This is so you can reassemble your consciousness when you so choose. Let's begin. Assume your Multiple stance."

I stand with my feet shoulder-width apart and put my hands together as if praying.

"Good, now when you split yourself, choose a visual to latch onto, and attach yourself with your multiple. If you are split into small numbers, it is not as important, but when you split into more than a handful, you risk losing track of yourself."

I close my eyes and feel the familiar ripping sensation of splitting my personality. I open my eyes and I become We.

"Excellent. Now, each of you assume the stance and multiply yourselves."

We each put our hands together in prayerful repose, and again, the tearing feeling allows us to separate. We open our eyes and see four of us standing together in a line.

"Good," says Claude. "Do you see your silver cord?"

We see nothing. "We can't see anything between the four of us. David? Claude, do either of you see anything?"

"No, only you can see your cord. You must create a visual that means something to you and embed it into your split each time. Remember, it's important to do this to bind all of you together. You must practice this on your own."

We reintegrate ourselves into one being. "Okay, I'll work on that. Thanks for the tip."

"Click, clunk," chirps the frog.

"Oops, my ride is calling me. Gotta go." I think of cinnamon and orange juice.

"Wait," says David.

I wave to them as I blink away.

~ ~ ~

Opening my eyes, I stared at a medical degree on the wall of Dr. Rami's office.

"Welcome back, Lucinda. I appreciate you staying connected," said Dr. Rami. "I trust you had an interesting time. You were talking to someone? I couldn't quite make out what you said, but you mumbled something about 'Learned', 'Multiple', and 'David'."

Glad I didn't mention Claude. "I was talking to David, and he told me about creating Multiples."

"Multiples?" Dr. Rami ripped his glasses from his face for effect. "Please tell me you haven't multiplied yourself."

24 – THE SHOWDOWN

I decided to listen to his explanation, but I knew Dr. Rami was overreacting about creating multiples.

"Why? What's the harm? A little split personality never hurt anyone," I said with a lopsided grin. "Look at Jekyll and Hyde, Professor Marvel and The Wizard of Oz, Miss Gulch and the Wicked Witch of the West, the Munchkins and the Flying Monkeys … need I say more?"

"Huh?" said Dr. Rami, his face screwed up in a knot, trying to figure me out. "The Munchkins?"

It's not going to happen, Doc, I thought. I won't give you the satisfaction of an easy answer. I'm coming into my own and doing things my way.

Dr. Rami twisted in his seat. "Look, I'm serious here. Creating multiples in your dream state is dangerous. If you do it wrong, you won't come back the same. I've seen it happen. You must construct—"

"I know. I know. I must construct the *Silver Cord of Lucinda*," I replied.

"Who told you that?" shouted Dr. Rami.

Whoops, maybe I revealed too much. "What?"

"The silver cord method … that's an advanced technique. Who on the other side have you been talking to?"

"Something David was telling me."

Dr. Rami shot to his feet, threw his notepad behind him on the chair, and pointed his red pen at me. He shouted, "Don't give me any more of this David crap. I want the truth. Who is telling you this?"

I was shocked at his harsh tone. "I … I don't know what you mean," I lied.

"Just because I'm old doesn't mean *I'm* stupid," he roared.

It was his turn to slip up. "You heard more than just a few random words, didn't you?"

Dr. Rami's indignant posturing soured.

I got off the couch and stood toe to toe with him. "Come on. Say it. You know more than what you're telling me. Don't come off holier-than-thou." I pointed at my chest and leaned into the conversation. "Scolding me like *you're* … my dad."

"I … I." It was time the Doctor felt some heat.

A commotion came from outside the doctor's door. The nurse yelled at someone that they couldn't come in there. Dr. Rami appeared more pale than normal. The voice I heard responding to the nurse chilled me—from my lips to God's ears. The door flew open, and Dad stood framed in the doorway. His hair stuck out in all directions. He panted hard with his head tipped down like a bull ready to rip a Matador's butt a new one. But his eyes—his eyes behind those glasses were squinted hard, laser-focused on Dr. Rami. He looked wilder and scarier than anyone I had ever seen.

"Oh … shit," I moaned.

"BOSCH. Did you forget what I told you if I ever saw you again?" Dad bellowed.

"Charles, this is not what you think." Dr. Rami put his hands out and backed up a couple of steps toward the couch.

My father resembled a crazed grizzly as he stomped forward a few feet, his arms held in a fighter's stance, fists clenched.

"You remember the protective order?" Dad yelled.

"Now wait … that was for your wife." Dr. Rami raised his chin and threw his shoulders back as if he had an argument.

"Wrong answer," growled Dad and charged Dr. Rami.

"Dad," I screamed.

Dr. Rami ran behind the couch. Dad came beside me and stopped. He acted like I wasn't there. He focused on one person—Dr. Rami. Dad proceeded to chase the doctor around the couch.

"Dad, stop," I yelled, but he was too fixated on catching the doctor.

He stopped and doubled back on Dr. Rami, but the doctor adjusted and ran the opposite way.

"Wait … let me explain," the doctor kept saying, sounding more out of breath.

Dad grunted and growled at each turn and adjustment, but he kept Dr.

Rami moving. It was comical, like two kids chasing each other around a parked car. Both men were getting winded. In a bold move, Dad attempted to leap over the couch's back to get to the doctor. He tripped, but as he fell over the couch, he smacked the doctor on the knee, knocking him down. Dad scrabbled after him and grabbed Rami's ankle as he tried to stand and run for the door. He crawled along the doctor's body as if climbing a tree, straddled him, and punched him hard across the face. The doctor flailed his arms, appearing dazed.

I grabbed my father around his chest from behind and tried to pull him off Dr. Rami. Dad resisted and fought to get in another punch. I dragged him enough away from the doctor that he missed.

"You SON OF A BITCH!" Dad screamed. "I WILL KILL YOUR ASS THIS TIME." He swung again, but I lifted Dad enough so that Rami wiggled and gained some distance. Dad's blows glanced off Rami's chest and stomach. A couple landed hard enough for Rami to gasp and grimace in pain. Dad struggled to get free.

Dad relaxed only slightly when two Dallas police officers burst into the office. Dr. Rami crawled far enough away and scrambled to his feet, backing into the police officers as they rushed into the office. The younger officer grabbed the doctor and escorted him to a corner away from Dad. The second, heftier officer lifted my dad off the floor. The nurse hovered at the door.

"What's going on here?" asked the officer with Dad. He was burly but seemed tough enough to handle the situation solo, if necessary.

"Doctor Quack here," said Dad, taking big breaths, "is making a move on my daughter."

"That is not true," said Dr. Rami, smoothing his hair down, straightening his bent glasses, and trying to tuck his shirt back in.

"Is this your office?" asked the burly officer of Dr. Rami.

"Yes. My patient, his daughter," said Dr. Rami, pointing at me, "and I was conducting a follow-up session when her father barged into my office and attacked me."

"Your patient? YOUR PATIENT?" Dad regarded me with a terrifying gaze.

"Yes, my patient," repeated the doctor.

"How long have you been her ... *doctor*?" hissed Dad through clenched teeth.

"A couple of months now, Mr. Locke."

"Bullshit," yelled my dad and struggled to get closer for another swing, but the officer restrained him.

"Sir, if you don't calm down right now, I'm going to cuff you."

"Officer, he's lying. If he's her doctor, then why haven't I received an Explanation of Benefits from my insurance company?" asked Dad.

The officers looked to Dr. Rami for his response. The doctor hesitated for a beat longer than he should have.

The younger officer with Rami asked me, "Is he your doctor?"

"Yes," I said.

"Has he been inappropriate with you?" asked Big and Burly, and immediately followed with, "Has he put his hands on you?"

"No. God, no. I understand the concept of inappropriate," I sassed the officer with my hands on my hips.

"Lip from you doesn't help," said Big Boy.

"Doctor, if she's your patient, then why haven't you billed the insurance?" asked the younger officer.

"I … I felt sorry for her. I did the work pro bono," stammered Dr. Rami.

"*Sorry?* More like *Guilty*. He's already killed my wife," said Dad.

"What?" I turned to Dad and stared. He knew I was looking at him, but he was locked onto Rami with a burning hatred.

"I did NOT … KILL … LARA!" shouted the doctor and lunged forward. "If you weren't such a horse's ass … It's *your* fault!"

"You sick bastard. Don't turn this around on me," screamed Dad.

I was speechless. I felt nested within my own reality: buried within a web of secrets, wrapped in a set of lies, inside of good intentions gone bad.

"Okay, cuff 'em both," said the burly officer.

"Turn around," yelled the young officer to Rami.

"You, too," said the other to Dad.

"Why are you—" started Rami.

"NOW," screamed the cop into Rami's face.

Once the cops had them cuffed, they seated them in Rami's high-back chairs across from each other. Both officers stood over them to prevent any more physical threats. I retreated and leaned against the wall near the door with the nurse. She was rapt with attention at all the proceedings, and I was sure she would have some great gossip for her book club.

"Do you two want to go downtown?" asked the big cop.

"No, sir," they each said.

"Good, 'cause I'm this close," the officer said, raising his thumb and forefinger with a sliver of space between them. "Believe me, you won't like it there. But if you can't calm down, then we're going to have to take both of you in to cool off. You're in luck. It's the end of our shift, and we'd prefer to skip the booking and paperwork."

"Yes, officer," they repeated.

"Do you want to press assault charges?" the younger one asked Dr. Rami.

"No," Dr. Rami replied.

"Do you want to press charges?" asked the same officer to Dad.

Dad shook his head.

The officer spoke again, "I don't even know what it would be: Medical Treatment of a Minor without Parental Permission? Joe, is that even a crime?"

"Hell, if I know," replied Officer Joe. "Okay, we're going to uncuff you both, and you, sir, are going to take your daughter and leave." Then, facing Rami, he said, "And you, Doctor, are going to stay in this office until they leave the premises. You understand?"

They both nodded.

"Any one of you so much as squeaks, I'm going to run you all downtown for processing. That goes for you, too, Missy-with-the-smart-mouth."

The officer uncuffed both men and escorted Dad and me outside.

"Mr. Locke, I don't want to see you here again, or we *will* go downtown," said Officer Joe.

"We'll talk at home," Dad angrily whispered as he left me to get into his car.

I took the long way home and drove slowly. I wanted to think about all that had happened and the revelation that both men blamed each other for my mother's death. I was on Dad's side, but I wanted to know what happened from each of their point of view and piece together the full truth. I pulled into the driveway and opened the garage door with the remote. I entered through the laundry room to the kitchen. The house was so quiet that it creeped me out. Going through the kitchen, I passed the dining room to the den. Dad sat in his favorite leather recliner, leaning forward with his elbows on his thighs and his fingers entwined together. He stared at his hands and did not raise his head to look at me.

"What the hell is going on?" he asked his hands in as normal a voice as I thought he could muster. He lifted his head and fixed his eyes on me. It felt like maybe he bore, not only his eyes but his soul, into me as I saw a mixture of fear, anger, and pain. "How did you get mixed up with that jerk? How did he find you?"

"He didn't find me. I found him. Remember the second week of school? I had the nightmare, and the next day I called you 'cause I was coming home early?"

He nodded.

"I had a nightmare during Spanish class and woke up screaming on the classroom floor. They sent me to the school nurse, and she told me she remembered you and Mom when you went there. She mentioned that mom had headaches and Dr. Rami helped her."

"Which nurse was this?"

"Ms. Dooley."

"That old bitch is still there? Figures. She was the one who introduced Rami to your mother."

I sat on the couch until I believed the silence had crept around us enough to the point of being uncomfortable and said, "Dad, I didn't set out to hurt you. I wanted to find out more about Mom." I reached out and touched the arm of the recliner. "I know talking about her hurts you, so I didn't want to bug you. But I need to understand. You say we are so much alike, but you won't talk about her. Dr. Rami would."

Dad took a deep breath and sighed. "Sweetheart, don't you know you're all I've got? You're my reason for living. When your mother … passed, a part of me also died. I'm so scared it's happening again. Soon, you'll be gone, too." Tears welled in his eyes.

"I'm not going anywhere. Now, tell me how Dr. Rami killed Mom."

He ran his hands across his head from forehead to neck and clenched his hands so tight I heard his knuckles pop. He opened them, leaned back into the chair, and looked up at the ceiling for a moment. "Dr. Rami didn't exactly kill your mother, but I blame him for pushing her to it.

"He had helped her with the headaches, and then he worked to hone her skills. She was pulled under his spell, and he became a kind of Svengali father-figure to her. He encouraged her to push the boundaries of her gift, and I believed he had too much influence. It didn't feel right to me. She gave too much emotion to their *professional* relationship." He used his fingers to put quotes around the word, 'professional.' "I'll admit I was jealous."

"She became more distant and lived more in her dreams than with us. I couldn't get through to her. She slept the days away, as well as the nights. We had you, and you were in second grade at the time. You wanted to do all these after-school activities, but it got to the point she wouldn't even wake up to get you from school. She got progressively worse until she never woke up. I can't sit idle and watch it happen again. When I saw him with you, I just lost it. All these negative memories came back along with an old anger. It's the same nightmare all over."

He put his hands over his face, and I knew he was crying.
"Dad, I won't let anything like that happen to me."
"Promise me you won't see Bosch anymore."
"I promise."
At the time, I fully intended to keep that promise.

25 - HOMECOMING

The explosive turn of events at Dr. Rami's office was put on hold. This was Homecoming Week. Life must go on, and as Maggie told me, this year had to be great. My personal school life had improved a bit with Evan and me being an item. We spent extra time together running over our lines for the play. It was a great excuse to call or stop by each other's houses. Evan had asked me to the Homecoming Dance right after we got our parts. That was a couple of weeks ago. Today was Thursday. Tomorrow was the big game, and Saturday was the dance.

Evan had bought me the most humongous, loud, dangly mum with all sorts of bells and rattling junk attached to it. It was the most obnoxious and obscene display of marking anyone as their girlfriend that I have ever seen or could remember.

It was awesome.

Maggie and I met in the lunchroom. She was already seated as I approached with my tray.

"OMG," said Maggie. "You look bent like an old woman. That mum's pulling you forward and sideways."

"Yeah, yeah. Yours is no better." I pointed to her mumstrosity and then carefully maneuvered mine in such a way that the streamers and stuff didn't dip into my plate of spaghetti while I ate. I imagined what it looked like to Maggie.

She covered her mouth with her hand and roared her laughter as if no one would know who was laughing. "You need to ask Evan to buy an extra ticket to the game ... for your mum," she managed to choke out between laughs. She was indeed tickled by my predicament.

"I don't care how crazy huge it is. Evan gave it to me, and I'm going to wear it. He spent a lot." I laughed as well, but I enjoyed the attention.

"I know. It just looks physically painful to wear."

I smirked and leaned closer. "It's almost unbearable."

"See what I mean."

"I said, *almost.*"

"Where's Brad going to take you for dinner?" I asked.

"Silvio's."

"Oh, that's a nice place."

"You and Evan can change your mind and join us?"

I fiddled with my food and didn't look up. "No, I think we'll do our own thing. Evan wants to take me to a certain place."

"Listen, I know Brad's been a little weird around you, but we can still hang out together. I convinced him the carny dude was a hypnotist and put all those thoughts in our minds. Once I fell from the stage and cracked my head, the carnies freaked and carried us out behind those buildings and left us there. He believes it, mostly, but I think he gets twisted around sometimes. He says he still has nightmares about it."

We ate a few mouthfuls.

"So, how have your nightmare friends been doing? You haven't talked about any new episodes since the Fair," said Maggie and shoveled in a bite of salad.

"I'm learning to keep them at bay, but I sense something's coming."

Maggie was silent for a minute. "Let me know if I can do anything. I hate for you to do this alone, but I'm not sure how to help."

"I've got it covered. Just help me hang on to my sanity." I motioned to the world around me.

"Okay." Maggie smiled and changed subjects. "So how late is Chuck going to let you stay out?"

"Midnight."

"Midnight?' Maggie set down her fork. "That's when all the fun starts."

"I know, but I don't want to push him too far right now."

"Why? What did you do?" asked Maggie with a wicked grin on her face.

"Nothing, really. He's just concerned about me being out on the road late at night with crazies like you driving around," I lied. I didn't want to get into Dr. Rami with Maggie. She and Dad were on the same wavelength when it came to Rami, and I didn't need any more grief.

"Oh well. We're going to have fun anyway. I'm so glad you got a date this year. I didn't want to go through anything like our freshman year."

"What do you mean? I came to the dance last year. I didn't need a date. In fact, the freshmen were discouraged to have dates."

"Yes, I know. But you were upset that none of the boys asked you. This year, you and I can tear up the dance floor 'cause we've got guaranteed dance partners." Maggie did a shimmy shake in her seat. "Does Evan like to dance?"

"I don't know. I think so. I'll drag him out there."

"Good. We can't waste one moment."

~ ~ ~

Friday, I arrived at Evan's house to pick him up for the game. His birthday wasn't for a couple of months, so I was the designated driver. He didn't mind. He was so laid back and easygoing. Maybe that was what I liked best about him. He was a good complement to the drama plaguing me—opposites attract.

He met me at the door, his aura beamed happiness. "Hey, you." He gave me a big hug but was careful not to crush the mum.

We both were casual tonight. Jeans and a polo shirt were our ensemble style. "Tomorrow, you'll be shocked," I said.

"Why?"

"I'll be wearing a dress."

"Looking forward to it."

I was about to query him as to whether he didn't like me in jeans, but I recognized my own insecure thoughts and let them pass. That's not what he meant. I'm getting better at this girlfriend thing. I just grinned back.

"I was going to get you a mum garter for your upper arm, but I figured you might think it was weird," I said.

"Yeah, not too hip on wearing flowers. Don't get why they're pushing them on guys now. I guess it's just more fundraising." Evan shrugged.

"Good, 'cause I need you free to help me negotiate through the crowd with this thing," I said, pointing to the mum.

Evan gave a twisted grin. He could have felt I was making a crack at the gaudiness of his mum, but he knew what I meant. It made me happy that he was also getting good at this boyfriend thing.

We arrived at the stadium, and Evan pulled out the tickets he'd bought. They were reserved but close to the general seating to our left. Maggie was already in her seat, waiting for the game to start and me to arrive. I sat next to her, and Evan was to my left in the aisle seat.

"Hey, girl. Is Brad ready to kick some butt?" I asked her.

"Oh yeah, he's ready enough," said Maggie, turning around and pointing at the players in their pre-game exercises. "Been warming up harder than I've ever seen."

The game started, and we got up by a couple of touchdowns. It looked like we were going to roll to an easy victory. We had the ball again, and Brad made a huge catch for a touchdown, but there was a yellow flag on the field. The referee conferred with one of his zebra brethren, I think he's called the side judge.

The referee stepped forward and announced, "Offensive pass interference, number 81."

"What?" cried Maggie. "I didn't see Brad push off the cornerback. Boo," she hollered along with the rest of the home team.

Brad seemed upset as he talked to his coach.

I sighed. "Too bad there's no instant replay."

Our team recovered from the penalty and got nearer to our goal line. It was fourth down, and our coach decided to go for it. A pass came to Brad in the end zone. He was about a second from making the catch when the safety blatantly pushed him down, intercepted the ball, and ran it back for a touchdown. We all waited for the flag. There was none. Brad hopped up and down, furious. His coach came off the sidelines toward the same side judge who stood with his arms crossed. Our coach railed at him, and the side judge pointed into the stands at the home side of the field. Then the side judge turned with his arms crossed and just stared into the crowd with a huge grin.

A chill crept along my spine. I felt the prickling tingles of adrenaline as it flowed through me. It couldn't be. No way, it could be. I couldn't see the side judge's face due to wearing a cap and the shadows on the field.

The referee called a penalty against our team for unsportsmanlike conduct, and we had to field the ball deep in our territory. We executed a couple of running plays and got close to a first down. The third-down pass was again for Brad. The cornerback stepped on his foot, and Brad went down. Clearly, it was interference, but again the cornerback caught the ball and ran it in for a touchdown. Pleas for football justice were met with indifference and what looked like more pointing into the stands.

This is what happened for the rest of the game. Anytime the ball came to Brad, he was fouled by the other team, and the officiating crew turned a blind eye. This continued until his coach had to bench him.

"Man, how much money did it take to pay off this crew?" asked Maggie, incredulous.

"And why do they keep pointing up here at us?" asked Evan.

I shrugged. I had a suspicion but no proof. I couldn't tell if any of the refs were from Koodzima.

Once the game mercifully ended, our team had been crushed. The score was 66 to 14. The players slogged with slumped shoulders, making their way to the locker room.

All three of us waited outside for Brad. He exited through a doorway off the side of the gym, his head hung low. Every other teammate that left after him gave him a look.

"What happened out there?" asked Maggie.

"I have no idea. It's like my worst nightmare come true." Brad threw up his hands. "Every time the ball came near me, I'd get fouled or get a flag, and then the other team would end up with a score. The refs refused to do anything. It was like they hated me or something."

"Why did they point up at the stands?" asked Maggie.

"That's the weird thing. When we asked why they wouldn't throw a flag, they'd just point up into the stands and said, 'Ask her.'"

26 – THE DANCE

Saturday was the Homecoming Dance. Blocking out the game on Friday night, I tried to start the day out fresh. I concentrated on the things I controlled, like having fun, enjoying my friends, and hanging out with my boyfriend. Who knew what this day would bring? I wasn't going to be the one to spoil it.

I had picked up my dress from the cleaners. Convincing Dad that a consignment store was a good enough place to find a dress, he mentioned, for some reason, I was God's gift to Fathers of Daughters everywhere. The dress was gorgeous, but it had a small stain on the hem. He insisted I take it to the cleaners and let them try to work the stain out. It was a chic black evening dress with enough bling to appease even Maggie's sense of glam style.

It felt strange gliding up Evan's walk in the thing, as I had never really worn a dress quite like this. My hair was tamed, pulled up, and back. Maggie had come over earlier and helped me with my makeup. I suspected that I looked nice since Dad appeared speechless. It felt like it took him over a minute to say anything. He just stood there, amazed, smiling, and shaking his head in disbelief. Then he held me hostage while he took pictures.

Evan greeted me at his door. He had the same reaction as Dad while his parents lurked close behind over his shoulder. They beckoned me inside and treated me like royalty. It was weird and cool at the same time.

"Oh my, Lucinda. You are stunning. Evan couldn't stop talking about you this whole week," said his mother. She was a petite woman with a wonderful smile. Her red hair was shoulder-length and hung straight. Now I understand why he liked redheads.

"Mom," Evan admonished.

"What?" his father asked, grinning. "She's a beautiful girl, and you like her, so what?" Evan's father was a rather tall and pleasant man.

"Thanks," I croaked and dipped my head from the attention as if I performed a small curtsy. I had met them before, but I continued my best Miss Manners impersonation. They would find out I'm not as girly a girl as they thought, but why not keep the facade alive for at least tonight? Hey, I looked the part.

Like my dad, they took numerous pictures. Evan asked them to take one with his phone, and he sent a copy to mine. The picture was great. And then I shared it with Dad.

We arrived at The Palacio, where Evan had made a reservation a couple of weeks in advance.

Evan pulled the chair out and seated me—such a gentleman. The waiter came and brought the menus.

"What specials do you have?" I asked politely.

The waiter sighed and then ran through his list. His posture suggested he'd rather be flossing. I decided to test him.

"Question?" I asked.

The waiter raised his eyebrows in response. "Yes."

"I was wondering about your seafood special. What kind of fish was that again?"

He closed his eyes for a long moment. "It's halibut," he said, enunciating each syllable as if I were deaf.

He had a creepy mustache like the ones serial killers wear. As a habit, I don't give service people grief as I know they're busy and trying hard to please everyone, but for some reason, this waiter bothered me. Our money was as good as everyone else's. Maybe he thought we're going to give him a crappy tip or something.

"Thanks. One more question?"

He sighed, and this time I detected a slight eye-roll. "Yes," he hissed.

"What's with the attitude?"

"Excuse me?" His eyes opened much wider.

"Yes, I will excuse you, but first answer my question."

He just stared back at me.

"Look," I said. "My boyfriend and I are going to drop about a hundred dollars tonight on dinner. We have agreed that I will take care of the tip." I pulled out three twenties. "I was prepared to give the whole amount to you. A sixty percent tip. All you have to do is make sure everything goes perfect." His attention was piqued. "It could become only forty," I said and put a twenty back into my clutch.

The waiter was interested.

"However, if we enjoy this meal with no further issues, then I'll give you the full sixty."

He gave a small laugh, smiled, and said, "Pardon me, ma'am. Do you have any other questions?"

"No, I do not. Evan, do you have any questions for ...?" I looked to our waiter to prompt him.

"Benjamin," he said.

"... for Benjamin," I finished.

"No, not now." Evan gave a small smile.

We ordered our meal without further incident and the waiter left. I kept the forty dollars on the table the whole time.

"How do you do that?" asked Evan.

"What?"

"Talk to adults that way? If I tried that, my tongue would get all tied up in knots. I'd be the one looking like an idiot, and they would feel certain I was just a stupid kid. But you're so smooth with a twist of wicked. It's fun to watch."

Flattered, I felt my face flush. "I find if I talk to adults like an adult, I get a better response. Also," I shook the two twenties for effect, "applying the appropriate level of capitalism never hurts."

Evan leaned forward. "We never discussed the tip."

"Yes, but he doesn't know that. I just want this night to be perfect. Dad gave me a little extra moolah."

The rest of the dinner went without a hitch. Everything was delivered on time and tasted great. Evan paid for the meal, refusing to take any of my money. I insisted on paying the tip. He agreed, and as we left, I put the third twenty on top of the others. Benjamin had recovered and did all right. Besides, you must follow through on your promises, or people won't take you seriously.

We arrived at the north side of the school. Evan produced the tickets. The music was loud and thrummed throughout the gym, breathing energy into the room. The DJ played a special mix of tracks. Opposite the DJ, a band had set up in the far-right corner for later in the evening.

"Hey, you finally got here," yelled Maggie over the thrashing music. She approached with Brad at her side. He seemed happy to see us, and I felt no negative overtones in his demeanor. All was cool.

"Wow, this place is crazy," I shouted, looking over the gym in pure amazement at the sea of students, in all manner of formal attire, undulating across the floor to the beat.

"Come on, let's dance." Maggie beckoned us to the floor, waving a hand to follow her and Brad.

Evan shrugged and appeared game to join in. We all found a place to stomp and shake. It was a blast, and the four of us danced near each other for several songs. A slow one finally came into the queue, and we could take a breather. It was a good opportunity to get closer to Evan. We assumed a slow-dance position: my arms around his neck and his around me. Evan looked great in his tux. There were a couple of beads of sweat on his forehead, and his breathing was slightly labored. I only perspired.

We danced close with our heads side by side. I had rested mine on his shoulder, and I felt him turn his head toward me to speak.

"Did I tell you how incredibly beautiful you are tonight?" he said in my ear, so only I could hear.

We now looked into each other's eyes.

"Sorta. Back at your house, when you just stared at me and said I looked great. That's all I needed, but a girl likes to hear it."

"I wish this night could go on forever," he sighed, with a dreamy gaze on his face.

"You're the best boyfriend a girl could ask for."

He smiled at me and, with a smooth, fluid motion, he moved in for a kiss. I met him halfway. Our lips touched softly and then again with more heat. I ran my hand through his brown hair, and he briefly caressed my cheek before we broke. We didn't want to attract the attention of the chaperones by locking lips for too long.

My senses tingled all over. Evan had a quiet strength about him that really did something for me that I can't really express in words, so I won't try. Once the song ended, we decided to go out into the hall for refreshments. Brad and Evan left to get Maggie and me some drinks.

Maggie sidled up to me. "You and Evan are working well together."

I laughed with embarrassment. "Yes." Now I felt the blood rush to my face. "I really like him."

"I could tell," said Maggie with a smirk. Then, in her best French accent, she said, "Oh … my darling, you are so handsome. I just want to run my fingers through your hair."

"Stop it," I giggled. "Don't you be spying on me."

"I couldn't help it. You two make a cute couple."

"Thanks. How was dinner with you and Brad?"

"It was good." She looked at her hands. "He's still a little freaked about the game. Has some confidence issues, but I'm working that out of him. He'll get over it."

"Sorry about that."

"Nothing you did. He's a big boy. He'll come around."

"Maybe I'll skip the next game."

"Uh, yeah," said Maggie, smiling. "That might be a good idea."

The boys came back and handed us each a plastic cup of punch. We sipped our drinks and savored the break. I felt uneasy being near Brad. Guilt gnawed at me that his football game may have been sabotaged by Rande and his freaky little friends.

The DJ came over the P.A. "Ladies and gentlemen, for the next set we will have a band perform. This group came in from out of town, and they were available for our dance. They come highly recommended. Please welcome to the stage, COBRA!"

My heart dropped a moment. I had to keep a positive attitude. This was not what I thought. No, I begged myself. From the hallway, we could hear the band tear into a frenetic beat and an electric guitar riff that sounded catchy, so people from the hall went into the gym to dance. The crowd moved us along. Plus, I wanted to relieve my overactive imagination.

The band had four members and appeared KISS-inspired. Their faces were painted to make them look like snakes. The bassist was also the lead singer. The group reminded me of something, but I couldn't tell exactly what. Brad must have had some memory sparked as he kept staring at the band while he danced with Maggie. Evan and Maggie were oblivious to anything being wrong. They just rocked out, and the band sounded great, so I put my imagination on hold and tried to enjoy myself.

They played for about an hour and were well received. The lead singer spoke for the first time. He sounded suspiciously familiar.

"This is the last song before we go on break. The following is a request for an original song for a special lady out there. Hope you enjoy it." The singer smiled knowingly and winked in our general direction. He grabbed the microphone with both hands, tilted his head back, and closed his eyes for dramatic effect. It was a slow ballad, and all on the dance floor embraced to slow dance.

"Lucy… Lucy… Lucy… Why are you so slow?

"Lucy… Lucy… Lucy… It's time for you to go."

The singer pointed at me.

Oh no. Who requested this? I thought maybe I was sleeping and pinched myself. It wasn't a dream. I saw Brad stiffen in place and stop dancing. Maggie glanced back at me with a questioning look. The song continued:

"Tried to warn you, but you didn't learn.

"Now it's time to burn… burn… burn."

Then the lead guitarist launched into a riff and blew a huge fireball over the crowd. A collective gasp fell over everyone. It was a bit of shock and awe that the band had managed to add pyrotechnics into the performance. I think the chaperones became alarmed, grouping together, and approached the DJ to discuss.

I saw them through the makeup. The lead guitarist was the Dragon. Rande was the bassist and vocals, and the carney dude was the drummer. I didn't know who the fourth member was. They wore smiles that seemed directed at me, and it seriously creeped me out.

"Holy Shit!" screamed Brad. He grabbed Maggie, "We've gotta leave … NOW," he shouted and dragged her through the exit.

Evan got a little weird. He stood mesmerized by the performance. They sang another verse, but I don't remember how it went as my senses numbed. The sound came through as if I were underwater—all muffled and unintelligible.

The band exited through a side door for their break. It looked as if Rande winked at me on his way out.

"Evan, I *need to* go to the restroom."

"Oh, all right. You need me to get you anything while you're gone?"

"No. Just wait here."

I exited the gym but took a left toward the locker rooms and away from the restrooms. I wandered down several halls and soon noticed I was alone. I found the men's locker room and entered. I could hear talking and laughter on the other side of several rows of lockers. Weaving through the labyrinth, I found myself standing directly in front of the band.

"Lucinda," said Rande, "before you do anything, let me speak."

I said nothing and just stared daggers at him.

"We did not come here to cause any problems. We wanted to personally ask you to reconsider our invitation to visit Koodzima. You might find the experience interesting. Who knows who you might meet there?" said Rande in a smarmy, slick voice. His eyes gleamed yellow in the fluorescent lights. The Dragon and the Carny snickered on either side of him. The fourth member was behind them, and I couldn't tell what he was doing.

"Randy, Randy, my slimy little buddy. Why do you continue to pester me? You're more like a mosquito than a cobra. I may have to swat you."

"It's Rande, the 'e' is silent," he politely corrected. "Now, before you get all pissy and banish us with your little trick, you need to consider the consequences of rejecting us. I'm trying hard to make this a peaceful transition. It will happen whether you accept it or not."

"Randy, I don't give a rat's ass about your consequences, but I do want you to tell me why you *need* me so badly."

"Need you? We don't *need* you. We want you to join us in the spirit of cooperation and goodwill. There is so much we can show you."

"If you just want to be *friends,* then why did you torture me in my dreams this past summer?"

"Torture?" said Rande. They all laughed. "That wasn't torture. Those were tests, which you passed with superb efficiency. You really should consider further discussions with us in our home universe. You would find it more than accommodating. We believe you have great potential."

"Look. Sweet-talking me won't work. You're not going to turn me into Darth Locke. That ain't happening. Your powers of persuasion are pitiful, so you might ask for your money back from whatever Koodzima Charm School you studied."

Rande appeared to stifle his anger and maintain his composure. "You are very funny, Lucy. I don't think you know how funny you really are. Your friend Brad is hilarious, and Maggie's got a lot of spirit. But Evan … Evan is not funny at all. Is he? He makes you all weak in the knees. Right?"

"Randy. Don't threaten my friends. This is my world, and you don't belong in it."

"Okay, okay. Don't get all feisty with us." He put his claws up as if to keep me away. "We'll go, but when you change your mind … and you *will* … come by and see us. Tootles y'all."

Rande threw his head back and laughed at his little joke. Then they all stared at me with menacing smiles and disappeared.

27 - SIDEWAYS

I dropped Evan off at his home. He wasn't exactly sure what was going on since I didn't think he noticed Maggie and Brad had left. It was like he was ignorant of what had happened. We kissed briefly in the car before he got out. Once I got home, I had to reassure my father that I had a great time, which was true up until the last thirty minutes. I didn't share those other details. He didn't need to worry.

David needed to know what was going on. Shirking my duties to connect with the other side, I consciously blocked myself from going there. I wanted to meet at our usual place, so I thought of our huge tree in the meadow—a peaceful place only David and I visited. It'd been too long since we were alone to talk together like we had the past eight years before I crossed my second multiple.

Settling into bed, I thought of the tree and David. Immediately, I felt myself drift …

~ ~ ~

I open my eyes, and I'm on my back. Above me, the beautiful green boughs of our tree splay out over me. Outside the shade of the tree where I lie, the sun is shining bright. The green grass around me feels thick, as if I'm floating. The branches sway in a cool breeze. I study the branches that spiral to the top of the tree, which is dark and full of shadows in the canopy.

In the darkness above, a familiar shape descends. I decide to relax and enjoy the moment since peaceful times like this might be hard to come by later. The shadow drops from the lowest branch and lands with a thump.

"Can I lie here beside you? I need a rest." David smiles down at me.

"Sure. Pick a spot. The grass feels wonderful. No mosquitoes, fire ants, or other creepy crawlers like back home."

David lies down in the grass beside me with his head next to mine, facing each other.

"I need to warn you," I say.

"About what?"

"Randy and his friends visited me tonight. He crashed my Homecoming dance and ruined my date."

"Date?" asks David. "I didn't know you were dating someone. Who is it?" He isn't good-natured with his questions but concerned.

"Why does it matter?" I ask.

"Oh, it's nothing. You never know what people are sometimes."

"Evan? I guarantee you don't have to worry about Evan. He's one of the coolest, sweetest guys I know." I almost laugh at the thought.

"Evan … Evan," David rubs his chin. "You've never mentioned him before."

"So? I want to keep both my lives as separate as possible. Didn't think you cared."

"Why did you try to hide him from me? Before, you'd tell me everything. Now you're keeping secrets." David doesn't look at me but stares up into the tree.

"Whoa there, Chief." I turn and prop myself up on my elbow and look at him. "I didn't think my love life was anyone's business but mine."

"Hey, don't *chief* me." David turns his head, and I see anger, or something, in his eyes. "It just surprises me you haven't mentioned him, is all."

I think I know what's going on. "Mmm, if I didn't know better, I would think you were jealous."

"Jealous? Don't be silly. I could care less about your … *sweet* Evan. Like I said, you should be careful of everyone. You don't know the intentions of people here *or* there."

"All I know is that I tell you Randy pays me a visit, and all you do is latch onto the fact I was on a date, and who it was, and what do I know about him."

"Okay, so what happened?" asks David.

"Nothing happened, but there was an implied threat."

"Tell me what Rande said, word for word." David appears interested.

I paint the scene and the dialogue exchange. "He threatened my friends."

"You can't go to Koodzima. It's a trap."

"I know it's a trap. But I have an idea how to do it kind of secret-like."

He raises his eyebrows. "Oh … how is that?"

"It's a secret. With Claude and everyone reading thoughts, I won't take a chance letting anyone know."

"Oh, so now I'm lumped in with the 'anyone' category?" David pouts.

"Hey, I'll let you know when the time is right. Why're you so pissed off? I don't remember ever seeing you this way."

David sighs. "Luce, I'm sorry. I … I just feel something bad is coming. It just sits on my shoulders, weighing on me, and I'm frustrated that I can't do anything about it. Claude is acting weird. The Collective is acting weird. You're acting weird. It's like I'm blind to everyone around me, and at first, it frightened me, but now it's just pissing … me … off."

"I understand. Now you know how I've been feeling the last couple of months."

"Yeah." David runs a hand through his hair. "I guess so."

I rise to my feet. "Hey, let's get out of here and go exploring. Get our minds off this stuff."

"Okay. Where?"

"What if we just climb the tree into the next place and then pick a different tree and see where it takes us?" I suggest.

"Sure. We just have to be careful."

We climb into the tree and into the high dark canopy where total darkness surrounds us. We climb through the layer, now we flip, and we're climbing down out of a tree into another place where it's night. The shadows are long and spooky from a full moon on the horizon. It's not our moon, but more like a light to guide our way.

I point out across the horizon to all the other trees there and say, "Well, which one do you want to try? Have a preference?"

David shrugs. "It really doesn't matter."

"What is your deal? Is there one we *don't* want to pick?"

"They're all potentially dangerous or interesting. No matter how you want to look at it."

"I'll mark this tree so we can find it again." I visualize a paintbrush full of white paint and mark the trunk with an 'X'.

"You vandal. Do you tag trees at home?" admonishes David. "You think we want your graffiti around here?" He serves up a minor scowl.

I look at the paintbrush and the mark on the tree. "Oh. I'm sorry."

He smiles. "Just messing with you. It'll wash away when you wake up."

We pick the closest tree and climb. We reach the inky, dark layer again, which we must crawl through to get to the other side. That's when I get an idea. David is ahead of me and disappears into the darkness. When I get fully inside the void, I wonder if I can go sideways. I reach out around me, feeling for anything besides the branches I'm holding. Deciding to take a leap of faith, I wander away from the tree. Part of me expects to fall and land with a crashing thud at the bottom but I don't. I travel within this darkness.

The dark space is cloying. As I wander farther away from the tree and David, I feel disoriented and hear muffled voices in the distance. I follow the sound, and as I do, I realize they come from all around me. Unfortunately, I'm traveling in circles and realize maybe I won't be able to find my way back. I concentrate on where the tree might be, based on where I last remember, but I can't find it. A vision of cave divers floats into my mind. Amateur scuba divers don't realize the danger of exploring caves. They kick up the silt, the water becomes cloudy, and they become blind. Some give in to the panic and become lost as they try to find their way back. They run out of air and drown. My breathing gets heavier as the possibility hits that in this reality, I might have done the same thing.

"David," I cry out. I only hear mumbling voices. My shouts attract them, and the voices get louder. "David. Help. I'm lost. David?" The voices home in on me. Their mumbling gets louder, and I almost pick up some of their words. Soon, I feel the presence of several entities near me.

One of them speaks. "Hello?" The voice is male.

I freeze, unsure if these beings are friendly or not.

"Hello, can I help you?" the voice asks again.

"Yes," I say softly. I feel it move closer to me. The panic of being lost outweighs my fear of the entity. It sounds friendly, like a guy, so that's how I will treat him.

"I heard you say you were lost," he says.

"I'm trying to find the tree."

"A tree? Did you really come from a tree?" The being sounds amazed and curious.

"Yes, can you help me find it?" I ask.

"Good Luck. I've been wandering here for what seems like forever, and I've never found a tree, let alone anything like you."

"Oh no, I'm that lost?" I sigh, and I'm sure he hears the despair in my voice.

"Afraid so," he says, and it feels like he is trying to comfort me.

"How did you get stuck here?" I ask.

"You know." I imagine him scratching his head. "I'm not sure. I just found myself here. I don't know how."

The other voices are crowding closer as if these other entities were trying to hear our conversation. "Everybody else here is in the same boat?"

"What?" His voice sounds shocked. "You're the only person here."

"You don't hear the others?"

"Sure, but I don't know if they're people." He pauses as if to think. "I sometimes hear faint whispers, but I chalk them up as auditory mirages from being here so long. Can you hear what they say?"

"Not sure. They sound muffled like someone talking from inside a box." I'm unafraid as his voice is calm, but the stark blackness of this place affects me, and I've only been here for a brief time. "Do you have a name?" I ask.

"Yes, it's ... it's James," he says as if this were a question he had to think about.

"Well, James, maybe we can help each other out of here."

"Sounds good." He maintains a conversational distance of about three feet away. I hear and feel the other voices still crowding in to listen.

"Luce?" I hear David's voice say behind me.

"David. I'm over here," I shout back to him.

"I'm not stepping into that. Follow my voice and come to me," David tells me.

"You hear someone else?" asks James.

"It's my friend, David. You can't hear him?"

"Nope," says James. I wonder why I'm the only one who hears David in this dark void.

"David wants me to follow his voice to the tree," I say to James.

"Can you lead me there, too?" James sounds hopeful.

"Sure, follow my voice." I walk toward David. "I'm Lucinda, by the way."

"Nice to meet you, Lucinda. To be honest, it's nice to meet anyone."

We continue to talk together as I move toward David's voice.

When I get closer, David says, "Who are you talking to?"

"A guy I met here named James."

"Luce, listen very carefully," says David in a very cool and even voice. "You need to shut up and run to my voice as quickly as possible."

"But ...."

"Luce, do it now. And don't lead that thing back here!"

28 – OPENING MOVE

I run fast to David, leaving the entity, James, behind me.
Fear of the unknown and the darkness spurs me on.

James must sense me disappear and yells, "Hey. Where are you going?" Waiting for my response, his voice follows me. "Don't leave me, please. I can't take this hell any longer." Then his voice sounds farther away. "Please help me. PLEASE!" He sounds so pitiful it breaks my heart.

I reach David in the darkness by the tree branches. He feels for my face and puts his hand over my mouth to shush me. I pull his hand away. I don't let anybody try to shut me up.

"Lucinda, please don't leave me. I won't hurt you. If you don't believe me, contact my parents: Jeff and Debbie … Kemper near … Sioux City, Iowa." James says the last part quietly as if he were begging the empty void around him to listen. "That is, if you're even from my world. Oh God, please help me."

"I will come back for you," I whisper and climb up the tree and out of the darkness, following David. When I look down, I see David descending into whatever new reality is there. I reach the bottom branches and drop beside him.

David wheels around on me as soon as I land. "What the hell are you doing? I tell you to be careful. Then you jump into one of the most dangerous places you can find. Does your soul have a death wish?"

His voice is wild with fear. The light in the day of this new reality casts a shadow over him, so I really can't see his face, but if I could, I would know how serious he is. I decide to take the tongue-lashing.

"I'm sorry," I say quietly, my head dropping down in guilt.

"You really scared me. Those voids are like the quicksand of this universe. Few enter, and until now, I know of only one to return. You don't know what things lurk in there."

"But you didn't hear him. He sounds like one of us, begging me for help. Didn't sound like any boogieman. Sorry. I had an idea, and I went with it."

"Luce, you have to promise me before you go with any crazy idea that jumps into your head, you first say, 'Hey David, I want to step into this eerie darkness and see what happens.' That would allow me to say, 'Luce, you know that's not a good idea because of this and that and the other.'"

"All right, I'll consult you before I leap into things." I glance at the ground. "Can I ask you something?"

David ran both his hands through his hair to pull it away from his face. I see his brow all furrowed and tense. "Okay, shoot."

"Tell me more about the voids?"

He sighs and remains silent a moment. "No one is quite sure what they are or where they lead. They're sometimes called the In-Between. Some believe it's a place of banishment—a proverbial hell if you wish. It's a crease, a stitch between worlds or universes. That's why, when climbing the trees, you stay on the branches. On the tree, you're safe and insulated from what lies between the two landscapes. But for someone like you, who can visualize things, it might allow you to create any number of horrible visions. Then you're locked in that darkness with them. Your imagination could take the form of anything you think up and literally kill you or anyone else in there with you."

"It's familiar somehow. I don't know why, but I think I've been there before. Like in a previous dream."

"I don't think that's possible. If you get stuck in there, your physical body dies no matter where it is, and your soul gets trapped. I doubt you were there in a dream or otherwise. Claude has explained that everyone is forbidden to enter the In-Between."

"Mmm, well, no one showed me that rule book. You really shouldn't have said anything. Now, I must go back. You can't expect me *not* to push the envelope."

"I'm serious. No playing around with this."

"Just messing with you." I smile, but in my heart, I mean what I say.

~ ~ ~

David and I decide to go to The Watch to find Claude. Maybe he has some insight. We both visualize the eye symbol and find ourselves on the lakeshore, but the water is not as crystal clear and blue as I remember. The sky appears heavy and dark.

"What's going on here?" I say.

David shrugs, glances behind him, and turns all the way around with his mouth hanging open. "Oh, no." He points.

I glance, and my eyes can't register what they see or what they fail to see. I turn around to look beyond the dunes to the lighthouse for The Watch. The whole top half is gone. Remnants of ragged wood and broken white stone are all that's left of the once majestic tower. It's as if the hand of a huge monster swiped the top off it. There's no sign of life. Claude doesn't wait at the crest of the dunes like I expect.

"No way," I mutter.

"Way," whispers David.

"Could this be ...?"

"Koodzima makes the opening move. I didn't think this would ever happen."

"Is this all because of me?" I feel a twinge of guilt, and I can't help but imagine there are angry people with my name on their lips.

"Let's see if anyone up there needs help," says David and runs up the dunes to the base of the lighthouse.

I follow him, and when we get there, the dunes are strewn with materials: stones, wood, chairs, tables, and books. As we rummage through the wreck, the crack of broken glass crunches under our feet. We find no one in trouble, just literally a shattered dream.

"Can Claude come, re-imagine the lighthouse, and fix this?" I ask.

David shakes his head. "Nope. The Watch was created by a superior being, and as such, it was endowed with certain protections. Something enormously powerful destroyed it, and it cannot be easily replaced."

"Should we go to NowHere and check it out?"

"Good idea," says David. "Let's head for the shack first." His eyes don't focus on anything. He looks like he sees something a million miles away.

We visualize the Shack in our mind's eye and transport there. The street of NowHere running outside of the Shack is empty. Every time before, it's teeming with robed figures traversing up and down. I look beside me, and David is split into Dave One and Dave Two.

The Daves also notice the street, and one says, "Not Good."

"Where is everybody?" I swing my head in both directions, squinting in the distance to see if there's any movement. "It's like a ghost town. Just waiting for a tumbleweed to roll by."

"Hey, don't you need to be split? I don't see how you get away with it. Just coming here forces the division on us," says Dave One.

"I don't like to split my consciousness. It makes my brain muddled. Besides, if I don't have to, why bother?"

"I know, but it's about fitting in and going with the flow," says the other Dave.

"You know me. I'm a non-conformist. Besides, I made a promise."

Dave One sighs. "That is so true. Look," Dave One says to Dave Two, "I'll stay here and watch the road and let you know if I see anything."

"Okay. Come on, Luce." Dave Two waves a hand for me to follow as he goes through the Shack door.

We walk along the corridor, which opens into the huge convention hall. Only a very few people move in specific directions. There's no milling about like I've seen before. We approach the Collective Circle farther in the distance. Not much activity appears to be happening there, either.

Claude appears. His cowl is down around his neck, and his face has an edge to it.

"I take it you didn't get the message," he says.

"What message?" I ask.

"The one to stay away. We are at war."

"We met at The Watch and found the lighthouse in pieces, so we came," says a Dave.

I step forward. "Are we really at war with Koodzima?"

"They destroyed several strongholds and have terrorized people throughout our universe," says Claude.

"Is anyone hurt?"

"Not in the traditional, corporeal way you think," says Dave Two.

Claude wrings his hands. "It's good you're here. The Collective wishes to discuss Lucinda. I think it is best she is here when they do."

29 – CAVING IN

"What do they want to talk about?" I ask.

"About whether they should allow Koodzima to borrow you," says Claude.

"Borrow?" I pause and cock my head to the side. "What kind of interest rate do I command? Is it simple or compound? I really want to know what the credit risk and opportunity cost are for this investment." I say this all Spock-like and cold, remembering it from an internet site I read four years ago, in sixth grade. I got an **A** on that paper.

Claude's face screws up into a knot. "I … I don't understand."

"Certainly, or you wouldn't have used the word. It's a word of convenience for you to avoid what you really mean." I stand up straight at attention. "You and the Collective are going to sell my soul to Koodzima," I spit out, completely un-Spock-like. "Tell me, Claude, did you do this to my mother?"

"No, I did no such thing." Claude looks to Dave Two for support.

"Don't look at me. I know nothing about any of this," says Dave Two.

"I cared for your mother. We were friends, colleagues if you will. I had nothing but respect for her," says Claude.

"What about them?" I say and point toward the gathering Collective. "Did *they* have problems with her?"

"I will say this: there existed a healthy counter-opinion for each of her arguments, but none that anyone found threatening."

"You were her friend, so what happened to her?"

"I cannot say, as I was not here when she departed." Claude tips his head downward.

"Who was?"

"I cannot say."

"Or you won't."

Dave Two is tense and doesn't appear too pleased with the direction this conversation is going.

Claude steps closer to me. "You are correct. *Borrow* is not the word I would have chosen, but that is how it was presented to the Collective, and why I used it."

"Oh, so Randy was here. How long ago?"

"Not too long. Lucinda, I'm on your side. I argued this was insane, but the Collective wants to debate it, regardless. I'm glad you are here to help talk some sense into them."

I realize maybe I'm being too hard on Claude. "Sorry, but I'm pissed they would bargain with me as if I were a thing rather than a being with my own sense of self. I'm also finding it hard to know who to trust."

"No, remain as you say, 'pissed'. That is what they should hear from you. Your spirit is what can save you," says Claude, his eyes showing concern. Other times when I would speak my mind, he would appear irritated, glaze over, or give a condescending look, but not this time. "Maybe you can save us all," he whispers.

Dave Two reaches for my hand and holds it in both of his. "I'm here for you, too."

"Thanks," I say, and look at them both. "Let's go kick some Collective butt."

In unison, we approach the privacy circle. We each mentally request entrance and are granted permission. I play my vision of a boat on a serene sea of glass. No waves: just a mirror to reflect anyone trying to read my thoughts. If they break through, then my brain has something squirrely queued up. It will drive anyone digging around in my head screaming for the hills. I dare them.

The members of the Collective sit cloaked and rigid in their rows of seats, with us effectively on the stage, looking up at them. Their cowls hang low over their faces, so it's hard to tell their demeanor.

I recognize the Chairwoman, Thekla, and the way her thoughts sound. "Lucinda, I'm surprised to see you, given how you left here the last time without permission: a general disregard for protocol and manners."

I decide to play nice until it's no longer effective. "I apologize for my previous abrupt behavior."

Silence. I do not break it.

"Yes," says Thekla. "The Collective does recognize the extenuating circumstances of your last visit and bids you welcome despite your singular form."

I bow my head. "Madam Chairwoman, I understand Koodzima has attacked and now demands my presence."

"This is true. We are prepared to only allow you to visit them for a short period."

"What makes you sure I will return?"

"The Rules of Palaver will protect you," says Roman.

"But the Rules of Palaver state provisions you mention are not guaranteed during wartime."

Roman grabs the large tome and flips it open and points to something there. "Palaver, Section 9870, verse 507, subsection A, states that a hostage cannot be taken at any time during war or peace."

"That's not exactly right," I say.

"Who are you to be questioning the Rules of Palaver?" asks Roman with indignation.

"Me, since I've read and memorized them."

Roman laughs and points at the large book in front of him, "This document has been drafted and amended for thousands of your years. No one could possibly digest, let alone memorize it."

"Well, I have. And you left out a keyword. It says that *emissaries* are not allowed to be taken hostage during a time of war or peace. I'm wondering why you didn't state that. You cheat by having the book in front of you, and you still get it wrong."

"I'm paraphrasing. Still, it does not explain why you claim to know something you could not."

"Turn to any page you want and begin reading," I say.

I feel Roman scowl through the darkness of his hood. He remains still, and his cowl stares at me unmoving for several long moments. "As you wish." He flips to nearly the back of the book and begins, "'Article Five, Section 20,023, subsection 9048: The amendment to the following— '"

I interrupt, "'... subclass is pursuant to acceptance of the proceeding Article Four, Section 17039, ratified and accepted by the Treaty of Leveling introduced by the Collective for the following Anwall.' Whatever that is, and it's followed by a strange symbol of a circle with two parallel lines drawn through it."

"Impossible!" shouts Roman.

"You like that word. Do you know what it means?" I quip.

He closes the book and turns to Thekla. "It is a trick. She reads the book from there."

I laugh. "That would be a rather good trick. Wouldn't you think? Now tell me why you read from that location? It's not exactly the main body of the document, but merely the reference section. Like I said before, you cheat, and asking me to recite from there proves it." I let the comment simmer a second. "What? Are you going to call me a witch, again?"

"Chairwoman, I say we ship her to Koodzima posthaste and be rid of her," says Roman.

I point at Roman and, in my best whiny voice and say, "You started it with, 'I guess someone needs to read The Rules of Palaver.'"

"Enough!" shouts Thekla. "This is not the time for us to fight with each other."

Claude puts a hand on my shoulder to try to calm me. I stop myself. So much for playing nice.

"Koodzima has made it painfully clear we are not prepared to deal with them as we once were. They are in a position to impose their will upon us, and we have no choice at this time but to comply with their requests until we are stronger," explains Thekla.

I shake my head. "I don't understand. You said our universe is full of light and power. They may want it, but the supreme being of this universe is stronger than theirs. How can we be weaker?"

Thekla tilts her head down slightly and pauses. "Our Supreme Being enters a much deeper state of dreaming. There is much more to manage in this universe. Koodzima is dark, lonely, and provides the breeding ground for envy and focused determination to affect change. Our Supreme Being requires us to be active participants in this universe and, in effect, help ourselves. We have become too relaxed, unfocused, and political. The depth of this dream state has rendered certain parts of this universe … vulnerable."

"I will consent to visit Koodzima," I announce.

"Luce. No," says Dave Two.

"What are you doing? I thought you were here to fight this," whispers Claude through clenched teeth.

"They want me to go, so I'll go. Besides, I could use the vacation. However, I do have two conditions."

"Let's hear them," says Thekla.

"First, I need some time to prepare."

"How much time do you require?"

"A couple of months of my time."

"I think that is the least that can be done. Besides, you may need it. What is your second?"

"I request as a protection; you appoint me as a special emissary for this Collective."

"We aren't allowed to appoint her as an emissary. She is not a member of the Collective," argues Roman.

I cross my arms in a huff. "Section 1089, Article 5, states, 'A special emissary may be appointed from outside the Collective and be afforded the same protection as any other representative.'"

"We cannot do that," rails Roman.

Thekla pauses. "We can and we will. It is not an unreasonable request considering what we ask of her. However, Article 109 of the same Section states any emissary must be at least a Level 8 to be a representative of this Collective. I understand that after Claude's training, you are equivalent to a Level 7. You lack an additional level." Thekla lifts her head to stare at me through her shadowed cowl. "You are not the only one with an eidetic memory."

So, I have a brown belt and I need a black one. I guess I could use some more training. "What does Level 8 require?"

"It requires you to work with our Senior Emissary."

Claude and Dave Two drop their heads.

"Who is that?" I ask.

"Roman," replies Thekla.

"Well, that explains it."

"Explains what?" shouts Roman in my mind.

"Explains this current situation we find ourselves. You must especially suck at being an emissary." Murmurs bubble from the rest of the Collective. I guess they're not used to an outsider talking to them this way. I don't care. They need me, and no one ever bothered to train me as a politician. "I don't trust you. For all I know, you could be setting me up. What could I possibly learn from you?"

"You could learn some respect for your betters," Roman hisses.

"Betters! You apparently don't read well enough to recite your own law," I return.

Thekla stands. "Lucinda, you will be silent. There is more to being an emissary than memorization of the Rules of Palaver. Roman, you will prepare her."

"What? That's impossible."

"There's that word again," I mumble.

"She's insolent, intolerable, and a professed know-it-all."

Thekla turns to Roman. "Good, then you two have something in common."

30 – LEVEL 8

Since I was about to enter a new stage in my development,
I decided that one last appointment with Dr. Rami was not only a
reasonable decision but a rational one. I wanted to connect some dots and
cram as much as I could into my bag of tricks. Feeling exposed and
uncomfortable with my situation, I considered my choices. One path
would be to just wig out, bury my head in the sand, and hope things
magically worked themselves out. Since *Hope* was not a business plan, I
had no other choice. I might be truly a dolt, but I didn't see any other way
to deal with this. The only plan I had was to rush in there, butt heads, and
take no prisoners. My methods came from a free mindset, but they worked.

I'd been trying to figure out one thing, though. How had my dad found
me at Rami's? I couldn't have him interrupting me this time. It was there
the whole time, but I hadn't put it together until I got the latest update for
my phone. There was a security flaw in the GPS, which was corrected in
the latest OS upgrade. It got me thinking, and once I did a little research,
I realized he had tracked me through my phone. Dads can be sneaky, too.

At school, I explained to Maggie about my dad's secret spy operation.
She was impressed, but she realized she was duty-bound to help me
circumvent my parental insurgency. If she had known it involved Dr.
Rami, she would have never agreed. I made up some story about meeting
Evan for a secret rendezvous. For that kind of sneakiness, Maggie always
approved. We swapped phones. She had nothing special planned and
decided to hang out at home. If I just disabled the GPS, it would tip off

my dad, and he would be suspicious. I told him I was doing homework with Maggie. Then, if he happened to check my location, he would see exactly what he expected. I even forwarded my number to Maggie's phone in case he called. Looks like Maggie's influence has made me a pretty good liar all the way around. I felt a twinge of guilt, but I knew what I had to do.

Dr. Rami's office was quiet. There was no office assistant behind the glass.

"Hello," I said through the opening. "Dr. Rami?"

A few moments later, the adjoining door opened, and Dr. Rami stood in the doorway. He held a subdued smile and wore a new pair of glasses.

"Miss Locke. How are you?" he asked with a polite purr.

"Fine. And you?" I asked.

"Better. Your father's not going to come busting my door down, is he?"

"No, he doesn't know. Nobody knows I'm here." After I said that out loud, it gave me the creeps. Dr. Rami pursed his lips and nodded acceptance.

The next thing I knew, I sat across from Dr. Rami in his high-back chair. He still appeared suspicious, and I caught him glancing at the door, expecting Dad to burst through.

"Lucinda, last time we were together, we practiced some additional techniques with your nesting abilities before we were interrupted."

"Yes." Did he forget he accused me of cheating on him with another mystic? I was afraid I had slipped up, and he would discover more about NowHere, and what was happening with me in that other reality. Obviously, my dad's antics had distracted Dr. Rami, as he did not pick up the conversation where we left it.

"Have you practiced creating a ghost version of yourself? Do you have any additional thoughts? Experiences?"

Those were loaded questions. I had to be careful what I said going forward.

"Actually, I haven't nested myself since the last time with you. It made me nervous, and since I've been a little stressed out, I didn't want to practice it." I was sure that was exactly what he wanted to hear.

"Probably a wise decision. You are right to steer clear of that technique. You may not understand this analogy, but you might have heard of it. Take a letter and copy it on a copier. Then make a copy of the copy. After each iteration, the copy becomes grayer, fuzzier, less defined," said Dr. Rami with an air of omniscience.

"Makes sense," I shot back.

"The issue is initiating multiples of yourself will blur you out horizontally, but being nested will blur you out vertically. Be careful not to mix them."

"Why?"

"It would be bad."

I'm hit with a scene from *Ghostbusters* where they're mixing the streams of their proton packs. "Like dogs and cats living together ... Mass hysteria?" I ask.

"Wha..."

"Like mixing drugs with alcohol?" I correct myself to make better sense.

"Yes. I guess that's right. Be careful not to do that. It makes your reality thin."

"Of course," I said aloud, and then to myself, I thought there would be no way to stop me from trying this. Once again, being an oppositional defiant girl had worked for me, and so far, I needed every advantage for the upcoming training and eventual duel with Koodzima. Thank you, Dr. Rami, for providing the inadvertent nugget of information I needed.

~ ~ ~

Level 8. Level ... 8. I wondered what I would need to learn to reach it. The next day after dinner, I told Dad I planned to do some homework and go to bed early. I had been reading through scenes with Evan for the play. We had been meeting up before school. Tomorrow, I would skip the drama workout in trade for tonight. I went to my room, shut the door, and cleared off all the homework papers strewn across my bed. Wanting no distractions, I changed into my nightclothes and crawled under the covers. I lay on my back and relaxed my entire body.

With my eyes closed, I summoned my mandala and focused on the eye symbol in the center circle. The Watch. As I stared into the mandala, the images came to life like a Hogwarts painting. The black and white bird in the upper left corner flew toward the Eye while its twin in the opposite lower right corner splayed wings and back feathers toward the Eye as if it were sunning itself. The bear reared up on its hind legs, roared, and pawed the air at me. The Twin Gates swung open. The dark Door to NowHere shimmered as it does when people cross through it. The light inside the Shack, leading to the Collective, glowed as if beckoning me. All the movement started in slow motion and sped up. The Eye in the middle blinked and did a 3-D effect, moving toward me from the mandala. Next, the whole thing spun slowly at first and picked up speed until I couldn't make out any details as it blurred. I followed the spinning wheel as it shrank away until …

~ ~ ~

I open my third eye, and I see the shores of The Watch. Behind me are the ruins of the Lighthouse. It reminds me of one of my favorite poems from Shelley, which ends, "Round the decay of that colossal wreck, boundless and bare. The lone and level sands stretch far away." That poem talks about earthly man-made things that time has destroyed. Our dreams also become lost due to time or the elements of this waking reality, which we believe is real. Neglect them and they become ruins just the same.

I turn back to the water and listen to the waves lap at the shore. I feel sand between my toes. It's wet and cool. Looking to my right down the shoreline further away, I see a small boat sitting on the beach. I meander down the shore toward it. When I am standing in front of it, I see a small note nailed to the bow. It reads, "Push the boat into the water and come to me."

I do what it says and slide the little boat from the bow backward away from the shore. The cool water rises to my knees the farther I go until the boat is floating. Jumping in, I look for an oar or something to row with but there's nothing. The boat floats away from the shore as if steering itself. I drift like this for a while. Closing my eyes, I picture this same boat with me in it, and the water has no ripples. This is my default preparation for mental battle with those who wish to gain access. I sense someone or something is about to come, so I get ready. I look inward to my third eye, pop myself up into the next level to become nested, and at the same time, I hold my hands together in the praying position to multiply myself. I chance the potential danger of splitting myself horizontally and vertically at the same time. I must see what happens.

I feel myself both split and pop up a level. It works. I am a ghost here, one level up, yet I have left my multiple behind as a mirror image of myself in the reality of The Watch. I float above myself, connected by the silver cord I conjure to attach to my split-self sitting in the boat within this reality.

"I look like I'm parasailing," I say to myself. I'm riding in a boat, smiling, and laughing out loud.

"How are you?" the Luce in the boat says to our collective minds. The reply is as clear as when I'm a multiple in the same reality.

"Good," I reply. "Just think of me as your spy. Where do you think we're going?"

"Who knows? Probably for the training."

"Who do you think set this up? David? Claude? Thekla?

"Roman. Watch for any of his tricks. We have a few surprises of our own."

"Yes, we do."

The boat continues to drift along. We close our eyes and float, concentrating on our collective thoughts and trying to anticipate what comes next. We lay down our trap and wait for the mouse. It doesn't take long, and we hear a booming voice.

"Who trespasses here?"

Ooh, I'm really scared. What is this, the Troll from Billy Goat's Gruff? He thinks he can bully me. I'll play along until the time is right.

We open our eyes, and we summon all our acquired acting skills and ask in a timid voice, "Who … who's there. What do you want?"

The boat lands ashore on an island in the middle of the Lake of The Watch. Ahead on the beach, there is a huge empty chair. The me in the boat steps out onto the shore and approaches the chair.

The voice says, "It is I, your worst nightmare. I am the Fear you keep hidden away and only dare to look at when you have no choice."

Paper or plastic? I snicker to my ghost self, floating above. We both laugh in our minds.

"What do you find so funny?" asks the voice.

Whoops, we laughed a little too loud in here. "Oh, nothing, sometimes when I'm scared, I tend to laugh. It is a weird response, I do," we recover.

"Come closer, have a seat, and let us talk."

I reach the chair. It's a huge red sofa seat—all soft, but four feet off the ground. I must jump up and crawl into the seat like I'm a little kid. Nice touch. I swivel in the seat with my legs dangling over the edge but not touching the ground. I glance up to look for my ghost self, but she is invisible. No matter, I see myself through her eyes. The me in the chair leans back, but the seat is so deep I must scoot myself to where my back rests against the marshmallow cushion. Nobody expects the Spanish Inquisition when sitting in a comfy chair.

It begins slowly at first. I sink into the cushion, as it's almost devouring me. A couple of months ago, I might have panicked, but Claude has trained me to master my fear. I freak out only for effect as the me in the chair whimpers a plea for help.

The voice snickers as if enjoying the perceived dominance. I wonder what a python would do if the rat it's trying to kill suddenly burrows into one of its coils and chews its way up and through to the snake's mouth.

We have a devious idea. Just a little closer. One more step. Try to come inside my mind and see what's waiting for you.

The voice says, "The next level requires you to protect your mind from all attacks. If you repel me, then you are worthy."

That's it? We adjust our plan. "No, please don't invade my mind. Not that," we say, then finish our thought—Brer Fox.

I ask my ghost self to search for Roman while I deal with him from the chair. The silver cord reels out to allow the nested Luce to search. I still see all that she sees.

I feel a slight digging at the corners of my mind. I don't fight it.

"Pitiful," says the voice. "I have received more resistance from a two-year-old."

"No ... Please don't." I don't even try to sound concerned. I feel him rooting around in there, but it's a special room I lock him into—a dark, empty place. He won't find anything. I let him wander about and rattle against the cage while I watch my nested-self search beyond the beach and up into the hills of the island. "Find him before he figures it out," I say to myself.

I watch through my ghost's eyes as she floats above the rocks and trees, searching for the monk. I see something suspicious to the right and ask her to check. There is a small cave there, and a robed figure sits cross-legged, deep in concentration.

"Okay, wait for my signal," I say to my ghost.

The rattling in my head becomes more violent as Roman realizes something's not right.

"What is this place? There is nothing here," says the voice.

I cackle. "Is w-ittle Roman w-ost?" I whisper. Panic bubbles up from within the dungeon of my mind.

"Let me out!" yells Roman, trying to mask his fear with authority.

"Sure," I say, and I open a door in my mind for him.

He steps through the door and into the light of a rolling green meadow with vibrant red flowers growing around him. I see it's Roman. His cowl hangs low as the robed figure wanders in the glen.

"What is all this?" he asks, looking at the flowers.

"I wouldn't be so worried about what's on the ground, if I were you," I whisper all around him.

Roman looks up, and a swarm of flying beasts descends on him. They beat him. Tear at him. He screams as if they're killing him.

My ghost sees Roman in the cave twitch and lets out a moan. She hears me say, "NOW." The ghost shoots straight into his consciousness and does her own digging while Roman is being attacked in my mind. She's quieter than him, and I'm sure she'll find some good dirt.

From within my mind, I have my beasts capture and fly him to me as I wait in a huge, dark castle. I leap from the chair and fly into the hills where I know Roman hides.

In my mind, I watch and see him struggle as the beasts carry him to me. I project myself with green skin, a huge chin, and a long hooked nose. I wear black robes with a black pointed hat. He thinks I'm a witch. Well, let's give him one.

They drop him at my feet. I shout the same words he said to me, "Who dares to trespass into my castle?" Roman tries to get up.

"Hold him down," I yell to my flying baboons. Their teeth are huge, bared, and ready to sink into him. They pin his arms and legs to the cobblestone floor. Somehow, his cowl is still in place. "I repeat, WHO ARE YOU?"

Roman's shaken but tries his best to regain composure. "You cannot treat me this way. I ... I am the Senior Emissary. Release me, now."

"You have no Collective or Thekla here to hide behind. It's just you and me. You wanted to train me ... so train me, bitch," I bellow.

"No one could train you. I ... I don't know what you are. You're a monster."

"Well, well, that is a step up from witch. Wouldn't you say? You want to know what I am? I'm the Wicked Witch of the Southwest." I raise myself up to my fullest height, "I'm a Texan!"

I twist my shape into a kind of horrible green lizard with fangs, and I hiss at him, "I'll get you my pretty and your little book of rules, too."

Roman appears to faint. I believe Roman is focusing on breaking loose.

It's good timing as now I reach him at the cave. I swoop down onto the sitting figure and toss his cowl back, then knock his Watch form to his back onto the cave floor. I sit on his chest with my legs pinning his arms at his sides. His features shock me. By all rights, he's a handsome man. Blond hair, majestic forehead, well-set eyes, simple cut nose, but his mouth has a wrinkled sneer, which makes him ugly. I release him from my conjured Oz nightmare, and his eyes flutter back to life. As they open, there is no recognition. Then I see the fire that I always imagine burning underneath his cowl in the Collective. His eyes radiate pure hatred.

"Hello, Roman," I say and smile my best I'm-a-nice-girl smile.

"Get off me," he says and struggles to get up.

"Not until you say, Auntie," I say.

He doesn't get the joke, so I stand. He throws his cowl back down over his face like poker-player sunglasses, attempting to hide his fear, anger, or shame.

"Sorry. I had to earn my stripes. I hope it wasn't too difficult for you," I explain.

"You've done nothing. You did not repel me from entering your consciousness."

"I allowed you to enter my trap, then I did something better than repel you." I let that simmer for a moment. "While you were busy, I snuck into *your* consciousness. I must say you're a naughty boy."

"Impossible," he mutters, and I imagine him with his mouth open in surprise.

"There's that word again. Look back into the deepest recesses of your mind, and there you will see me staring back at you."

Roman pauses a moment and looks inward. My ghost self sees him coming and holds up a few choice images that she has collected. She waves them at him like gruesome trophies from a battlefield.

Roman screams. And screams again. Then screams several more times.

31 – THE PLAY

I still had the play, *Our Town,* to provide a blessed distraction from Koodzima. The premier would happen at the Park North Auditorium this weekend. For the past couple of weeks, posters have been placed around the school, and signs have been in the schoolyard and street medians for the cars passing by. I was excited because we had all worked so hard. Maggie was the Stage Manager, a multi-faceted role of narrator, Mrs. Morgan at the soda fountain, and the minister marrying George and Emily in the second act—played respectively by Evan and me.

All three of us had some of the largest roles to play, and we knew our lines. I had the whole play memorized during the first read. The more esoteric items, like emotions and stage presence, were more difficult to master. Those were the things that made a good performance. It went beyond just the words; I had to make the audience believe I was Emily.

Ms. Thatcher, Maggie, Evan, and the rest of the class put in a lot of time with me to master expressing all those softer subtleties. Somewhere during the process of preparing for the play, along with the difficulty I had showing my emotions, I realized I'd become hardened. I didn't know if it was losing my mom or a collection of other things causing this. Dad was no help because he had his own issues to sort through. I knew who the guilty party was every time I looked in the mirror. I vowed to do a better job as a daughter, friend, and girlfriend. But of most importance, I promised to be a better self to myself. Avoid being so tough on myself when I get things wrong. Allowed me the luxury to make mistakes and gave myself the latitude to laugh them off. I had adopted more of this attitude since Homecoming.

It was now mid-November. The wet October led to a vivid autumn where the red oaks lived up to their names and mixed with dappled yellows and oranges. I had realized that with the turning of the seasons, I also had changed. The people around me weren't acting different. They were the same; it's the way I reacted to them that was different. It's a reality check dealing with multiple realities. Maybe this was what they called, *Enlightenment*. Still, if anyone wants to get up in my grille, they will receive no quarter from me. Ask Roman.

Maggie and I met while heading to Theatre I. Ms. Thatcher was strict about being late, as we couldn't waste any time so close to the performance.

"Are you nervous?" asked Maggie.

"A little," I said. "It's only the thought of all those people."

"I know. There'll be so many. What if I get distracted by something and totally blank out?"

"You'll be fine."

"Yeah, but I don't have your steel trap of a memory."

This was the first time I had ever seen Maggie doubt herself. She was usually the one full of confidence. I understood since she had the most lines of any character. She had several long passages to learn.

"Just *be* the Stage Manager. Feel it like Ms. Thatcher taught us," I said.

"Yeah," She stopped in her tracks and clenched her fists. "Oh, I wish it were opening night already. The waiting is killing me."

We moved again. "Take each day as it comes, sweetie," I said.

Maggie laughed. "What a role reversal. You sound more like me than I do, and lately, you're even dressing better."

"What, this old thing?" I pointed to my blouse I had picked up last weekend. Dad had seen me sifting through my simple wardrobe for something to wear. When I told him I couldn't find anything I liked, he promptly took me to the mall and bought me clothes. He let me take my time and took me to several stores until I found the pieces that symbolized the new me, rising to the surface. They felt good. Something new clothes had never done before.

"It's not a T-shirt, is what I'm saying." Maggie crossed her arms, cocked her head, and waited for my reply.

I shrugged at Maggie. "I'm upgraded."

"Huh?"

"You're looking at Lucinda 2.0. It's the same me, but with some extra features."

"Luce 2.0, eh? Funny. I've got to remember that one," laughed Maggie, as we reached the classroom door.

Ms. Thatcher had us gather, and she ran through the schedule. "Okay, Thursday night is the dress rehearsal. Be here at six, sharp. We'll run through the entire play top to bottom." She walked to the far part of the room and brought back printed sheets that had all the details. "Take this home and share it with your parents to remind them of our schedule this week. Remember, your family and friends can still purchase tickets, so be sure to get them soon."

We spent the rest of the class delving into certain scenes that Ms. Thatcher felt were still rough. It amazed me that no matter how many times we went over things, there were still details to improve.

~ ~ ~

Dress rehearsal went well for everybody except Maggie. She had a couple of pauses where she had to wait for her lines to bubble up from the back of her mind. Only someone who knew the pace of the play would notice.

"Oh, snippety snap," Maggie said. She had been trying to curb her cursing.

"Ooo, 'snippety snap'. Nice one. You're not gonna bust any curse jar with that," I said, trying my best to make her laugh.

"I'm so embarrassed. I flubbed my lines."

"That's why this is called a *dress rehearsal*, so if you make mistakes, you fix 'em. Look, just get to bed early and get plenty of rest for tomorrow night," I said, and put a hand on her shoulder and patted.

"Yeah, I guess you're right."

"Of course, I'm right. I'm Miss Know-It-All." I twisted my index fingers into my dimples, trying to be cute, yet deprecating.

Maggie raised her eyes and laughed. "Yeah, I guess you are."

~ ~ ~

Performance night. We showed up early to prepare and get into our own Zen grooves. Before we knew it, Ms. Thatcher pulled us together for the curtain call. I peeked through the side of the curtain and saw my dad on the front row—the perfect fan.

Maggie strolled out on the stage. She explained the layout of the town of Grover's Corners, New Hampshire. There was no real scenery, only her description of where everything was: Main Street, railroad line, churches, school, town hall, etc. She was great. The right inflection with a touch of a northeastern accent, as if she had grown up there.

Evan as George, and I as Emily came on stage for the first time. We had a casual discussion about school, how George needed some help with math, and how I could help him since his aspirations were only to be a farmer. The lines came easily. We blocked out the crowd and focused on each other. The audience chuckled or commented approvingly to each other, and in my mind, it was like hearing a laugh track of an old show. I kept my place firm within the character of Emily. We finished up the first act with the characters, Emily and George, standing on the ladders that represented them talking across the second-story windows of their neighboring houses.

We all headed backstage for a breather while the stagehands removed the simple props.

Ms. Thatcher gave us a brief pep talk before the second act. "Beautiful, just beautiful. Great job, everybody. Way to stay in character. Let's keep it up, two acts to go."

The second act opened with Maggie as the Stage Manager, explaining it was three years later. It showed George and Emily falling in love and the families planning their wedding. The whole second act flew by, as if in a dream. Our words and our actions flowed from us, and we were Emily, George, and the Stage Manager, along with the rest of the cast. We were all in this beautiful moment of make-believe, which felt so real. All the daily burdens: the Koodzimas of our world, school, etc., all faded away, and we lived in the Now. The second act ended with George and me saying, "I do" with rings and a kiss. M marries N and all. I melted into George's eyes, and I believed Evan was George. I was married and filled with amazing bliss.

After another pep talk and encouragement from Ms. Thatcher, we entered the emotional third act. As I sat in the chairs of Grover's Corners graveyard, conversing with my fellow departed, I was overwhelmed with the scene and was able to touch my own mortality; it shimmered and shook within me. Like Emily, I returned to her past, visited her family, attempted to recapture her former life, and tried to rekindle something lost. I realized at that moment, I was Emily. I truly felt her, embodied her pain, and bewilderment of the living. I couldn't tell where Emily began, and I ended. I had somehow ascended into that character, and I was she, and she was me. My tears, pain, and ultimate realization were real to me, and I couldn't doubt their sincerity.

When I said my final goodbyes to Grover's Corners and the world of the living, the curtain came down. I was ripped from my trance and was Luce again. The audience roared with applause, as did the rest of the cast for themselves, as it was clear our production was a success.

Ms. Thatcher praised us, and the curtain came up for our final bow. The audience reacted again with a rousing response. Evan and I came out for our final bows together. He bowed first and then passed it to me for the final individual bow. The loudest response was saved for me as a huge explosion of applause blasted from the audience and backstage. Once I looked back up, I saw my father with tears and a huge grin, clapping as if he were one of those toy monkeys banging their little cymbals together, loud and unconcerned for the noise. As I looked out across the audience, everyone appeared to tear up or had recovered from it and clapped wildly. There were shouts of praise as well. Ms. Thatcher took a bow and extended her arm to the cast. We bowed in unison to further applause. The curtain fell for the last time.

We retreated backstage to undress. Still, in a state of shock, I lived within this play just as if within an out-of-body experience. It was weird and yet exhilarating.

Evan found me and gave me a huge hug. "That was amazing. You were incredible." He gave me an emotion-filled kiss somewhere just outside of the we're-at-school category.

"No. You were great. Not a better George could have been played." I hugged him hard again.

Maggie ran up and grabbed us in a three-way hug, screaming with excitement, "Awesome. Better than anything I could've possibly imagined."

"Your delivery was flawless, Maggie. You handled all those mini-speeches with ease," I said.

"*You*, my little fairy princess, have been holding out on us," Maggie said, after stepping back away from me.

"Wha…?" I asked, shaking my head in disbelief.

"You were on another level, Luce. Your performance was so real. It was right in front of me, where I could touch it. Perfection."

"Yeah, I was sorta feeling it tonight," I said, thrilled someone other than me noticed.

"Truly mesmerizing," added Evan. "I had to be careful not to get lost watching you."

"Come on, guys. Really, you're starting to embarrass me."

"No, Luce, you were really that good," declared Maggie.

Then the rest of the cast and Ms. Thatcher came to me, saying similar things. It was the best night I could remember. It was my night—Our night in Our Town. No one could take away the memory or how it felt running through my arms, down my legs, and coursing through every part of me.

32 – COLLECTIVE, MY COLLECTIVE

This night, I dream myself to the Shack. Claude is there to greet me just outside the door to NowHere. I guess an alarm warned him of my arrival. He stands with his hands behind his back. What they say is true: Black does make you look slimmer. His dark robes mask his girth. His cowl is down, exposing his big pumpkin head while wearing a grin.

"Claude, I didn't know you had such a great smile," I say.

His lips push forward around his teeth, and the moment passes. "I smile," he says, all serious.

"I'm not messing with you. I'm glad you're happy."

"Oh." The smile comes back. "I have some good news." He stops and waits for me to ask.

"What?"

"You might be released from your dealings with Koodzima." He spreads his arms out as if this is an Ah-Ha moment.

"How do you mean?" I ask slowly.

"We have word Roman is meeting with them now, and he may have successfully negotiated a truce."

"I bet he has. Look, Roman is not exactly what he seems. You really don't know him." I shift my weight to one side.

Claude's face twists into a knot. "I don't understand."

"Let's just say I did a little investigating. You'd be surprised what I … dug up."

"What did you find?" he asks.

"Maybe I should wait for a more appropriate time to discuss this in front of the Collective." I put my hands behind my back and dip my head in a pensive stance.

"Good, then we should get moving as they are meeting soon."

We meander through the hallway of the little shack and emerge into the enormous gathering within NowHere. The expansive courtyard is full. The crowd isn't bustling about as before, but all stand still and look toward the Collective chambers, its members settling into their seats. The silence bubble traps any sound the Collective makes. It's as if they anticipate some announcement. As I get closer, I sense everyone moving out of our way. The vibe of this place contains no fear. When we reach the privacy circle, I hear a voice even before I request entry.

"Enter, Lucinda." It's Thekla, calm and cool.

I step inside the circle, but Claude must request permission for himself. He appears pleased at this minor slight to his position—whatever that is.

Stepping forward to the center, I keep my eyes trained on the figure of Thekla, her cowl staring at me. The rest of the Collective is still gathering. I stand in silence. I feel no intrusion into my thoughts, so I keep my shields down.

"Welcome," says Thekla when I reach the center. She's as pleased to see me as Claude. Roman is absent.

"Thank you, Chairwoman." I place my arms at my side. "I hear rumors there might be a truce."

"Yes, that is the report we have received. Why are you here?"

"I have come to be appointed as Special Emissary," I say.

An uncomfortable pause of silence settles. "Considering the impending peace, I don't see how your services as an emissary will be necessary."

"Well, I hate to be the bearer of bad news, but whatever truce Roman negotiates will be fleeting," I say with no malice.

"How so?"

"I know the Emissary of Koodzima and his kind. He's playing a game. They won't stop until they get what they want. But as soon as you give it to them, Koodzima will demand more. To quote something from my other reality: 'You cannot negotiate with terrorists.'"

"We understand, but we cannot assume the worst. We must be vigilant in our hope for peace."

I maintain my cool. I must help them understand. "Keep the fires of hope alive, but I respectfully request you temper it with a dose of realism." I had to catch myself from laughing at my ridiculous choice of words—*realism*. I'm amazed at how fancy I sound. "Koodzima will not stop until they control this universe and this Collective. You can't reason with the *unreasonable*. I believe I can help. Koodzima thinks they can force me to assist them in some way or provide them a solution against you. I'm prepared to go along with them to figure out their motives and neutralize the threat before it happens."

"Lucinda, your words trouble me." Thekla holds a hand up to prevent my response. "Before, you gave us the impression you had only disdain. Now, you sound as if you are ready to fight." Thekla cocks her cowl a minor stitch to the side. Under the darkness, I imagine a questioning face. "What has changed?"

I tip my head in thought for a moment. "Thekla and Collective. It is true, I have been mistrusting of this council, and that frustration has caused me to misplace my emotions against you all. For that, I apologize. I see now the true threat is Koodzima and all those who serve it. They have been the ones who continue to haunt and cause fear. With Claude's training, I have conquered those fears, and now I want to rid Koodzima's influence from my soul and from our universe. I humbly request that you allow me to help. This is my universe, too."

Thekla appears to measure her words internally. "Lucinda, your thoughts are true, and your heart is pure. I feel this. However, I am inclined to wait to hear what Roman has to say before I decide."

"I will speak," comes Roman's voice. He strolls out from the side.

I close my eyes as I know the kind of acid that will drip from his mouth.

"Roman, when did you return?" asks Thekla.

"I arrived before your conversation, but I wanted to listen in secret." He climbs up to the section with his seat and sits. "I did not want to influence the exchange in any way."

"How do you mean?" asks Thekla, turning to look at him.

"I wanted to hear her words when she thought I was not here."

"What do you mean?" I shoot back.

"Collective, I have heard her words, and ..." Roman adjusts himself into his seat.

Here it comes, I think to myself.

"I believe this Collective should consider her request," he finishes.

"Roman, we thought you were close to an agreement," says Thekla.

"That is what I initially thought, but negotiations broke when they became overly aggressive. I saw their true intentions, and her assessment is correct," he says with his cowl pointing to the floor ever so slightly.

Well, feed me gumbo and call me Cajun. I can't believe what I'm hearing.

"They broke negotiations?" asks Thekla.

"Actually, *I* broke them when I had to flee. I think they wanted to harm me."

"You believe she is ready?" asks Thekla.

"Yes, she is. I conducted her training, and she is more than qualified to be the Special Emissary. I must admit she outmaneuvered me. She is extremely capable of dealing with them."

"In light of what happened to Roman, would you truly send her there?" Claude asks Thekla.

"It is that, or we go to war," she responds.

"Then we go to war," yells Claude. "We cannot sacrifice one of our own. Soon there will be no one left to stand in their way."

I am truly touched by Claude's sentiment. "It's okay, Claude. As Thekla said, this universe needs to borrow some time to prepare. I believe I can cause enough of a disruption to give them fits. I have that effect, as you well know from personal experience," I smile.

Claude whips around toward me. "Why are you giving in so easily? Are you not a fighter?"

"Exactly. I am a fighter. They think they have the home-field advantage, but that's where their arrogance will fail them, and when it does, I'll be ready."

Claude drops his head as he knows arguing with me is futile, and regardless, the Collective wants to send me.

Roman adds, "I agree and believe focusing on Koodzima is an appropriate response."

The backhanded compliment smacks me upside my head, but it satisfies me that Roman wants me on his side. He'd rather not have me rummaging around in his head, but I will continue to keep an eye on him.

"Very well," says Thekla, turning from Roman to face me. "Lucinda Locke, on behalf of this Collective, I am appointing you Special Emissary of NowHere. Please make your final preparations for your visit."

"My Collective, I appreciate the trust you have placed in me. I will do my best." It sounds a little corny, but I believe what I say.

"Remove the Dome of Silence," says Thekla.

As if a soundproof door opens, we hear murmurs percolating within the crowd of monks, patiently waiting for an announcement.

Thekla stands. "Attention. We are still in negotiations with Koodzima. We have appointed Lucinda as Special Emissary to conduct further talks. We wish her well on her journey."

Claude and I turn and leave the Collective area. The monks outside the circle in the courtyard now move out of my way and each bows to me as I pass them. A hush falls over the crowd. It's as if their idea of applause is utter and complete silence.

33 - SIDEWINDER

Something had stuck with me ever since I met James during the sideways trip into the dark void within the realities of my dreams. His pleas for help were so genuine; they haunted me. His last name was Kemper, and he said his parents were Jeff and Debbie. I developed a theory that they might be able to help me prove or disprove.

I pulled out my laptop and connected it to the Internet. I did a look-up for Jeffrey Kemper near Rapid City, Iowa. There were only two Jeff & Jeffrey entries found in the state. I found one where Deborah was at the same address and wrote down their phone number. In seconds, I managed to creep this information. The world was indeed a smaller place with everyone only a few mouse clicks and a cellphone tap away.

I set my outbound number to anonymous and called the number for James's parents. It rang several times until I got an answer. This was too easy.

"Hello," said what sounded like an older woman's voice.

"Hi," I said and paused. "Um, Is this Debbie Kemper?" I asked.

"Who's calling, please … who is this? If you're trying to sell me magazines or a car warranty, I don't want any," she said with a harrumph.

"No, I'm not selling anything. I'm looking for information about someone. Do you know a James Kemper?"

There was silence and then a quiet response, "Jamie? How do you know Jamie?"

"Is he your son?" I was stalling for time as I hadn't role-played this phone call and had just dived in.

"Yes, he is. Was … was he a friend of yours?"

Oops, I was unsure what I stepped into here. "In a way. He asked me to call you."

"Is this some kind of sick joke?" The words were said with a harsh edge.

"No, no. Please, I'm sorry." I could sense her about to end the call. "Don't hang up. I … I—"

"Just say it. You're killing me. You know that?" I heard the faint beginnings of her breaking down into tears.

"No, I'm not trying to hurt you. I talked with him, and it's a little strange—"

"Damn straight. My Jamie's been dead for over three years now."

The response, although a possibility, also shocked me as I had held out hope that maybe he might be a dream traveler like me.

"Who put you up to this?" Anger now crackled in her voice.

"I spoke to him in a dream, and he asked me to call you."

"Wha… Spoke to him in a dream?"

"Yes. In my dream, I spoke to this man, who said his name was James and he gave me your and your husband's name and said you lived in Rapid City, Iowa."

"What else did he say?" I heard desperation seeking any information, no matter how small.

"He wanted me to call and tell you he loved you. He was a little lost for a while but would find his way." I didn't have the heart to tell her his soul might be trapped, and he had begged for my help before I abandoned him. I felt such guilt, but I hadn't forgotten him.

The floodgate of tears flowed from the other end of the phone. "My poor, Jamie. My poor, poor boy."

"What happened to him?" I asked.

"Iraq. Killed by an IED." She hurled the words at me.

"Oh … I'm sorry. I didn't know."

"You said he came to you in a dream?" she asked. I hesitated to answer as I found myself lost in the possibilities before me. She followed with, "Are you some psychic looking for an easy mark? I'm sure anyone could find all of this information online."

"No, I'm not psychic, but I would never do anything like that. It was just … he seemed so real that I had to see if he existed or if it was only a dream." When I felt this poor woman's pain, I realized I was causing so much more.

"Did he look well?" she asked in a timid voice. "… in your dream?"

Feeling the additional harm I might cause by the slip of the tongue, I said, "I … I'm sorry. I shouldn't have bothered you. Please, forgive me."

Just before I disconnected the call, I thought I heard her say, "Wait."

~ ~ ~

That night, I focused on the big tree where David and I had always met, but I didn't add him to my thoughts 'cause I wanted to do this solo. I felt I needed an investigation of my own to check out a theory. Besides, I would be the one running into the dragon's maw. I drifted …

~ ~ ~

I see our giant tree in the perpetual spring of this reality. Not waiting to see if some invisible alarm summons David, I quickly leap into the tree and climb to the top. I reach the inky, dark layer that is the In-Between and climb up into the emptiness. My idea is to explore from a level up. I'm a creature of habit. If something works, I repeat using it until it doesn't, or I find a better way. I roll my eyes back and focus on my third eye, and I pop myself up a level to a ghost of myself. Staying at the tree, my ghost-self ventures forth into the dark using the silver cord that ties us together, and I belay her out. Later, she can find her way back, or I could reel in the cord, if necessary.

She glides through the In-Between, and I already feel the presence of many beings, peoples, and things. I'm not sure exactly what they all are, so I'm reluctant to think of them as monsters like David wants me to believe. Instead, I visualize them as people, like me, somehow lost. Just as I see through the eyes of my ghost, I also feel what she experiences. I ask her to speak and see if anyone comes to her.

"Hello? James Kemper?" my ghost asks. I'm not sure if anything hears us when we're nested a level up. We do sense others feel our presence as we hear mumbling and murmuring getting louder. They converge on us and some even pass through me, but it looks like they cannot affect me. "James Kemper," I yell louder into the void.

I feel someone beside me. "Yes, you asked for me," a quiet voice says, almost in my ghost's ear.

We turn but see no one. "James, it's me, Lucinda."

"You sound different, somehow."

"I'm sure I do." I step back to give some personal space. "Do you remember what you asked me to do?"

"I asked you to call my parents, but I didn't know if you even understood what I was saying. They're from someplace in my old memories."

"Well, I do. I'm from Dallas."

"Dallas? The name rings a bell, but I don't know why. The longer I'm here, the more I forget."

"Do you remember Jamie?"

"Sure. That was the name of a young boy on a farm in Iowa. It's been forever since I heard it spoken. It's what my mom called me. How did you know?"

"I called her as you asked."

"You found her? How is she?"

"Good. She misses you, though."

"You talk to my dad?"

"No, not yet."

"Anything you want me to tell them?"

"Tell them I miss driving the tractor on the back acreage on those cool spring days with the wind ripping through my hair. I especially miss the sun beating down on me in the summer. I somehow believed I had to get away from the tedium of running equipment up and down that property. But it's the happiest memory I have. Ask them if they've removed the stump that put the wobble into the front wheel of the old combine. I loved that beautiful, decrepit thing."

"What is the last thing you remember?" I ask.

"I'm in my Humvee with my unit, and we're going somewhere. There's a huge flash and then I'm in darkness. A light comes for me and leads me here. The light goes away, and I'm left alone in this dark place. Am I dead? Is this Hell? I'm no saint, but I wasn't bad enough for this."

"I don't think this is Hell, but it's certainly a place I've heard called the In-Between." I wasn't sure how to answer his questions without dashing any shred of hope.

"You didn't answer my first question: Am I dead?"

"James, your mother said you were killed by an IED."

"I thought as much. Are you dead, too?

"No, I dreamed myself to this place from my reality, where I am very much alive."

"Are you sure?"

"Yes. James, I need you to concentrate. Can you tell me what happens here?"

"Nothing happens. Sometimes it feels like I have been here for an eternity, but other times it feels like yesterday. It's dark, except every now and then, a light comes from somewhere behind you, hovers around, and then it goes somewhere behind me. It lasts for only a moment, but after it leaves, more entities appear."

"Do you interact with the other entities here? Argue or fight with them?"

"It's only verbal. Most of the time, you can't understand what they're saying. It might be another language, and other times, it sounds, unlike any tongue a person could even speak. There is no physical interaction with anything. If you get too close, you are repelled, kind of like when the same poles of two magnets get close. I'll show you."

I feel him reach out for me, and his hand touches me. There is some resistance, then it passes through me.

"Weird, I know you're there but…" I feel him take a step closer. "But you aren't there. It's like you're made of water. What are you?" he says.

"I'm sort of a ghost. The real me is behind us. This form allows me to explore this place and not get lost." I almost sense I'm confusing him. "It's a little hard to explain. Listen, I'll get you out of here, but right now, I need to investigate where the light disappears."

"I wouldn't do that. It's where the Reapers come."

"Reapers? What do you mean?"

"Aw, that's just what I call them. We hear them coming and then they disappear, but so do some of us."

I know I must explore the far reaches of this place. My theory is gaining new substance. I still need to check this out and have an idea. My ghost-self grabs the silver cord that attaches us. She holds it out to James. "James, reach out your hand, do you feel this?"

I sense him reaching forward, his hand touches the cord, and passes through it as well.

"Um, yes, I think I can."

"Follow this line back to my other self, standing near the tree. There you can escape this place."

"Are you still going to follow the light?"

"Yes, but I'll be all right 'cause I'm not really here or there. Just follow this and you'll find me."

"Lucinda, thank you."

"Thank me later in person." I turn and head in the direction he says the light comes and goes.

"Be careful," he says.

As I glide forward through the air, I hear others and try to go around them, but I zig and accidentally zag into them or them into me. As they pass through me, some tense up and others don't notice at all. They feel full of fear, anger, or anxiety. As I get closer to where James said the Reapers come, the entities become sparse.

Before me, the dark void expands from the tree into a large, cavernous space, but after a while, I feel the dark layer narrow. The cord is still connecting us. The ceiling slopes down, and even though I'm a ghost, I am bound by this void. I stoop to get through this dark, constricting layer. Lower and lower, until I'm crawling. I get to where I'm lying flat on my stomach and scoot along until I suck in my gut to wiggle further. The crushing darkness and the echoing sounds around me trigger an old fear I had forgotten. I'm claustrophobic.

The sounds get louder around me. I don't know if they are echoes of the entities, but it sounds like they are right beside me. My breathing gets labored. It feels like the entities have followed me as the chittering in my ears grows louder. I'm being pushed by my feet and getting wedged into the crease. I panic and ask my other self for help, but even though she is standing up and holding a tree branch far away from me, I realize she is locked into the same moment with me. We are paralyzed together.

I want to scream, but I can't get a full breath into my lungs as they are crushed. It doesn't make sense 'cause this is not real. I don't need air, here. When my hands reach forward, the darkness dips a little. I twist myself sideways to the lip of the void on which I perch. I'm able to slip my thigh through to the other side. Then my head, shoulders, and upper torso get free. My panic subsides. Now only my butt is caught. I always thought it was too big, and this confirms it. How I wish I could distribute some of that upstairs. I yell a battle cry, "Less Ice Cream!" as I pull myself through.

I glide forward. It's slick in here, and the chittering and murmurs are gone. The darkness dips down here almost like a slide. I fall and slip through it. As a ghost, I should have no mass to act on me. I should be in full control, but it's as if there were a force like gravity pulling me down deeper. As I come to a leveling, the darkness lightens only a shade. It's dim, but I'm able to make out a bleak landscape. I step away from the void and look up at the sky. Only a few stars are shining. I could count maybe only a hundred or so. There is a tiny moon or huge star, I don't know which, that gives off enough light to see only various shades of gray. The cord still connects me. We are still experiencing this together. There is a long black void spanning out across the horizon where I just exited. I float above the ground. My ghost-self can fly. Looking to my left, a dark shape rises from the horizon above everything else. I fly toward it, hoping there might be answers there.

The thing is huge, as it takes me a long time to reach. It must be a mile high and cut into a rectangular box—such boring architecture. There's a gaping dark hole there, and I enter. It's cylindrical, so a fair bit more interesting. The ceiling is high enough that I can fly straight through. The tunnel is only about a hundred feet and on the other side, far below me, is a huge mall of grays and blacks. I slide by and see some shapes in white robes shuffling about in all directions. The ceiling is thousands of feet from the floor, so I fly down to just above them, avoiding any inadvertent collisions.

Robed entities gather in a square off to my right. There is a huge empty space outside of them, so I figure I'll do a little spying. In my ghost form, I am invisible. I creep closer to see if I can overhear anything.

Only one voice speaks. It's not English, but for some reason, I understand what it says. "We must strike soon. They are weak and so is their Dreamer. They will never release her to us. It would be foolish and reckless of them."

I sense something beside me and feel a scaly claw clamp around my wrist.

A robed figure holds me in its grip and yells, "I got one!"

And at that moment, the cord connecting my ghost-self to the me holding the tree branch contracts. The reeling only takes a second, and then when I look again, I have now nested down a level. My ghost is gone, and all that's left is me. The robed figure lifts me off the ground by my arm and turns me to face it. I see a hideous visage within its white cowl. It's so gruesome, I can't describe it.

It draws me near and hisses, "Welcome to Koodzima."

34 - INTERSECT

The Koodzima creature sets me down but continues to hold my arm in the air.

"It's her. It's her," it yells toward the crowd. A wall of white-robed monstrosities turns to investigate the ruckus. They all converge on me with ghastly, greedy faces. I try to stay calm as I know this is only a dream, but I keep hearing Rami's and David's warnings about how I can lose my soul.

"Release her," comes a familiar voice. The crowd separates, making room for the speaker. It's Rande, also dressed in a white robe with his cowl down, exposing his snake-like head, all scaly and gross. He stands at the top of a dais with his fellow monsters. I'm still in the grasp of some nasty Koodzima freak. "Zuk, please let go of her."

Zuk sneers and, with reluctance, releases his grip but remains poised to strike if I try to flee.

"Ah," sighs Rande, in what sounds like relief. "Apologies for the mess. I was not told of your departure, and consequently, I had no opportunity to make plans. I hope you will forgive us." His claws rest on his hips with a whimsical air of nonchalance. He reminds me of an evil metrosexual. "Oh, how rude of me. Everyone, this is Special Emissary, Lucinda Locke. Lucinda, everyone." He smiles and extends a claw toward me and flicks his scaly digits, inviting me up the dais.

I'm frozen in my tracks. I summon all my nerves and swallow my fear. The fear is what they feed on. Am I to be served up to them there? It takes me a moment to find my legs and move forward. I climb the three steps to the top of the dais where Rande waits.

Stopping a couple of feet away from him, I say, "Randy, thanks for welcoming me to your … ah …." I glance around. "… humble, dark, and foreboding abode." Sometimes I just gotta be me to get through certain situations.

Rande's eyes gleam with the same intensity as his pointed, toothy smile. It's as if he knows I'm trying to suppress my fear. "Such a wicked sense of humor you have. You'll fit in nicely." He stands at attention, claws at his sides, and says as almost a declaration, "You have nothing to fear as you are our guest."

I hear this but remember when Roman said that he had to escape when they got aggressive. Rande leads me to the center of the dais and stops.

He looks about himself and points to the muted darkness of grays around him and says, "Lucinda, this is the Grand Hall. This is where we conduct all our meetings. It's not as fancy as where your Collective meets, but it is home. I take it Roman gave you the required directions to get here?"

He must not know I found the backdoor they've been using to come into our universe through the In-Between. I play along.

"Yes, you know how I can be: always independent-minded. I wanted to surprise you."

"I take it the rest of the delegation will be along shortly?"

"Um …" I stall for a moment. Maybe I'm not supposed to be by myself. "For the time being, I'm alone."

"My, you are braver than I gave you credit. To come here for the first time and unescorted at that. It is a bit … foolhardy." Rande cocks his head to the side, his snaky eyes twinkling with evil mirth.

Immediately, I feel a host of twitching weirdo things all around me. They gather in close as if to smell me like I produce a wonderful aroma, which I cannot decide whether it's pleasant or tasty. I sense he's digging or thinks he knows something. I smirk and stare back. "Well, I'm adventurous to a fault."

"Ah," he nods, and there is an uncomfortable silence. "So."

"So, what?" I respond.

He raises his claws, questioning. "What did you want to discuss?"

"You summoned me. I figure you had an agenda." I sense my voice rise an octave.

"Mmm, nope. We are at war. There is not a whole lot to talk about. At least, not for this cycle."

"All right, then. When is the next cycle?" I ask.

"Soon."

I know where this is going. "What should I do until then?"

"We have very nice accommodations for you while you wait." He clasps his hands.

"Am I your prisoner?"

"No, of course not. Don't perceive it that way," he demands in his sultry way. "Come."

Rande leads me down from the dais and along a white gravel path to a dark room. There is enough light reflected off the white walls to see a gray table and chair in the middle. It's very spartan. My guess is everything is different shades of white as an attempt at colors, since there is only the spectrum of the night. The whole reason for white robes, tables, chairs, everything, must be to reflect what little light exists. It's not a simple matter of white being the good guys and black being bad. This is a matter of perception.

"Um, thanks. This will do fine, I guess."

"Good, I will retrieve you once we are about to meet."

Rande throws a smirk and leaves through the square portal cut in the room. There is no door. I follow him to the portal, but as I poke my head out, a couple of creepy, robed things step together to block my way.

"Emissary, do you need something?" one hisses.

"No, nothing at this time. Just curious." I step back into the room, sit in the chair, fold my hands in front of me, and close my eyes.

When I sense there are mental sharks in the water sniffing at my thoughts, I conceal myself and opt for the mental spigot approach as opposed to the serene boat visual. This way is much more fun and irritating for them. Aloud in my mind, I play all the old sitcoms as they seem to send those curious diggers into my mind, running away. I play through them all in the order I had seen them, which provides a jumbled mess to anyone eavesdropping. At the same time, in a mental background process, I recite the Rules of Palaver. That should sufficiently frustrate them, I chuckle to myself.

I don't know how long I'm in this state, but it feels like a while. I hear a voice. It's Rande.

"Lucinda, it is time."

I open my eyes and see Rande standing on the other side of the table. He doesn't appear as smug as before. "I trust we weren't boring you."

"Nope, just watching some TV, Randy." I smile like a Cheshire cat. He and I know full well his cronies had no luck in penetrating my mind.

"You seem pleased with yourself." He purrs and places his hands on the table, leaning toward me with his own flashing grin. "You might take a note. Things here are not the same as where you come from. For example, your travel here as a ghost does not work. We see you either way. Your little mental games, although effective, are not foolproof. We saw all we needed. And ... nobody knows you're here."

I try not to show any reaction and put on my poker face, but the statement chills me. What if he can read me? I continue to smile and call his bluff as I have no other choice.

"Yeah. Interesting, Randy. Did I let you *think* I'm a fool? Or is that by my design?" I stare, unmoving. His smile fades a fraction, but I know he is now double-thinking everything.

"The Ministry is convening for this cycle and requests your presence. I caution you to hold your tongue. They are swift to cull out any contemptuous behavior."

"I will carefully regard your advice." I fight to keep an impish smile from curling my lips.

He leads me through the portal and onto the pathway back to the central dais. As I approach, a crowd of grotesque manifestations assemble around the base and separate to allow me access. Rande and I climb the three steps to the top. Two entities wait for us in the center of the square. Their cowls, like those of the Collective, are pulled up over their heads, and I only see darkness where their faces should be. They stand silent. One has its arms behind it, and the other has its hands tucked into both sleeves of its white robes. I can't tell if they hold concealed weapons, nor can I read their eyes to assess their intent.

"Lucinda," says Rande in his most smarmy voice. "These two are Orators: Gles and Mour. This is the Special Emissary." They make no effort to move but stare silently. I believe I hear some light breathing, almost like a wheeze.

Less is More, I say to myself, to remember their names. "Charmed, I'm sure." I bow my head slightly, and I imagine that I'm wearing a twisted smile.

Rande lurches with my sarcasm, but the others don't appear to notice. He continues, "As I promised, she is here at our request."

I hate it when people are full of themselves, especially inter-dimensional demonic twits. I'm here because I choose to be, and unfortunately, I tend to underestimate things. Deciding to let it slide, I say nothing.

They continue to stare as if waiting for me to speak. I hold my ground and give them nothing but the same empty stare. It's then I realize I have no fancy robe, just wearing a T-shirt and jeans. I'm feeling left out. Since

I'm also a member of the Collective, I conjure a robe like theirs—a roomy black one with a huge cowl of my own that I pull over my head and hide my face deep into it like a turtle. I can play this game, too.

This must cause an effective blink in our staring contest because they are the first to speak. I win.

"Welcome, Emissary. We have greatly anticipated the opportunity of meeting with you," says the one named Gles, I believe. His voice is exceptionally soft, and I strain to hear it.

I'm unsure how to respond. I don't want to offend anyone, but I have impulse control issues, so I try to keep it simple. "Thank you."

The shorter one with the hands in its sleeves moves its head ever so slightly and speaks, "Are you familiar with our meeting protocol?"

"The Rules of Palaver? Yes, but I am new to my Collective, so it is possible my understanding is limited," I lie.

"You understand why you are here, do you not?" asks Gles.

"Um … not. I understand you have summoned me, but for the exact reasons, I don't know."

"We want to recruit you from your universe, as you have a certain characteristic we require. You have a light about you. As you see, this is a dark place and we desire to understand you better," says the shorter one, Mour.

"So ... you think I'm bright and want to get to know me better?"

"No, we believe you possess light within you. Can we perform a small test for ourselves and demonstrate the light we believe you possess? Unless you feel frightened or you do not wish to show us," whispers Gles.

I can't resist the urge to show off. It's a weakness of mine. "Okay, I'm game. What is this test?"

"Within your mind, imagine your core as a burning flame … a star if you will. Now project that from yourself as if a light," says Mour.

"Okay, I'll try." I close my eyes and focus them on my third eye. I concentrate my mind on a picture of the full moon, so I don't overdo it. I visualize pulling it from the sky and into my head. I hear several gasps around me, so I open my eyes. It's as if I were a giant light bulb shining out of my cowl like a flashlight. I turn to Rande and the Orators, who each put their hands up to block the brilliance. I look across the crowd, and several Koodzima entities fall to the ground and scrabble away from the beam of light I shoot at them from my cowl. There are cries of fear as well.

"Very good. Put out your light. We are not accustomed to it."

I douse it, and I see Rande appears pleased, talking with Gles and Mour. I think I hear him whisper to them, "Did I not tell you she was more powerful?" The Orators nod.

"You did very well with little preparation, Lucinda," says Gles and turns to Rande. "You have found a replacement even better than expected. You shall receive the reward agreed upon."

Rande appears elated.

"Replacement? You say that as if you're filling some position. I hate to disappoint y'all, but I am not taking up a permanent residence in Koodzima."

"Ah, but you will," says Rande in his silky voice, and then he laughs. "If you do not submit to us, then we will destroy all those whom you care about within all the realities of which you belong. You know we can. What if we make a visit to the dreams of your friend, Maggie, or your special boy, Evan, not to mention a visit to your father? We could scare them literally to death if we so choose. Then there is Claude and David …."

I feel the cold grip of reality sink into me as if I've stepped barefoot into something especially nasty in this yard. I've been a fool. I didn't see this coming.

"The Rules of Palaver, Section 7634, verse 1987 states that you are prohibited from kidnapping or holding any emissary by force," I say.

The three of them laugh with mild snickering from the crowd around me. Some even shake with glee at my entertaining arguments.

"Lucinda, we are not holding you for ransom or against your will. You may leave at any time," says Rande with false kindness. "We have merely, with systematic aim, charted a course within your universe, discovered your weaknesses, and now we wish to reap our harvest. You, your family, and your friends are so predictable and weak. It is such an easy game to play. Almost like cheating, the way you care about each other. You are like little marionettes. Pull a string here and there, and you jump as high as we want." Rande's face shines supreme in his pride of intellect and his ability to maneuver.

Fear for my family and friends courses through me. It might cause me to tremble, but I refuse to give them the satisfaction. I know they, indeed, have this power over me. They control me through my love of others, and I'm powerless to resist. I did see them attack Maggie, Brad, and Evan at the Fair. They can do this to anyone.

Rande continues, "Your universe is too weak to even help you. They are too busy running around, like how would you say, 'Small Chick.'"

"What?"

"You know. 'The stars are falling … the stars are falling.'" Rande is rolling his hand as if trying to help me remember.

"Chicken Little. The sky is falling, you twit."

"Yes, Chicken Little. Your universe is pitiful. So much power at its disposal but no focus. Sorry, my dear lost Lucinda, it appears that you and your magnificent universe are the twits."

I remember there was to be a trade. "My condition of arrival was you provide the Star of Larissa. Do you have this, or will you again find a loophole to hide behind?"

"The Star of Larissa," muses Rande. "This should be interesting. Please summon the star."

A blast of a high-piercing horn reverberates through the hall. Everyone is staring out through the large dark opening near the ceiling where I flew in during my attempt to spy. I turn and stare for what feels like several minutes.

The opening glows, and soon, a point of light floats into the hallway above everyone. As it flickers, it is a giant point of illumination for everything. There's enough light that I believe I see some color dotted in amongst the crowd. It's the same light I imagine they see in the In-Between. The star comes over the dais and slowly descends on top of us. As it sinks and lands in front of me, I see a figure within the sphere of light. I gasp with recognition, and tears bubble up.

35 – THE STARS OF LARISSA

"MOM," I cry.

My mother wears a blank face, staring forward and devoid of any emotion or recognition. She wears a flowing white gown and stands within an egg-shaped cage of light. The strawberry-blonde tint of her hair is as familiar as the lines on her face. She appears just like I remember her when I was eight, but she's sad and broken, like a mindless Glenda the Good Witch of the North.

"Mom!" I cry out again and approach her. I get close enough to touch her, but the egg of light won't let me pass.

Rande sidles up and says, "I'm sorry, but she can't hear you."

I turn on him, fists clenched at my sides so hard I feel my nails dig into my palms. "What have you done to her?" I hiss through my teeth.

"Nothing. She serves the Grand Hall. She is here of her own free will."

"I presume you made her the same deal you made me. One she couldn't refuse?" I believe all the pieces are coming together.

"As a matter of fact, yes, we did." Rande puts his hands on his hips again with that aw-shucks look on his face, and before I can stop the impulse, I stamp my heel down on his foot. I hear something pop, and Rande doubles over in pain, grabbing his foot. I figured it might make him back away from me, but I appear to have hurt him. Good, I hope he limps around in this hellhole for all eternity.

Gles and Mour move toward me. "You are not permitted to strike anyone under the Rules of Palaver," says Gles.

In my mind, I search through the rules. "I am within my rights to defend my … personal space. See Section 1230, verse 303. I was encroached upon, so I am within my rights as Emissary."

Gles and Mour glance at each other as if they are not sure of the interpretation, and too proud to look it up, they appear to defer to me.

Rande stops his dance of pain and limps back to me. "You have hurt me," he rages in my face.

"Too bad, so sad. Invade my personal space again and I'll crunch the other one."

Rande warily takes a step outside my range, anger seething in his eyes.

I stare into my mother's soul and cannot help but feel unbelievable sadness for her—for myself. I feel abject hatred at Koodzima for holding my mother and for using her to deceive all those souls in the In-Between, making them prisoners to this horrible, dark universe. Gathering my rage up into a tight ball, I stuff it deep within myself.

"You want me to be your new star," I say while looking into my mother's lifeless eyes. "Answer me this question first."

"Ask," says Rande.

"What do you do with the souls you reap from the In-Between?"

Rande's eyes open wider. "Oh, you know about them. I guess it doesn't matter since you are bound to us and will never be able to share our little secret. We harvest them. Once they are ready, they are our source of recruitment. They are like our children waiting to be reborn. But first, we have to work them until they are bound to us like you are."

"You trick them and then mold them with fear. They're not supposed to be in there."

"You think we follow your sense of what's right. WE don't follow your rules; WE do what we want." Gles and Mour relax, and Rande paces with a limp outside my reach. He stops and crosses his arms. "Will you bind yourself to our service?" he asks.

"Yes," I say.

"Will you collect all those we require?" whispers Mour.

"Sure. Let my mother go first."

"Your words bind you through the Rules of Palaver, Emissary," says Rande with his toothy grin.

"Let her go," I say, suppressing my rage to a minimum.

"As you request," says Rande, and then stands orthogonal to me before my mother. He says, "Larissa," and holds up both his claws high over his head and mumbles unintelligible words or incantations to her.

The cage of light around her dims and dies. She remains standing in the dark void with me. Her eyes are still dead. With the force of the light gone, I touch her. I conjure my robe away so I'm back into my jeans and shirt, so maybe she will recognize me. I place a hand on her shoulder and gently jostle her. I'm amazed at how much we look alike, except I stand a couple of inches taller. I cup my hands around her face, hold her head, and make her gaze into my eyes.

"Mom," I say and caress her face. "Mom, wake up."

Her eyes flutter, and I see them focus on me.

"Mother?" she manages to say to me.

"No," I stroke her hair with my hand, "It's me, Lucinda."

"Lucinda, but … you're so grown up," she whispers in awe.

I can't resist any longer, and I throw my arms around her in a tight embrace. To hear her again and to feel her hug me is beyond belief. "Oh, Mama, I missed you so much." Tears flow as never before. It all comes pouring out of me, and I rock back and forth on my feet. She hugs me as well. After what seems like forever, I pull away from her. She, too, has tears streaming down her face.

"It's you," she says, in amazement. "I dream about you, and here you are."

"I hate to break up this little reunion, but we *must* maintain schedule," says Rande, tapping at some invisible watch on his wrist.

It snaps me out of the moment with my mother and to the reality of the bigger picture. Mom gasps as she recognizes him and then notices the hosts around her. "Where are we?"

"Koodzima … We're in the Grand Hall," I tell her.

"Oh, dear God," Mom says, and covers her mouth. "How much of that was real?" she asks herself. "Why're you here? Tell me you didn't promise them anything," she pleads, grabbing my shoulders.

"Enough of all this," says Rande. "We relieve you of your duties. You are free to go. Bye-bye." He waves his claw at my mom. The egg of light surrounds her. I see her mouth form the word, 'No' from her cage as she rises above the dais, and with a shot, is gone through the opening.

"Wait … Mom … wait." I whip around to Rande. "What did you do to her?"

"As agreed, she's been returned," says Rande, palms up.

I calm myself. "So how long did you plan this?" I ask, and I'm patient to listen to his ego speak.

"Mmm," purrs Rande. "Ever since we employed your mother, we knew about you. It wasn't until you approached your second multiple that we took notice. I had to convince the Ministry that you are more powerful than your mother, and we should harvest you. That's when I put together the whole idea of a war to lure you here."

I'm in shock. "This whole idea of war between our universes is imaginary?"

"Of course. You think we really care about your stupid NowHere?"

I notice Gles and Mour move toward Rande. It was as if he said something. There must be a loophole. I continue to listen to Rande gush about his superiority, and in the background, I search the Rules of Palaver.

Rande continues. "I must admit, I didn't expect you to give in so easily. I cannot tell you how hard it was to orchestrate this. But it could not have come together any better. Your dreams were a perfect vehicle for me to enter your universe, spy, and prepare you. It was perfect –perfect."

I replay the conversation in my mind and analyze the words spoken. I think I have part of it solved, but I need clarification.

"Impressive, so let me get this straight. You conduct surveillance on me, my friends, and my family, and then *pretend* to start a war. All this for little ol' me?"

"Yes, and you and your silly universe fell for it."

Got him. "Okay, thanks for the job offer, but I decline. See ya." I turn to walk away from the dais.

"You are bound by the Rules of Palaver. You can't leave," laughs Rande.

I spin back to him. "Oh, but the Rules of Palaver don't apply. You admit you spied on me, and you admit that this war is not real. That implies deception. Under Section 4901 verse 1, 'Any agreement built on false pretenses is null and void, and any representative who willfully deceives is subject to punishment.' That wraps up this little story nicely. You and your fat mouth have cost you a star."

"We don't care about the Rules of Palaver. You will remain bound to us, or I will personally enjoy destroying your friends and family. Surrender to us. You have no other choice," says Rande, while limping back and forth in front of me.

"The Rules only apply to Koodzima when it's convenient?" I look at Gles and Mour, "You really need to put a leash on your dog," I say, pointing at Rande. "He keeps putting his foot into his mouth."

"Lucinda, my sweet, your insults cannot save you," drips Rande.

He chants. I feel a pressure wave strike and wrap itself around me, trying to crush me to its will. This must be what he did to Mom. I visualize a protective force field emanating from me, and the pressure loosens. Rande looks annoyed; he's not winning as easily as he expects. He chants louder as he tries to subdue me.

I realize I cannot allow this to go on. I don't want these freaks threatening me and hurting everyone I love. I can't passively accept this; I must act. These Koodzima creatures are a bunch of assholes. My body shudders as I know what I must do. "I AM NO LONGER BOUND," I shout to them all.

"Ah, but you are. You just do not know it," says Rande.

"I'm not talking about you, but about me. *I* am no longer bound by the Rules of Palaver." I smirk at Rande, holding his spell off me with ease. Rande gets a confusing twist to his face. "I was named Special Emissary on the premise we're at war. The agreement with NowHere exists under false pretenses and, therefore, is worthless. As Emissary, I swore to abide by the Rules of Palaver. I'm forbidden to attack you except to protect myself, like when I stamped on your little piggies, but now I am no longer bound as Emissary, and I'm free to do what I want. And what I want to do is PUNISH you." Turning and directing my voice at all the grisly crowd surrounding the dais, I shout, "PUNISH YOU ALL for what you did to my mother. Punish you for the souls you steal." Then I point at Rande. "And punish YOU for even thinking of messing with me."

The anger rising within me, I pull out that ball of rage I set aside. The heat pours out. For the first time, Rande appears worried. His eyes bug out, and he moves away. Gles and Mour take a few steps back, and the crowd around me chitters with anxious fervor. I close my eyes, stare into my third eye, and visualize the sun.

Then a hundred suns.

Then a thousand-thousand suns.

I pull all this light into my core—my very soul—until I can barely stand to contain it. Next, I put my hands together as if in prayer, and I stand, vibrating and trembling. I visualize myself splitting in two. My consciousness splits, and there are two of us. Then I visualize each of me, in turn, splitting into multiples. Again, and again, this is repeated like cells dividing, but at an exponential rate until there are millions of me.

We open our eyes and shout in unison, "We are the Stars of Larissa. You want light. Choke on it."

36 – SLUMBER PARTY

Millions of me spread out over the dais and throughout the hall. We outnumber and surround every nasty entity, monster, and creep. We unleash the light within us and burn as bright as the stars we represent. Some are brighter than others, but the intensity is overwhelming to our Koodzima hosts. We illuminate every darkened cowl to reveal each gross, disgusting thing that hides within it. Their faces are wrenched open in terror. Eyes burning. Faces glowing. They howl and scream as the light is too intense—the campers are standing in the campfire. We don't care. Not even their robes protect them from the light of the heavens we pour onto them.

I saved Rande for the first two originals of me. His face is melting, his mouth in a huge scream. We deploy the tactic we've all declared. We leap at him, shove our hands into his mouth to pry it wider, and climb inside of him as we visualize ourselves as brilliant, burning balls of light and fly down his throat. In unison, the rest of us do this to every Koodzima creature lurking in this place. We tear into their gaping maws and illuminate them from the inside, burning as we go, as if we were making them swallow molten gold. Their choking screams are muffled by our burning rage of light, as we exact our judgment.

A voice, deep and powerful with commanding force, says, "ENOUGH." The voice reverberates through our minds and souls. "BE GONE," it commands, and we are vomited out from our creepy hosts and flung far away into the deep recesses of darkness and space.

We are fractured. We split ourselves so many times that our minds are now thin. We are too far away from each other to reconnect. The silver cords of Lucinda have been snapped, and we each become one individual shard of the smashed vase that was once Lucinda, flying back into our home universe.

I'm one Lucinda and see the familiar swarm of galaxies around me. I am home, but weak. The dark weight of my smashed soul makes me lose consciousness. I'm dying. It's a peaceful sleep, warm and comfortable. Trying to fight it, but it's too heavy.

A happy thought comes from protecting everyone in all my realities. But I'm sad about having to go. Appreciative of the magnitude of the loss of oneself, I fear for my poor soul. Have I lost it by shattering it into a million pieces? Humpty Dumpty sat on a wall …

The memory of the play, *Our Town,* floats up, and now I understand why my character, Emily, reacts the way she does to her passing. The final thoughts I have are my own personal homage to the play, which flows through my mind.

"Farewell, Park North High School.

"Goodbye, Mom and Dad. Whatever is left of me will always love and need you.

"Take care of yourselves, all my friends—especially Maggie and Evan. And goodbye to all those I didn't realize were my friends.

"So long, Earth. You were more beautiful than I really knew.

"Oh, my universe, you were the grandest and most beautifully brilliant of all. I only got to sample a small taste of the wonders you possess. Forgive me for not staying longer.

"I will miss you all."

~ ~ ~

“..
....
....
....
....
....
....
....
....M......
....
....
....
.......................D..
....
....
....
.............................C..
....
....
....D...........................
....
....
....
R...
....
....
...............M..
....E”
“Where are...................you? ....”
“Luce...”
“Lucinda...please”
“LUCINDA...”
“Lucinda, sweetheart.”

"I've got some of my World-Famous Pancakes waiting……………………………"

"You should have seen it……………..."

"We were so embarrassed…………………………"

"We'll be back…………………………………………"

"Hello, Miss Locke. I have something for you. Just a sec."

<Flash>

A tiny stream of sunlight shines down. It's only a small cone that illuminates me—everything else remains dark. The cone widens; it imparts warmth. The scene is a familiar one. It's our oak tree. The huge branches sprawl above me, and I lie in soft green grass. I see a familiar shadow high in the tree descending from the branches. Wait, now there are two shadows. I get up and stand by the huge trunk, anticipating.

David lands with a thud beside me. He looks different—wiser somehow. He wears his trademark smile with dark slacks and a white shirt. He stares into the tree, and from the boughs, my mother slowly floats to the ground in front of me, wearing the same flowing gown she wore when Rande dismissed her. She reaches her arms out, and I run to her and hug her so tight I fear I may crack her ribs in this reality. I sense David embracing us both. We stand together, not uttering a single word for the longest time until the need to speak overwhelms us and we separate.

"How did I get here?" I ask.

"What do you remember, sweetheart?" says Mom.

Reaching up, I touch my forehead. "I remember Randy sending you away, and they tried to trap me into being their new star. Then I got super pissed and split myself into a million or so multiples." I look back at my mom and drop my hand as I remember. "I cooked the bastards until they hurled me away from them. I thought I was dead."

"In a way, you were. And it was more than a million," says David, scratching the back of his head. "It was more than double that, to be honest. It explains a lot."

"What do you mean?" I ask.

Mom touches my face, cradles my chin, and lays a hand on my shoulder. "When Rande released me, I flew out across the desert plains and into the gap of the In-Between. I shot straight through to where the trees are. I climbed up and down them into all the different realities for the longest time, looking for someone to help me until, at last, I found David."

David takes a step closer. "We didn't know what had happened to you.

We got reports that the Grand Hall was burned by intense light. We weren't sure it was you until your multiples began raining down all throughout our universe."

"There were pieces of me scattered all over?"

"Yeah, but you were like dead. It caused a huge uproar as all the pieces of you just lay there. Nobody could wake you up. Dead Luces littering the cosmic countryside." David gives a twisted smile. My recovery gives him permission to kid me.

"I was dead? Then how—"

"Sweetheart, you fractured yourself so badly and got scattered so far, you could no longer connect and pull yourself together. All those individual pieces of your mind were too weak to function by themselves. They just went to sleep," says Mom.

David adds, "Then Claude gets a visit from an old friend who suggests an integration exercise to pull you back. We gathered up all the Lucindas we could find and began to integrate you. You slowly came back."

Mom strokes my hair. "But not completely. You appeared to be alive, but you were in a deep sleep. We knew that there were more of you we needed to collect. We searched all over and did find remnants of you stashed on an obscure asteroid here or tucked away in a remote forest in some distant reality over there. It was an overwhelming and slow process. We didn't know how to proceed."

"Until I reached my multiple," says David. "It raised me to a new level in my abilities. Since I know you best, I could figure out how to fix you. We separated you into eight Luces. I split myself into eight Daves and each of me took one of your multiples into the far reaches of the universe. As each of the eight Lucindas got close to other multiples, they would fly back and merge with you—like steel to a magnet. I did this until I had all eight of you as full as I could possibly get and brought all of you to our tree to complete the integration. I had just left to get your mother and bring her back here."

"Wow," I say, and stare at the ground, trying to collect my thoughts. I look at David and give him a quick hug. "Thanks", I say to him. "You're better than all the king's horses and all the king's men."

I think he got the point. "You're most welcome. Wait 'til Claude sees you. He's going to flip. The Collective's been buzzing ever since they found out you went to Koodzima and spanked them."

"Have you heard anything from those jerks?" I ask.

"Nothing but silence. No one knows exactly what is going on with them," says Mom.

"Click, clunk. Click, clunk," rumbles through my mind. It's my special wake-up call.

David sees my face. "What's wrong?"

"I think I'm waking up. Dad's going to be so pissed that I slept the weekend away."

"Lucinda, sweetie." Mom grabs my arm. "Come look for me." She's smiling, her face as serene as an angel's. She looks to David as if she wants him to say something.

"I'll see you soon," says David with a wry smile drawing across his face.

Before I can speak, I spin away from them, and when I smell orange juice and cinnamon, I know for sure I'm coming home.

37 – AWAKENING

I took a deep breath and let it out slowly. My eyes remained shut, and I sensed that I was lying in my bed. But then I heard something that didn't sound right. There was a beep sound every few seconds, mixed with some other faint noises. This was not my room. Opening my eyes, I gazed at a white ceiling with fluorescent lights. Beside me, an ECG machine monitored my pulse with wires running over to me. I opened my mouth to speak, but I made only croaking sounds like I hadn't talked in days. What the hell? I must have been asleep for so long that they've stuck me in an ICU at some hospital.

It was as if someone sat on me or I had gained a hundred pounds because when I tried to lift my head off the pillow, I could barely raise it. I ran my hand up to my chest and felt a tube running into it. The tube had white liquid, and it ran up beside me to a machine that clicked and burped. From there, it connected to a hanging IV bag full of the same white fluid. I tried to move my legs, but they were heavy, too. What's going on here?

The door was closed, so no one could hear my pitiful squeaks. I sifted through curly locks of red hair and traced one of the wires to my chest and peeled it away. Nothing. I removed more wires until the monitor alarm went off. That should bring someone.

Shortly, a nurse came into the room. When I wiggled my fingers at him, he almost had a heart attack.

"Oh, dear Lord," he said as if he saw a ghost. "I need to get a doctor." He was about to leave the room but rushed to my bedside, placing a reassuring hand on my arm. He silenced the monitor, smiled at me, and said, "Are you okay? Do you need anything?"

"Yes," I managed to croak. "Where?" I added.

"You're in St. Mary's Medical Center LT Ward. Listen, I just need to notify the attending physician. You'll only be alone for a couple of minutes. I'll be right back."

I nodded, and he shot out the door. While waiting, I scanned the room. Old flowers in vases and some get-well cards were stacked on the nightstand. Tacked to the wall near the foot of my bed was my mandala.

A doctor stormed into the room, and she was followed by the same nurse. She flew over to my bedside and asked, "Miss Locke, how're you feeling?"

"Tired," I muttered.

"I would assume so. You've been through quite an ordeal." After reviewing the monitor's report, she turned back to me, "May I examine you?" I nodded. She plugged in her stethoscope and listened to my heart and lungs. "Sounds pretty good in there." She pulled the bed covers from my feet. "Wiggle your fingers and toes."

I moved them all. Things were a bit slow but worked.

"Can you move your legs?"

I moved my legs side to side like I'm making a snow angel, but I felt something strange. "Something weird there," I said, and looked at my groin.

"Oh, it's probably the Foley. You have a catheter," she said.

Joy. I point at the tube going in my chest.

"TPN feeding tube," the doctor responded. I must have given the doctor a confused look because she continued, "It's feeding you intravenously."

My vision blurred as I sank deep into thought. She asked me a series of questions: my name, how old I was, where I lived, where I went to school, blah, blah, blah. I answered them all to her satisfaction.

"Okay, enough excitement for now. I'll let you rest a bit and notify your father immediately."

I snapped out of it. "How is he?"

"He's been worried about you. But he'll be happy to see you."

"Good." Realizing how weak I was, I slept.

~ ~ ~

The next time I opened my eyes, Dad sat in a chair beside me, holding my hand. He stared at me with happiness mixed with pain. It looked like he'd lost twenty pounds. His face appeared gaunt, with his eyes recessed and dark. His hair seemed to have more gray.

"Baby, are you okay?" Tears welled in his eyes.

"Mmm-hmm," I nodded.

He jumped up and put his arms around me in a half-hug. Fat tears splashed on my face. When he pulled back, he couldn't tell if he had cried on me, as my tears had already mixed with his.

"Daddy, I really missed you." My voice was weak but audible.

His smile broke wide, and his eyes sparkled bright and wet. "We were worried to death."

"I'm sorry, Dad." I'm thinking I must have been out for weeks. "Tell me I didn't miss Christmas," I said, hoping he would smile or laugh, but he didn't.

"Sweetie," he glanced at the door and back at me. His eyes relaxed. "You missed three Christmases."

The room swam. Something was wrong. I replayed everything I'd heard recently. When David told me he reached his multiple floats up, I knew that was it. His multiple was nine, which meant he was now eighteen. Which meant I was eighteen. OMG, I've lost two years.

My face must have shown my distress as Dad tried to comfort me. "Don't be upset."

"Too late," I said, staring at my mandala and noticing nothing else. I was a zombie. "What month is it?"

"February," he said.

"Of my senior year?" I cry in my best froggy voice. "I've lost over two years?" New tears for myself flowed from my chin and dripped onto my gown.

"You don't understand," Dad said and grabbed my arm, tight for effect. "I thought you were dead." His eyes welled up again. "For a while, the doctors told me you had no brain function. NONE. They removed the ventilator once they realized you could breathe on your own." His eyes focused on mine and burned intense. I froze. "That's if—IF you ever woke up ... you would be one step up from a vegetable." He paused to let the comment sink in. "Today, thank the Lord and the lucky stars above, you're awake. Up there." He pointed to my head. "Your beautiful brain is working. It's nothing short of a miracle." He sat there looking shocked that I was complaining.

"Well, when you put it that way, I guess I feel stupid feeling sorry for myself." I was lucky to be alive, but still mourned the loss of time and over half of my high school experience.

"Try not to get hung up on what you lost. Think about what you gained," he whispered.

"Okay," I squeaked. "Dad, can you hand me a mirror?"

"Why?" he asked with a worried face.

"Because you just responded with 'why' and your face is pinched."

With a look of wonder, he said, "You *are* back."

~ ~ ~

The day after my awakening, a physical therapist visited me with a new regimen of exercises to build muscle. They had moved my limbs while I was in the coma. You take for granted all the muscles you use for simple things like talking, sitting, walking, and standing. My whole body had atrophied. I looked like a skeleton, and when I tried to stand, I fell back into bed. I did some isometric exercises to flex my arms and legs as I lay in bed to build myself up quicker. I didn't want to be a bedridden slob, drooling on myself. They started me off slow with a liquid diet. The doctors said my stomach needed time to adapt, and I had to move along in steps.

Lying in bed, deep in concentration on my exercises, I heard a knock. Looking over, Evan and Maggie stood in the doorway staring at me, eyes bugging, and mouths opened into huge grins of shock.

"LUCE," they shouted in unison and scrambled over. They each, in turn, gave me a hug and then pulled up chairs to sit beside me.

Maggie looked so mature. She had grown her hair out longer and spoke first. "Girl, when Chuck called and said you were awake, I couldn't believe it. I made him tell me twice, and the whole time, I pinched myself to make sure I wasn't dreaming." She gazed at me and waited for me to respond.

Evan jumped in. "We visited you every day for months. Then every week. Chuck just knew you could hear us and wanted us to talk to you every chance we could. We told you about everything that was happening with us." He finished and stared at me. I didn't respond. They looked at each other and held hands as if they thought maybe I was somehow damaged.

I'd let them stew long enough. I looked to Evan and said, "Since when did you start calling my dad, Chuck?" I broke out my best smile, which ended their worries.

"You cheeky devil. How long were you going to let us drone on like that?" asked Maggie.

"Until you gave me a moment to speak, I was just soaking in the sight of you two."

We all laughed and talked for hours. They tried to catch me up on two years' worth of drama at Park North and did a fairly good job of filling in the gap.

I could read their body language.

They did not broach the subject that they were a couple. The old me would have gotten angry, mentally beaten them, and guilted them. The new me understood that I had been gone for two years, and my tragedy was what brought them together. I chose this fate for them, and it was the cost of doing business with Koodzima. I couldn't blame them. They made a cute couple.

After Maggie and Evan left, I missed them already. I wanted to chase after them and talk some more, but I'm not supposed to get out of bed without someone's help. This was to protect me from falling. The nurses had issued me yellow non-skid socks and told me they didn't want to catch me out by myself until I graduated to blue.

I pulled out the mirror and the brush the nurse had brought earlier. I did need a haircut, I mused. My eyes were deeper set with dark rings around them. I looked like a raccoon. My cheeks were sunken as well, but I felt better every moment I was awake. I glanced at my mandala hanging on the wall. I had decided to take a break from visiting my dreams for now. First, I needed to spend some time in my homeroom reality to get a firm grip.

I wanted to get back to my life as much as possible—as soon as possible. That required positive thinking, and I willed myself to take only that first day awake to wallow in sorrow. That was it. I wasn't wasting any more time on what was.

I needed to concentrate on what is.

EPILOGUE

It'd been about a month since I woke up. My physical therapy had progressed well enough that they moved me out of the long-term facility into a transitional one. The doctors declared me fully recovered, at least from what they could tell, and I'd be going home in a few days to finish my rehabilitation. I was still deciding what to do about school. Part of me wanted to get the textbooks from Maggie and read them, so I could take the final exams. Math may be a little more difficult 'cause reading it and understanding it are two different things. Maybe I could just study for a GED.

The last thing Mom told me was to come and find her. I had been overly cautious in my dreams since then. I'd done some looking around, but she hadn't appeared. I showed up every night at our tree for one week and waited for her or David. I called out to them for what felt like hours. Nobody came. Don't know why, but my gut told me she was all right, so I'm not going to worry. She will be found when she wants to be.

I washed my face in the sink of the little bathroom off the side of my hospital room. The cool water helped to wash the sleep from my eyes. The mirror has been slightly kinder since I put on some weight. My face was filling out, and I looked more like me, albeit still a little Dickensian. I imagined how I must appear to others like an Oliver Twist holding his empty bowl. "Please, sir, I want some more."

When done, I flipped the light off and stepped back into my room, and saw a doctor seated in the guest chair with his back mostly turned toward me. Something felt familiar about him—the way he held himself, the way he read his newspaper. He clicked his red pen, and I knew. Rami.

"Lucinda," said Dr. Rami. He stood to greet me and tucked his newspaper under his arm.

"Doctor," I said, and approached him. We shook hands. "How'd you know I was here?"

"I have my sources." His smile betrayed that he was glad to see me. "I've kept my distance, though I wanted to visit you sooner. Charles was so stressed; I was worried the sight of me might make him spontaneously combust." He chuckled at his own little joke.

"Are you allowed to be here?" I asked.

"Technically, no, but I wanted to speak to you. This was the only surreptitious way to make it happen." He pointed to my bed. "Have a seat." He sat back in his chair.

I sat and worked to keep my posture. Slouching will quickly turn to pain if I'm not careful.

"You appear to be making good progress since the last time I saw you," said the doctor.

"When was that?" I asked, curious.

"When I clicked the metal frog and waved a cup of orange juice with two heaping tablespoons of cinnamon under your nose," he said with a straight face.

"How…?"

"I suspected you were all jumbled up and needed a way to organize yourself. Pop you out of whatever multiple, parallel, nested states you existed within. So, I mixed the metal frog clunking with your trigger scents to realign you. I thought it might be a winning combination." He waved his hands like a magician. "Viola! And as usual, I was correct."

"That was you?" I asked, surprised.

"Who else would it have been?" asked Rami, now leaning back in his chair. "It certainly wouldn't have been David. Yes, I know, he was able to integrate you and all, but that only got you so far. Your mother was still recovering, and Claude's such a linear thinker, he wasn't going to figure it out. I just needed to push you over the hump a little. Get your wheels moving …." Dr. Rami gazed at me with a smile of pure satisfaction and clicked his pen a couple of times.

"Claude. How do you know about Claude? Was I talking in my sleep?"

"Your mandala told me everything about where you'd been: The Twin Gates, The Watch, NowHere, the Magpies. I suspected someone like Claude was teaching you these techniques because it sure wasn't me.

Frankly, I did not approve. And from how the last couple of years have gone, I was right in my assessment."

I imagined my mouth hung open, and my head spun around like some possessed doll in response to his revelation. He sat there smug and waited for me to speak. I decided to take the high road. "Thank you," I said.

He seemed ready for a verbal sparring match, and then his eyebrows raised for a moment. "You're most welcome. You know … I was worried about you, too." His face softened.

"You're a little creepy sometimes," I said, with a twisted grin.

"You know, that's not the response most people give me after helping them."

"Well, I'm not most people. Maybe that's why some people think I'm creepy, too."

"That is so true," laughed Dr. Rami. "People tell me, all the time, how creepy you are."

"Funny." I ran my fingers through my hair.

Switching to a quiet voice, he said, "No, but seriously, you're not like most people. You *are* special. But you're not as powerful and smart as you think you are. You need to be careful and heed my counsel every now and then."

"Okay, message received." I placed my hands in my lap.

Dr. Rami stood up. "I probably should go, as I'm here under false pretenses."

I stood up from the bed and, instead of giving him a handshake, I hugged him.

He pulled away first. "Don't want anyone getting the wrong idea." He patted my upper arm, put his pen in his pocket, and sighed as people do when there is nothing left to say and it's time to leave. "Oh." He pulled the newspaper out from under his arm. "There's an article in there I thought might interest you." He handed the papers to me with a grin and sauntered out of my room with a whistle.

I shook my head. What a strange bird. Opening the folded newspaper, I saw it was from the *Chicago Tribune* about the same time I awoke. Flipping through the pages, I searched until I found it. The title was circled in red ink, "Boy Wakes from Eleven Year Coma a Man." I read the article with trembling fingers:

```
Winnetka, Illinois - Eleven years ago, the
Greeley  Elementary  School  second-grader,
```

David Rodrigues, fell into a coma. Dr. Thomas Robertson was at a loss to understand any medical reasons for his condition.

"For over a decade, David has been in a vegetative state. His recovery is atypical," said Dr. Robertson. "Usually, coma patients wake up slowly over days or weeks, but for David, it was immediate. We have always been unsure of the extent of his brain function and his capabilities."

David's father, Raymond Rodrigues, commented: "The first word he spoke was 'Mom'. She just happened to be visiting that day. For so many years, we had given up hope he would ever wake up, let alone speak. Now, we can't shut him up long enough to get him to rest."

David has a long physical recovery ahead of him. His doctors believe his chances of a full recovery are excellent. The greater Chicago medical community is...

The article showed a picture of David at seven before the coma. I said to the picture, "I'd know your smile anywhere."

I sighed out loud to myself and dropped into the chair.

"Looks like I'm going to Chicago to see my boyfriend."

The End

ACKNOWLEDGMENTS

I'd like to thank my family and friends for their support in the creation of my second novel, *Dream Across This Mortal Coil.* This novel has been rattling around in my head for several years. I believed I finally reached the point where I could write well enough to capture the story the way it deserved to be told.

I especially want to thank all the members of the Lesser North Texas Writers for their insightful critiques, opinions, and friendship. I thoroughly enjoy our Thursdays together. I read chapters to them for almost two years. They kept up with it and provided great feedback on the voice and the encouragement to continue. Any author would be hard-pressed to find a better group from which to learn and share. Big shout out to Gerardo Delgadillo, Lyn Levin, Carol Woods, Virginia Boylan, Robert Young, Carolyn Fitz-Gerald, Laura Seaborn, Terry Mills, and Andrew Matthews for being trusted sounding boards.

My appreciation for my high school English teacher, the late Dr. Elizabeth Van Hamersveld, from Trinity Valley School. A tough critic, she always demanded the absolute best from her students.

Mom and Dad, I save the best for last. Your support through encouragement and education gave me a solid foundation to express myself through writing. Thank you.

ABOUT THE AUTHOR

Duke Droste was raised in Fort Worth, Texas, and now resides in Richardson, Texas, with his wife, two children, three cats, and a bird who doesn't believe in the Oxford comma.

Writing has become a creative outlet since becoming a software development manager. His style leans toward the metaphysical, where his main characters are driven with a sense of hope.

Come visit my website/blog at:
DukeDroste.com

REFERENCES

If you would like to understand more about the concepts and works referenced in this novel, please refer to the following:

Michael Talbot, *The Holographic Universe*
(Harper Perennial, 1991)

Malcolm Godwin, *The Lucid Dreamer*
(Simon & Schuster, 1994)

Thornton Wilder, *Our Town*
(Harper Collins, 1994)

Percy Bysshe Shelley, *Ozymandias*
(1818)

www.ingramcontent.com/pod-product-compliance
Lightning Source LLC
Chambersburg PA
CBHW051048050726
47592CB00002B/437